Camellia Season

Camellia Season

A NOVEL

NATASHA PETERSON

THE PAPER HOUSE
PUBLISHING

To Scott and Miranda

Contents

Camellias do not come true from seed, meaning that the resulting seedling often looks different from the parent plant. According to the American Camellia Society, superior camellias are rarely produced from seed.
–Steve Bender, "The Complete Guide to Camellias," *Southern Living Magazine,* 2023

Camellias are both gorgeous and strange.
—Honoré de Balzac

CHAPTER 1

August. 1965. The Wordless Diary

CHERIE TURNED the key in the front door lock very slowly, and she flinched when it clicked. She opened the door carefully and looked in. Cherie's mother, Paulette, was on the phone in the kitchen, her voice piqued with giggles. She knew the flirty tone in Paulette's voice. It meant a man was on the other end of the line, which made it easier to sneak in.

"Oh, George! You are such a bad boy," Paulette chastised playfully, her French accent on display. Cherie listened. There it was. The high-pitched laugh that punctuated her mother's words like three beats on a snare drum.

All clear. Cherie entered on tiptoes, closed the door behind her, and spirited through the living room avoiding the spot where the floorboards always creaked. She darted down the hall into her room, shut the door, and hid in the closet, where it was dark and silent.

I did it! Cherie sighed with relief as she curled up in the corner. She closed the closet door from the inside by pushing a sneaker outside and then pulling on the shoelace. She kicked aside the mess on the floor, shoes, clothes, books, pictures torn from magazines, pens and pencils, notebook paper with wishes and curses scribbled on them, little junky things dumped out of her plastic purse, and a few pennies. Cherie felt around the floor and found her flashlight. The light was yellowish and dim. She tapped it to make it brighter. *C'mon*, she coaxed, *shine for me*, but to no avail. The battery was going. Still, there was enough light to see the treasure she snuck in without her mother knowing it.

It was a blank book. It had a dark blue hard cover and binding like an actual book. It was smaller than a spiral notebook but larger than a paperback. The pages were soft, thicker than notebook paper and unlined. Looking closely, Cherie could see tiny streaks of wood pulp in the paper, kisses from the tree that created it. Attached to the binding was a gold brocade ribbon for a bookmark. Cherie counted the pages. There were 100 pages, and with both sides, that meant 200. *If I draw the numbers small*, she supposed, *it will be enough*. She put down the flashlight and felt the fabric on the cover. *You are my Wordless Diary*, she told the book as if it had a soul of its own.

The Wordless Diary was Cherie's birthday present to herself, even though she turned thirteen in late spring, and now it was late summer. It took that long to scrape up enough money to buy it. Cherie first saw what would become her Wordless Diary in a French Quarter shop with her friends. And now it belonged to her.

Finally! Cherie reveled. She was thrilled to hit her teens. The more she could be on her own, the better. She bit her lip and chanted, *All I have to do is last five more years. Five more years. One thousand, eight hundred and twenty-six days*, she had figured out. If she could last all those days, then she would be 18 years old and leave home. Five more years pointed the way to a future unformed as outer space to Cherie, yet as real as stone. It made her feel like growing up was a good thing.

Cherie's Wordless Diary would be her countdown; it would

help her remember her wishes and prayers, be the thing she could talk to, and to what she would build childlike, petal-strewn altars.

Cherie had tried keeping diaries before, but it never worked. It was impossible to keep them out of Mama Paulette's prying hands, resulting invariably in what her mother referred to as "a good laugh." One time, her mother even shared Cherie's diary with her then-boyfriend. They sat on the couch drinking wine and laughing at what Cherie wrote.

It made Cherie cry and hate herself for not hiding her diary better. "Stupid! Stupid!" she sobbed into her pillow and bit deep marks into her hands.

Cherie's words did not work. They could not be kept safe.

Cherie determined her Wordless Diary would be coded, her countdown numbers disguised, drawn in strange ways like hieroglyphics. Mama Paulette could hunt it down, stare at it all she wanted, and still not know what it was.

Mama will just think it's a bunch of scribbles, Cherie told herself.

She found a pencil in the clutter on the closet floor and began her first entry. She drew a tall candle with a triangular flame for One. Next to the candle, she drew two balloons with long strings, one on top of the other. That was Eight. Then, a snake with a dragon-like ruff and feathered tail for Two. Cherie liked it; it looked like a Loch Ness monster. She finished with another candle with concentric circles at the bottom, which looked like a crazy eye. 1-8-2-6. Cherie felt hopeful. No matter what, when everything was jumbled in her brain, she could draw her numbers at night, kiss her Wordless Diary *Sweet dreams,* and know that Mister Sun would rise and shine in the morning.

CHAPTER 2
Devil Woman Betsy

FOR AN ENTIRE WEEK, Cherie and Mama Paulette and everyone on the Gulf of Mexico from Houston to Tampa were glued to weather reports about a wild storm in the Caribbean. The weatherman on TV called the storm Hurricane Betsy. "This one's a bit of a devil," the weatherman said, "No one knows where she'll be heading next."

Paulette and the other renters in their four-plex house on Annunciation Street asked the landlord about boarding up the windows, but he shrugged it off. He told Paulette through the window, "Don't you worry, honey, Hurricane Betsy's going west of here."

He was wrong.

Hurricane Betsy grew to be Category Four devil woman. She wielded chainsaw gusts at her fingertips and ripped up every dead and living thing in her path. Her banshee winds wailed with murder.

It was early September 1965 when Betsy rose from the sea full force, chewed up the Bahamas, and ravaged the Florida Keys. At that, she straightened her bra straps and flicked flesh off her high heels. She looked toward the mouth of the Mississippi River. Ninety miles upriver lived the Delta Lady herself, lovely New Orleans. Wild with jealousy, Betsy ground her teeth 'til they sparked lightning bolts and took off.

Hurricane Betsy gained strength over the Gulf of Mexico. She sucked up shark heads and bit their tails. She twisted and zig-zagged, and eight massive oil rigs and all the men working on them flipped into the sea. Betsy slammed into New Orleans dead of night. She beat the Delta Lady to her knees, grabbed her head, and held it underwater.

"Mama, the front door!" Cherie screamed. The whole house shook as Hurricane Betsy's ugly growl drowned out Cherie. She shoved the heavy couch in front of the clattering door with all her strength.

The electricity gone, Paulette appeared ghostlike in the archway between the living room and the kitchen. In a lightning flash, Cherie saw her mother holding a box of matches upside down. Matches fell to the floor. Paulette ran to help Cherie with the couch but tripped straight into the coffee table. "*Merde!*" Paulette cried out in pain against the thunder.

Cherie and Paulette madly pushed everything they could in front of the seizing door: the couch, the coffee table, the TV set, the little bookcase, but they couldn't budge the big, old armchair, which was stuck on the rug. Mama Paulette limped across the room and plopped down on the armchair, cursing the storm and her bloody knee.

A loud thud and the shatter of breaking glass came from the kitchen. Cherie and Paulette screamed at the noise. "What the hell!" Paulette railed. "Now what do I do?"

Cherie could feel the rain fly through the kitchen to where she stood. Lightning struck, and she saw a garbage can caught halfway through the window over the sink; its innards of smelly diapers, beer bottles, and food spewed all over the kitchen. Cherie fled.

She felt along the walls until she reached her bedroom closet, pulled it shut with the shoelace, and curled up. She tore down clothes off the hangers to cover herself. Her foot pushed up against the Wordless Diary. She grabbed it and held it tight.

Cherie covered her ears tightly and sang. She sang all the rock songs she could remember, their familiarity and conviction comforting as prayers through the fearsome night. She shuddered with relief as Eric Burdon's voice echoed in her head, and he sang to her, *"Now my girl, you're so young and pretty"*... to the chorus, *"Girl, there's a better life for you and me."*

Missy Ruby Dawn showed up gray and sad, exposing all the ruin even before Mister Sun took over. Miles and miles of the city had drowned. Hundreds were dead and injured, and thousands no longer had homes. Massive, old trees were snapped apart, wires were down, chimneys, steeples, the levees, all crumbled. Alligators munched on floating corpses which, but a few hours earlier, were real people trying to stay alive.

The Delta Lady clung to life in fetid water as her babies cried and grabbed onto her tatters.

As for Hurricane Betsy, she didn't look back. She pulled up her stockings, reapplied her red lipstick with a loud smack, and headed northeast. By the time she reached the Tennessee border, she had dissolved into a lovely autumn rain, proud to have earned the title *Billion Dollar Betsy*, the costliest storm in United States history.

CHAPTER 3

Shut Your Stupid Mouth

NOBODY alive in New Orleans could remember worse. For weeks, tourists boated into wrecked neighborhoods and gawked at homeless people in their camps. Charitable folks brought food, clothes, and blankets. Eventually, dead bodies stopped showing up, and hurricane funerals ceased altogether, except for broken-heart attacks and suicides.

Fix-up plodded along, the sound of hammers and drills in every corridor. The citizens of New Orleans prayed with all their hearts the authorities knew what they were doing, but underneath, nobody believed they did.

It was long gone on the national news. The people of New Orleans agreed it was time to go back to school and work and quit the complaints.

Cherie sat on the front steps of their new place, an old two-story house on Octavia with four apartments. She was absorbed in her copy of *Tiger Beat* magazine with the Rolling Stones on the cover.

Cherie was used to moving from place to place, this last time because of Hurricane Betsy. After six weeks, the kitchen was still boarded up, and Paulette refused to pay the rent. She had a big fight with the landlord, and they had to move, but not before Paulette poured a bottle of glue down the bathtub drain.

"There!" Mama Paulette exclaimed, staring at the tub, the handiwork of her revenge complete, "That will fix that little bastard!"

In the place before Annunciation Street, Paulette and the landlady had a big fight about Paulette making eyes at the landlord, and they had to move again. Cherie asked her mother what happened but got the irritable hand wave, which meant *Shut up.*

Before that, three places ago, they lived on Plum Street. Cherie loved being on Plum because she was extra close to her friends Estelle, Marlene, and Katherine. An extra bonus was that they lived upstairs. Cherie had a little corner room with shady trees next to the windows. It was as good as air conditioning when she opened the windows on both sides.

When Paulette when out at night, she could sleep over at Marlene's. Katherine would often join them, and sometimes Estelle if she could. There was always a birthday or holiday the little girls could celebrate.

They would drink coffee and then dance around wild to loud music and holler Cajun yells. Baking was part of the ritual. Together they'd make brownies stuffed with pecans or pineapple-coconut cake and proceed to destroy their creations play-fighting and stuffing chunks in one another's mouths. Late at night, they'd watch an old horror movie on *Morgus Presents* holding on to each other during the scary parts. And share stories until they fell asleep. Cherie described to them, her eyes wide, after a weekend in Pensacola.

"There was this place down the road that was supposed to be like a zoo but just farm animals. There was this box with chickens painted on it. Mama's boyfriend, well he's not anymore, made me put a dime in the box. Then, part of the box opened up and a real, live chicken came out and danced to "Old MacDonald." Katherine jumped up, "Cluck, cluck," and did the chicken-scratch dance. Marlene joined her. Estelle clapped her hands, singing, "And a cluck, cluck here, and a ..."

"No! Stop! It was creepy," Cherie protested. They stopped. "Yeah," Marlene nodded, "Poor chicken." "Poor chicken," they all agreed.

"You won't believe this," Cherie continued, "I was at the beach in the water, and I saw a real seahorse. It was tiny, but I know that's what it was. I was the only one that saw it."

Come Monday morning, they walked to school together.

Now, Cherie was thirteen and lived on Octavia Street, a little more than two miles away from Marlene's house and close enough to St. Charles Avenue to hear the streetcar.

"Cherie!" Paulette's snare-drum call was so sharp it split the humid air molecules.

Cherie didn't move. Her mother had been calling for her all day, and she pretended not to hear the latest summons. She wanted to read. She didn't want to run to the corner store or any place else. Her hands clenched the magazine as she waited for the next ratta-tat call.

Cherie sensed somebody close by. She looked up to see five kids from the neighborhood sizing her up, the new girl on the block. The leader of the group looked older, maybe fifteen. Her blond hair was teased up, and her white shirt was tucked into a black straight skirt. She wore pointed black flats on her feet. The flats were too small, and it looked like her little toes would pop out. She held a cigarette.

Teased-Up broke the ice.

"Where y'at?"

"Good," Cherie replied, "Y'all?"

"Good. You a hood or a frat?" Teased-Up ordered. The kids beside her stared at Cherie as they waited for the answer.

"I don't know. Neither."

Teased-Up didn't like that one bit. She rolled her eyes at the other kids, and they all smirked.

It was true, though, Cherie was neither. She wore red Keds with her jeans, not penny loafers like frat kids. Yet, her dark brown hair was waist-long and silky, not curled, teased, or tied up like a hood girl.

"What does your daddy do?" Teased-Up continued her third degree, determined to get to the bottom of it.

Cherie shrugged, and the group nodded with understanding. They knew it meant no dad.

"Your mama?"

"She's a secretary."

Teased-Up looked Cherie over, thinking about it. She wasn't from doctors, bankers, or teachers. That made her way more hood. She read *Tiger Beat*, though. That was a frat magazine. It was hard to gauge.

Teased-Up resolved the mystery with the tell-all question, "Who do you like more," she commanded, "The Stones or Elvis?"

When Cherie didn't answer, the group shook their heads *no*, and Teased-Up called it. "You're a frat!" she concluded, and with that, the whole Y'at pack turned and walked away.

Cherie called after them, "But I hate frats. You mean like fraternities? They're just a bunch of jerks that pay money to have friends."

Teased-Up cut her off, "Shut your stupid mouth! You're definitely a frat."

Cherie sighed. She had her own friends. *I'll see them at school.*

Giant live oaks lined the street. Their branches intertwined, forming shady tunnels. Cherie was grateful they had survived Hurricane Betsy. The houses were painted in pastels, yellow, peach, and lime, and the street had an enticing name, Arabella.

Down St. Charles Avenue, a group of streets on the other side of Jackson Avenue were named after the nine Muses of ancient Greece: Melpomene, Terpsichore, Felicity, Erato, Euterpe, Thalia, Urania, Calliope, and Polymnia. Cherie thought it was so cool. *All you have to do to memorize the Muses is take the streetcar.*

Cherie loved the Greek gods and goddesses. She wished they were real. *Myths of Greece and Rome* by H.A. Guerber was her favorite book, and it had survived all the moves. She found it in a box of books her mother brought home from somebody's house way back.

Cherie turned back to her magazine. Ten seconds later, there it was.

"Cherie!" The next one was louder still. "Cherieeeee!"

"That woman is fever pitch," Cherie recalled the Pensacola boyfriend saying. *Fever pitch,* Cherie whispered to herself when he said it. When Mama Paulette watched the evening news, she saw misery in everything, no matter what was reported. She thought happy people were ignorant, and she hated religion. If Cherie said, "Thank God," Paulette would snap at her, "Who are you thanking?" Even so, Cherie secretly refused to convert to atheism. *Maybe there is God or even a bunch of them*, she told herself.

Paulette had been in America for twenty years but still spoke English with a thick French accent. She pronounced *this, that,* and *thing* like *zis, zat,* and *zing.* Cherie knew never to correct her. However, her mother said it, *zat* was *zat.* The same rule applied to the flying hand-whack, which meant *Enough!* It was slightly different from the *Shut-up* hand wave, except it stung when it landed.

Paulette appeared at the top of the landing, "Are you deaf? I swear I'm going to get your hearing checked! I can't find the tweezers. Did you take my tweezers? Run to the drugstore and get me tweezers." She handed Cherie some money. "Hurry up! Fix yourself before we go."

Cherie didn't reply but got on her bike and headed for Prytania Street. She turned the corner and broke into *Hail, Prytania!*

CHAPTER 4
A Slab of Beef from Texas

THAT AFTERNOON, Cherie accompanied her mother to the French Quarter to visit Shannon O'Brien. Paulette loved Shannon because she was exactly the hard-drinking career girl Paulette wished she could have been. They both liked parties. Sometimes, Paulette would take Cherie with her rather than walk in alone. At times, Cherie was the only kid there.

It made Cherie feel older than she was as she observed all the sexy behavior and chatter about Freud, Fellini, and the *mondo bizarro*. At times, she found the adult world cringe-worthy, especially when Paulette would get drunk, dance around doing the Can Can, and throw up.

Cherie grew up watching her mother's flirty antics with men and how much they liked it. Paulette was curvaceous and dressed in tight clothes with silky fabrics and heels to go out. She never left the house without red lipstick.

When she was little, Paulette let her men carry sleepy Cherie back home from the neighbor's couch after a date. The next day, Paulette would ask her, "Didn't it feel good when he carried you to bed like he was your daddy? He said he would adopt you in a second!" Cherie never replied. Instead, she stared at the floor and prayed, *Thank you, God, thank you, God, and all the saints, Zeus, gods and goddesses, angels, and fairies for keeping Mama's boyfriends away from me!*

They headed into the French Quarter to Shannon's loft apartment near the deserted Ursuline Convent. They stood at the tall, iron gate by the carriageway until Shannon buzzed them in. In the courtyard was a fountain with marble birds, streams of water trickling from their beaks.

They walked to the far side of the courtyard where the slave quarters over the stables had been converted into apartments.

Shannon's place didn't fail to please. They walked into a main room with a high ceiling, and best of all, at the back was a twisted metal staircase that led up to the loft bedroom. Instead of paintings on the walls, there were baskets, brightly colored tapestries, and folk instruments from other countries. Jazz played on the radio.

Another fixture in Shannon's apartment was her boyfriend Wayne. Wayne was a slab of beef from Texas with greased-back dark hair and narrow blue eyes. Like his girlfriend, he was divorced, and unlike her, he had a child, a daughter a little younger than Cherie, who lived in Houston.

Even though it was noon, Shannon greeted them in a red silk kimono, prompting Paulette to apologize profusely for arriving too early. Cherie watched as Wayne lumbered down the twisted stairs in his boxers and drawled, "I hope you made the coffee strong. Yesterday, it was so weak, I spit it out."

"I made it strong," Shannon replied dryly as she turned down the radio volume.

Paulette piped in sarcastically, "Ohh, Wayne, you poor boy. You are the only man in New Orleans with a girlfriend who cannot make coffee."

Shannon rolled her eyes, "I don't know what he's talking about."

Wayne homed in on Cherie and spoke directly to her, "Well, good morning, sugar. You're Cherie, right? You want to go with me up to Cafe Du Monde and get some real coffee and beignets? Get away from the coffee klatch?"

Cherie shook her head, "No. I'll just stay here."

Shannon leaned in and whispered to Paulette and Cherie, "He feels bad today because it's his daughter's birthday. Cherie, why don't you go? It will make him feel better."

Then Shannon offered brightly to Wayne, "I've got an idea, honey. Why don't you take Cherie for a swim over at Martin's?" And to Paulette, "It's just a few blocks away, they have a nice pool in the courtyard."

"Yes, we can park her there for a while," Paulette replied. Cherie hated that expression, being parked.

"I can't. I don't have a suit with me," Cherie protested.

"That's okay," her mother's friend replied with a twang, "I have one that shrunk in the wash. It will probably fit you just fine."

"Especially because neither of you has anything up here, hahaha," Paulette chuckled as she patted her ample bosom.

Cherie flinched but didn't argue. If she countered Paulette's sexual talk with so much as an expression, Paulette would get mad. "Oh, what an American girl, a real puritan. I don't believe I raised such a stupid, close-minded creature." Cherie knew that being close-minded was one of the worst things you could be in her mother's eyes. It meant you were stupid and old-fashioned.

Cherie didn't want to go, but Paulette insisted.

Shannon's bathing suit was a little big, but she could get away with wearing it. It was a navy blue two-piece with a white stripe on the side. She wore her skirt and top over the bathing suit. In a sing-song Texan drawl that sweetly reassured Cherie, Wayne said, "Let's

15

go," and he pulled her by her hand out the door. Cherie was unsure, but beignets and a Quarter courtyard pool were a real treat, so maybe, she hoped, it would be okay.

They walked the few blocks to Cafe Du Monde, and when Wayne noticed scattered folks waiting for tables, he huffed, "It's too crowded. We don't need this." He gestured to Cherie to follow him as he left the Cafe. She did. "Sorry, sweetheart," he said.

A half block down the street, he turned into a bar, ordered a double-something, and threw it down his throat. When the bartender looked obliquely at Cherie, Wayne threw back another double-something. He emphatically repeated, "This is my daughter. See? I'm divorced, and this is my daughter, and it's her birthday today, right? And I've got her here with me today, right sugar?" He shot a big smile at Cherie.

She noticed the bartender glower at him as they left, Wayne with a bottle in a paper bag. Her stomach started to twist.

"I want to go back!" she blurted out.

"Hey, don't you want to swim? It's right around the corner." He took her hand and pulled her along.

When they arrived at Martin's apartment, Martin wasn't there. Wayne found the key under a flowerpot by the banana tree. He gave Cherie a towel. She took off her clothes over Shannon's suit and jumped into the water.

Hurray! A real swimming pool, she thought as she relished the cool water. She swam from one side to the other, darted down to the bottom, and did a handstand in the shallow side. She did a somersault underwater, then swam straight up, bursting out of the water like a dolphin. She did it again and again until she looked up to see Wayne standing on the second-story walkway. He yelled to her, "Hey, watch me do this!"

"Don't do it!" Cherie yelled.

He climbed onto the railing and, a second later, cannon-balled into the pool. Cherie barely had time to get out of the way. Wayne hit the water hard and started flapping in a heated butterfly stroke. Cherie hurried out of the pool.

"You're crazy!" she yelled at Wayne. She dried off and headed into the apartment.

As Cherie looked around for some soda in the kitchen, Wayne came in. He made a beeline for his paper bag. He poured some light brown liquor into a glass with ice and stood next to her against the kitchen counter.

"I think it's time for us to go back," she said, but Wayne didn't respond. He was looking her over. "Why do you have that suit pulled up to your waist? It makes you look like a little girl, and you're way past that."

"But that's how it goes," Cherie defended.

"No, look," in a split second, he grabbed the suit and folded the bottom down so it looked like a bikini. "There, look." He grabbed her arm and pulled her into the bedroom, where one wall was covered by a big mirror. "Isn't that better?"

"I guess so," she responded. It did make her look more grown up. The curve of her waistline was clearly evident.

He slipped an ice cube from his drink down Cherie's bathing suit bottom, laughed, and snapped his fingers as she jumped and got it out. "That's not funny," Cherie snapped.

"Oh c'mon, quit being a baby," he spewed. He put his drink down on the dresser and whistled a few notes. Wayne grabbed Cherie's hips and pushed them around as though she were a puppet. Cherie tried to pull away, but he held both her wrists behind her back with one hand and clutched her with the other arm. She couldn't move at all. He jammed his mouth on hers. He tried to push his tongue into her mouth, but Cherie clenched her teeth, so he just mashed his mouth on hers. Finally, he released her. Cherie wiped her mouth.

"I don't think you should have done that!" Cherie said to him.

"Oh yeah, and why not?" he replied, taking a swig.

"I think you should apologize to me!"

Wayne burst out laughing. "Apologize to you!" he chuckled, "Apologize to you! If that's not the cutest thing I've ever heard. You really are cute."

"I'm going back," Cherie put on her skirt and shirt and started for the door.

Wayne shoved her into the open coat closet stuffed with clothes next to the front door. He was behind her. He had both arms around her and pushed her into the hanging suits. Her face was pressed into them.

Cherie's "Stop it, stop it!" was sorely muffled by wool even though she shouted. One of his arms was across her chest, and the other snaked down her. He grabbed her thigh. She couldn't move. He humped her and drooled into her hair. She smelled the liquor and felt his hard thing against her backside.

His grip tightened. Tears ran down her face, mashed against the scratchy wool, and she began to choke. Still, he pushed on her, making noises, *ungh, ungh, ungh,* with each thud. One more long *uunnggh* and it stopped. He let her go, ordering in a low voice, "Wait for me by the door," and he went into the bathroom.

Cherie took a step and fell to her knees. She was shaky but got back up. She wiped the tears off her face and bit her lip hard to stop crying.

Her mind raced. *I have to figure out how to get back. Where are we? What's Shannon's last name? I can't look it up in a phonebook without her last name. Oh God, some of it's on me!*

She grabbed a towel and wiped off her leg. *I can get someone to give me money. I'll take the streetcar home. I can't open the door. I can't open the door...*

Wayne reappeared dressed, his hair combed. "Where are you going?"

"I wanted to wait outside," she said. The words barely stumbled out of her mouth.

18

"Just a damn minute, Cherie, you listen to me." He took her arm and pointed his finger at her. He spoke flatly, "Now, I'm going to tell your Mama I kissed you, and you asked for an apology. But there's nothing else to tell, right? Because nothing else happened, did it?"

Cherie stood there; she prayed to leave. She could hear her heart beating.

"Did it?" He raised his voice, "Did anybody take your clothes off? No!"

She shook her head, no, but Wayne still wasn't assured of his innocence. He continued his barrage.

"Hey, I thought you were a smart girl. Are you smart or dumb? Are you going to be a dumb baby about this or a smart young lady?"

Cherie was frozen to the spot. She hated him. The voice in her head rang loud and clear, *Play dumb. Agree with everything he says.*

"Nothing happened for you to go crying to your Mama about! I'll tell her I hugged and kissed you. I'm not ashamed of that. So, what are you going to do? Upset her? You going to worry her as hard as she works, scraping by and raising you." He tightened his grip on her arm and raised his voice, "Nothing happened here. You got that?"

"I got it." She forced the words out sweetly, "It's not a big deal. I'm not going to say anything." He let her go and opened the door.

Back at Shannon's, Wayne went straight to her liquor cabinet. Cherie went to the bathroom and washed up. She got dressed in her own clothes. She threw the bathing suit on the floor and stomped on it.

In the living room, she shrunk into a corner easy chair.

Cherie looked at a *Cosmopolitan* magazine while Wayne regaled the two women with his cheerful story about the kiss, the apology, and how cute Cherie was, which made Paulette smile.

Cherie stared blankly at an ad for pink nail polish called Max Factor's 3 Little Bares. The three models were all in pink bikinis. Her mind was going round and round: *Maybe he was right. Nothing really happened. I hate him. Gross! But he didn't stick it in. Maybe it wasn't a big deal. Was it?* She knew what dry humping was.

Still, she knew she shouldn't have gone with him at all. *Why did Mama make me go? I'm so stupid. I should have refused, made up something.* But Cherie knew acting perfectly in front of Paulette's friends was really important.

Wayne, the drunk skunk, jumped up from where he was, grabbed both of Paulette's hands and announced, "I'm taking us out to dinner! Let's go to Felix's!" He did a little tap dance while he whistled and, with one finger, traced Paulette's neck right into her tight blouse that had the two top buttons opened, displaying her cleavage and the top of her bra. Paulette pulled at one of the buttons and giggled, "I train them to do that!"

Wayne said to Shannon, "Do something with Cherie. She can't go to dinner like that."

Paulette approached Cherie with an excited gleam in her eyes. "Oh, I love you, I love you, I love you," Paulette cooed. She planted a big, wet smooch on Cherie's face, and then she laughed as she rubbed off the lipstick with the palm of her hand. Cherie was used to the gesture.

Paulette stopped and looked at Cherie. "What's the matter with you? Are you okay?"

Cherie shrugged.

"He's taking us out to dinner. Don't you want to go?"

"No. I want to go home."

Paulette roiled, "Oh, here we go again. You're such a party pooper. C'mon, let's go get ready."

Cherie followed Shannon and her mother up the twisted metal stairs to the loft bedroom. With every step, she chanted to herself, *I hate that pig, I hate Shannon, and I'm going to barf.*

They went through Shannon's closet, picked out a pink cotton dress for Cherie, and added a belt. Then Wayne's girlfriend teased Cherie's hair, pinned it up, and put eye shadow and mascara on her. The women agreed Cherie looked better with makeup on, and it was time she should start wearing it.

There were five different lipsticks on the vanity. Shannon decided on a light pink one with frost and dabbed it on Cherie. Then Shannon gave it to her. "You keep it, darlin'. It's prettier on you than me."

They left for the restaurant. On the way out, Paulette sang a song from a popular film, *"Gigi, am I a fool without a mind ..."*

Wayne's jacket got ripped by the corner of a low-slung air conditioner in the walkway. He attacked it, cursing, and kicked it in, leaving deep dents. At dinner, he got mad at the waitress. Cherie sat silently at the table, wishing he would keel over and die.

Back on Royal Street, Wayne was all over Shannon trying to kiss her, who called to Paulette over her shoulder, "Better go. I'll call you tomorrow. Kiss. Kiss." The women kissed the air at each other with loud *Mwah* sounds.

Cherie finally got to go home. Neither she nor Paulette ever said another word about that day.

She ferreted out her Wordless Diary from its hiding place. She slowly drew the one all zig-zag, the seven with teeth coming down off the top, and the two sixes were eyes. 1-7-6-6.

The bruise on her arm faded. It was over. But the whole thing sometimes barreled into her head round and round. *Why won't it go away? Forget it, you!* She fought with herself, the voice in her head yelling, *Forget it!*

21

CHAPTER 5
Mrs. Skillet's Hot Stove

"MAY I TRY IT?" Cherie eagerly asked as she joined Devin and Garrett by the back entrance of their middle school.

"Sure," Devin replied, generous enough to share the treasured Pall Mall swiped from his father. He held the cigarette up and instructed, "Now, when you breathe in, try to hold the smoke in your mouth, but if it goes down into your lungs, just relax and let it blow back out. That way, you won't cough."

Despite his wrinkled cotton shirt and dark blond hair that fell into his blue eyes, he explained his newly found skill with a deliberate, gentlemanly air, true to his southern upbringing. He handed her the cigarette. "Hold it like this."

Cherie pushed her long hair back behind her shoulders and awkwardly held the cigarette to her mouth. She tried to look cool, took a puff, and coughed like hell.

The boys burst out laughing. She dried her watery eyes on the sleeve of her print shirt. It was early November. You could wear long sleeves again without roasting.

"Let me try it again," she sniffed. This time she managed a nice puff and, having conquered it, handed the butt back. "It's stupid."

"Yeah, but it looks cool," Devin said.

Nearby, transistor radio on high, a group of girls tuned in "Stop! In the Name of Love" on Bob Walker's morning show. They sang along and imitated The Supremes, palms straight out, then folded their hands over their hearts.

The bus stopped at the corner, and students poured out of it. Most Catholic and private school kids had their own buses, but public school students took city buses and the streetcar.

Katherine got off the bus. Cherie and the two boys waved her over. She limped slightly to where they stood. That wiped the smiles off their faces.

Garrett liked Katherine. He walked over and put his arm around her. She smiled at him. From inside a copy of *The Good Earth*, Katherine pulled out a few pages of notebook paper covered with Cherie's even script.

"Did you get your paper done?" Cherie asked, taking the pages. Katherine shook her head, no, her shoulder-length, honey-colored hair shaking with it. Her light brown eyes with a glint of amber in the sunlight were tinged with red like she'd been up all night, and her lip was swollen as though she had bitten it.

"Why are you limping?"

"It's okay." Katherine looked away, recalling her mother's temper tantrum the previous night. It ended when her mama's boyfriend came over with sleeping pills, but not before Katherine twisted her ankle when she dodged the alarm clock her mother threw at her.

Garrett gathered up his books plus the paperbacks he secretly read at school. On top of the pile was *Black Like Me* by John Howard Whit. Cherie recognized it. All the progressive families, known as *Pinkos*, had a copy. It was written by a white journalist who dyed himself black to see what it was like. When the Ku Klux Klan found out what he had done, they set out to castrate him. Author Whit and his family had barely escaped their wrath.

23

"It's twenty after eight," Cherie announced, "We have ten minutes left."

Ten whole minutes before school started! Ten whole minutes to be with your friends before you barreled through another eighth-grade day. Ten whole minutes before they had to face another gut-wrenching social studies class with Mrs. Skillet.

A convoy of military vehicles trolled up Claiborne Avenue. Some of the kids cheered them and saluted.

"What's that about?" Cherie asked. She turned to Garrett for the answer.

"It's the US Army Corps of Engineers. They're going to rebuild the levees solid so it never happens again." His N'Orlins accent was less evident than his friends, but there was, still, that *little bit of extra sound* that hung off the ends of words, less than a drawl and purely unique to New Orleans. "But they're not going to fix the pumping stations," he added with a shrug. The group groaned in response. The pumping stations were something only New Orleans people understood. They were old. When bad storms hit, they got overloaded and couldn't pump the water out.

"Look at 'em all," Cherie said, amazed by the line of Army Jeeps.

"No shit," Garrett agreed. He added bitterly, "The oil companies can't afford another Betsy. That's the only reason."

They watched the convoy drift away. Federal attention in New Orleans. Folks were surprised. They remarked, "Now that's something you don't see too often."

The school bell rang with rigor. Cigarettes were squished out; radios were silenced. Girls who wore makeup put on more lipstick.

"Let's just skip," Garrett said to Devin.

"Can't. Did you bring lunch? I'm hungry," Devin replied.

"Here." Garrett handed Devin some change for a cafeteria lunch.

"Thanks, but I'm giving this back if it's ham and collards. That shit makes me throw up. Can I have your *Black Like Me* when you're done?"

"Yeah, man. I'm almost done."

Everybody filed into Eleanor McMain Secondary School, a grand, three-story art deco building built in 1930. It was painted light blue with graceful features such as stone carvings over the entrances.

They ran into Marlene on the second floor. The sunlight hit her blond hair as it poured through the windows, and she stood out in the crowd. She whispered to Katherine, "Everything okay?" Katherine shrugged, "Doesn't matter."

Seconds later, Estelle ran up to them with a big smile, breathless, her thick, dark brown hair over her shoulders. Her face featured perfect skin with a tinge of olive in it, high cheekbones, and brown eyes. She ran right into Cherie and almost knocked her over. "Hey!"

"Hey!" Cherie glanced at her, startled. "Oh wow, Estelle, you look so cool."

Katherine and Marlene gathered 'round. Estelle's hair was parted in the middle instead of on the side.

"Let's *all* do it," Marlene enthused.

Cherie, Katherine, and Marlene awkwardly retrieved their combs as they walked down the hall, parting their hair in the middle to look like Estelle. They reached Mrs. Skillet's classroom.

"See you later." Marlene chirped sarcastically.

"Yeah, have fun," Estelle grinned.

Cherie and Katherine made faces like they were gagging. Katherine started to laugh. Cherie thought how good it was to see her laugh.

They followed Garrett and Devin in, taking their seats seconds short of the late bell.

On the first day of school, Mrs. Mary Skillet stood before her advanced social studies students and stared them into silence. They looked up to see a short, pudgy teacher with beady eyes obscured by eyeglasses. Her grayish brown hair was puffed up in front and pulled back into a chignon. She wore a dark blue suit and leather loafers. Then she spoke.

"You see that greasy smudge on the floor?" Mrs. Skillet asked in a pinched accent laced with traces of the other Louisiana outside the city limits.

They shifted in their seats to look.

"That's you. Now, do you see this?" She pointed to a double-ax brooch pinned to her blazer.

"That's me. Are there any questions?"

Year after year, Mrs. Skillet devoted herself to turning out citizens who held to the nation's manifest ideals, except for discussion or dissension.

Mrs. Skillet was famous in certain circles for her participation in the local chapter of the Daughters of the American Revolution. In Louisiana, the DAR tended to serve as a front for the Confederacy, which often moved their Yankee sisters to hair-pulling at national conventions. "Why don't they just join Daughters of the Confederacy and leave us alone?" the Yankee ladies groaned in frustration.

To her students, Mrs. Skillet was anything but an old teacher. They knew she was capable of transforming comic-book style from teacher to creature. They knew the transformation was imminent when her eyes narrowed. It gave them a moment to grip their desks before an onslaught of flesh-burning words flew out of her mouth.

It wasn't long before Mrs. Skillet realized there were strange critters in her class. When these critters trumpeted the God-given

American ideals of free speech and civil disobedience, as in, "the Vietnam war is a big, stinking lie," Mrs. Skillet took to battle.

Mrs. Skillet would smite what she called a Baby Agitator. She knew how those things grew. They were mutants, podlings from another dimension that, left unattended, would grow into giant alien enemies that threatened the American Way.

Not on her watch.

Mrs. Skillet passionately made it her mission to pluck out any leftover socialist tendencies from her students' continental ancestors.

Mrs. Skillet complained about the Baby Agitators in the Teacher's Lounge, where McMain's teachers in desperate need of a smoke and a nip were trapped on their breaks. Mr. Reynolds, the science teacher who fought in WWII, read his newspaper, and tried to ignore her, only to dryly quip when she left the room, "Lord, help the child stupid enough to say *counterculture* in that woman's class."

Cherie and Katherine were in for it. They had immigrant mothers with foreign accents. Aha! Mrs. Skillet caught them talking during class.

"Katherine, Cherie — stand up!" They did as the eyes of their classmates burned holes into them. Katherine stared down, but Cherie made the mistake of glancing at her teacher.

"Don't you look at me, you look at the floor!"

In her peripheral vision, Cherie saw Garrett and Devin shoot Mrs. Skillet the bird under their desks, and she bit the inside of her mouth hard to keep from smiling. She thought defiantly, *Mrs. Skillet thinks she's ferocious, but she's nothing but a dried-up old hag, just like that ugly pin she wears.*

Cherie shivered. *Why? Why is Mrs. Skillet always picking on me? There's no way she could know Grandpa Henri was a commie. How could she know that?*

Cherie's handsome grandfather, Henri, was a French

Communist sympathizer in Paris. During WWII in France, the Nazis killed him and other political activists early on, even before Jews, gays, and gypsies. Cherie's mother knew how to sing "The Internationale," the commie anthem. Sometimes, when Paulette was drunk at parties, she would stand on a chair and sing it with an exaggerated flourish, then burst into tears because of her beloved lost papa. She would slump down, almost as if to fall, and people at the party would gather around to catch her and offer comfort.

Cherie was named after him. Her real name, which made her cringe, was Henriette. It wasn't so bad pronounced in French, which sounded like *awn-ree-ette*, but in English, it was different. *Yuck. All the beautiful French names for girls*, she thought, *and I ended up with that.*

Punishment spewed from Mrs. Skillet's mouth at Cherie and Katherine. They stared at the floor.

"Well now, don't you two think you're something. You think you're so smart, don't you?" She paused, then continued, "Well, I don't think you have anything to be proud of. Not. One. Thing! You're not one bit better than anybody here. In fact, you're worse. Right, class?"

Frightened students responded in little voices, "Yes, ma'am."

Cherie endured Mrs. Skillet's insults. She stared at her hands and made herself think about nail polish. She worried for Katherine; *Mrs. Skillet's whipping is the last thing Katherine needs.* Cherie hoped that after school, they could go to Marlene's.

"Nothing to be proud of at all," Mrs. Skillet repeated. Then, the wrap-up, "Look at the two of you, a sorry sight if I say so myself. Too stupid to know how stupid you are. Just two stupid little girls." Finally, with volume, "Sit down and shut up so I can teach my class. Maybe you'll even learn something!"

Cherie and Katherine flopped into their desks. Behind her back, Cherie spelled out s-h-i-t in sign language. They used it to talk across classrooms and help each other on multiple-choice tests.

Nobody told their parents what had happened. Teachers had authority. They were mentors at one end of the learning continuum and abusers at the other. Being insulted, slammed against a wall, paddled, or smacked by a teacher was as much a part of a jolly school day as being complimented, hugged, and invited out by one. Teacher's pet or pest, their call.

It was Devin's turn to deliver his book report. He went to the front of the class and muttered the title and author.

"My report today ..."

"Speak up!" Mrs. Skillet interrupted.

"My report today is on *Das Kapital* by Karl Marx," he croaked.

Cherie gasped and covered her mouth with her hands. *Oh no. Devin's gone insane.* Garrett tried to stifle his laughter and sputtered all over his desk. They knew what that book was about. It was the commie bible.

Mrs. Skillet stood at the side of the room, lips pursed. Staring. Turning red. Devin was as good as dead.

Barely minutes into his book report, right after, "And then he talks about how workers are exploited and used ..." Mrs. Skillet cut in, "Do you even know what *exploited* means?"

"It means the bosses are taking advantage ..."

Mrs. Skillet didn't let him answer. "Okay, that's enough. Leave your report on my desk. Class, open your text to page 40."

Devin did something unforgivable in Mrs. Skillet's eyes. He went off the recommended book list and read a dangerous book. Without proper guidance, she believed, he could be lost forever. Mrs. Skillet didn't understand that Devin was curious about communism.

Since the day he was born, he heard so many terrible things, like how commies would attack America and turn the survivors into robot slaves.

New Orleans wasn't that far from Cuba, and he remembered crisply the nerve-wracking atomic bomb drills during the 1962 Missile Crisis three years back. The bells rang unexpectedly, and the principal would yell over the PA, "Everybody under your desks! Crouch down, arms over your head! Stay there, and don't move!"

Who is this enemy, and why are we fighting them a million miles away in Vietnam? Devin thought. Boys in his neighborhood had been killed. *Will I die there, too, in five years when they draft me? Will I lose my legs like Albert?*

Albert was in his early twenties, a black guy who worked at Langenstein's Grocery Store. They sent him to Vietnam, and one of his legs got burned. When Albert's leg healed, he was sent back again, and that's when he lost both legs. Now, Albert was in a wheelchair forever.

Terrifying thoughts floated around Devin's young mind. *Why do good guys like Albert have to end up crippled or dead? Mom believed Jim Garrison. She believed JFK's assassination was a conspiracy to keep the Vietnam war going. Lots of people did. Or are commies really that bad? Do they really want to kill us?*

Mrs. Skillet declared war on Devin. She was determined to break him, take the wayward wind out of his sails.

Over the following weeks, Mrs. Skillet repeatedly humiliated Devin in class to reduce him to tears because being a crybaby at school equaled death. Then, when he yelled at her, "Why don't you leave me alone?" she sent him to the vice principal's office to get paddled. Garrett banged his head on his desk, and Cherie could hear him cursing. She threw a pencil at him, and when he looked up, she whispered, "Stop it, or you'll go, too. Bite the inside of your mouth."

Mrs. Skillet made the class watch a film about communism

that starred the *Father Knows Best* actors from TV. It was called "24 Hours in Tyrantland."

At lunch, huddled around a back corner table, Estelle told them what they were in for.

"I watched it with my brother. It was on TV late at night. What happens is the big daddy in the TV show tells the kids that the whole house will be communist for twenty-four hours and he's the dictator."

"Okay, Daddy Dictator. Why?" Garrett asked, disgust in his tone. Estelle continued.

"Father is angry that his three kids don't want to sell US Savings Bonds, and he's going to teach them a lesson. So, he takes away all of Bud's, Princess's, and Kitten's freedom, listens in on everything they say, and makes them work around the house all day. The kids all put up with it and just count the minutes to midnight when it's supposed to end, but then..."

They all stared at her, waiting for the punchline, so Estelle continued.

"The Daddy Dictator turns back the clocks, extending the twenty-four hours indefinitely. That causes the kids to totally freak out, and Princess starts crying."

"Whoa, what a creep," Devin chimed in, "He made Princess cry!"

Katherine added, "And Kitten pee in her pants." That cracked them up.

Later, as they sat in the back row of the AV room where educational films were shown, Garrett whispered, "If I had a piggy bank, I'd break it open and buy a Savings Bond!"

Mrs. Skillet's desiccated voice sailed through the air, "Would you want to live that way?"

Then, a miracle happened. With Estelle and Marlene pushing him, Devin confessed to his brother what he was going through, and he called their dad. Their dad, who golfed with police sergeants, got angry about what he was hearing. He called McMain's principal, who called in Mrs. Skillet. Devin's ordeal was over.

Devin's father wasn't crazy with joy that his younger son read Karl Marx, but he didn't think Devin was *The Bad Seed* either. If anything, he blamed Garrett.

"He's trouble, that boy!"

Cherie ended up in detention for sassing a substitute teacher. Garrett was stuck in there, too, because he wore a button to school that he had found on the ground at Tulane University that read, "The Great Society: Bombs, Bullets and Bullshit." The words on the button satirized the words of President Lyndon Johnson, who had coined the phrase, The Great Society for America.

Garrett was reading *All the King's Men*. He yawned loudly like a lion, distracting Cherie from her homework.

"What's it about?" she whispered.

"Governor Huey P. Long."

"Like the bridge?"

Garrett nodded. He put his head down and closed his eyes. He drifted off, his voice trailing, "Huey P. Long, man of the people. Louisiana Robin Hood."

Cherie smiled, thinking, *Louisiana Robin Hood. Cool.*

It was an extra dark night. Mizzy Moon teased the Delta Lady with her cat whisker from behind the clouds, and more folks than usual put on their porch lights.

Paulette showed up all smiles at the foot of Cherie's bed. She held an old cardboard box. "Wait till you see what I have for you!"

she sang-song. A man she was dating gave her some sweaters his daughter didn't want anymore. Cherie was used to her mother showing up with hand-me-downs for her. Sometimes, there were nice things.

Cherie looked through the box. They were pretty. She tried one on and then another, tearing them off in turn. "I'm sorry, Mama, but they itch!" she shouted. She scratched her arms furiously, leaving bright red streaks. "They're wool!" A *closet full of woolen suits.* A surge of prickly energy coursed through her. She dragged her nails over her limbs and tore at her skin.

"What the hell is the matter with you?" Paulette moaned, "These are beautiful sweaters!"

Past midnight and covered in calamine lotion, Cherie listened as she stared at the ceiling. She heard a dog bark and another one answer it, a train slowly chugging along on the other side of Tchoupitoulas Street along the river, some shrieking birds, and a couple arguing. She sat up and retrieved her Wordless Diary from where it was hidden.

On a fresh page, she fashioned her numbers and kissed them goodnight. The first was a tall, thin, snow-capped mountain. The second became a cloud wrapped around the mountain. Next was a stairway, the last was a shooting star with an arching tail and flying bats underneath. 1-7-4-2. That's how many days she had left to go.

CHAPTER 6

Estelle and the Prince of Broadway

THE PARADE on Canal Street to benefit the Tuberculosis Foundation was small but mighty. It had four marching bands, a decorated truck from the Mardi Gras club called the Krewe of Thoth, and Shriners riding their motor scooters.

The Shriners brought comfort to the people of New Orleans, and folks were always glad to see them. They helped children from struggling families who were injured or hospitalized with rare diseases. They also owned the colorful Shriner Auditorium called the Jerusalem Temple on St. Charles Avenue. Even though some of the Shriners were old and overweight, they drove their motor scooters in full formation as they wove back and forth and around each other. It was an amazing sight. Nobody crashed into a fellow Shriner or into the crowd.

From the sidewalk, Cherie studied their romantic regalia with fascination. They wore gold pants with red stripes down the sides, green cummerbunds, and red jackets over white shirts and white gloves. They also wore ties in the same light green color and, best of all, tall red fezzes with the Shriner symbol.

Cherie anxiously looked for the car that would carry Estelle. Her very own friend was the Tuberculosis Foundation honoree.

As the Furies had wickedly conspired, both of Estelle's parents were stricken with tuberculosis. It was a heartbreaking thing. Estelle's mother and father lived in their beds in the family's shotgun-style house along with Estelle and her two older brothers, two little sisters, and a baby brother. The family survived just barely on Louisiana welfare and one of President Johnson's new programs called Subsidized School Lunches. Welfare. It was a word rarely spoken and only in hushed tones and once said, not repeated, like *jail* or *cancer*.

Estelle's father had worked in the Gulf with the oil companies doing oil rig architecture. He caught TB from a work crew and gave it to Estelle's mother. The children were all healthy, though. It was a problem in port cities like New Orleans, diseases that didn't show up in other places.

Epidemics flared up now and then — sleeping sickness, polio, TB, malaria — and keeping everybody safe or vaccinated wasn't easy. Many locals hated vaccines; they thought they were communist plots, and the city didn't have the money to vaccinate everybody anyway. Instead, the mosquito trucks would go around at night and spray pesticide when it got really bad.

The brunt of keeping the family glued had fallen squarely on little Estelle. Extended family helped. Her aunt would take her food shopping every week, but nobody lived with them.

Day after day, as Estelle's pretty mama and handsome daddy lay in their beds praying for mercy, Estelle saw to laundry, grocery shopping, meals, and the little ones. Sometimes, she would hit them and then feel bad about it. Her older brothers helped by taking care of themselves and lending a hand.

Estelle especially enjoyed a routine with her oldest brother when they did the dishes. They'd sing the Righteous Brothers'

"You've Lost that Lovin' Feeling." At the end, Estelle would sing the bass, and her brother would do the falsetto.

"Ba-hey-by," Estelle would sing in a low voice.

"Baby!" He would sing back in a squeaky high pitch.

When he got to *"I need your love,"* he'd screech it until Estelle was in hysterics.

Estelle and her siblings were off-beat, fitting for blood relations of the famed French impressionist painter Edgar Degas.

Degas' mother was a New Orleans girl, and a large part of the family lived in New Orleans. Estelle was named after her great grandmother Estelle Angelina, Degas' most fancied cousin. Edgar Degas had done famous paintings of Estelle Angelina and New Orleans. He loved visiting his mama's hometown. The most notable was "Portrait of a New Orleans Cotton Exchange," which hung in France. France coveted this masterwork and wouldn't lend it to New Orleans even for a limited exhibit. The Cabildo Museum in the French Quarter, just blocks from Degas' ancestral family home on Esplanade Avenue, did not have even one of his paintings.

Estelle's best friends were Cherie, Marlene, and Katherine. They loved her. Once, they went to the movies and fought over who got to sit next to her. Her favorite flavor from Plum Street SnoBalls was black currant. Plum Street had 100 flavors, and they made their snow balls with real fluffy snow, not chunky, crushed ice like the rest of the country. Donovan was her rock idol. His music and his voice soothed her.

The drums got closer, then the music. A group of majorettes held banners announcing the Tuberculosis Foundation, followed by clowns that handed out candy.

Treats and tokens were a parade requirement in the Crescent

City. No organization would dare put on a parade without them. If they did, the crowd would turn on them and start booing. They'd yell, "Stingy! Go home."

The Krewe of Comus, which always paraded on Mardi Gras night before it met the Krewe of Rex for the grandest Mardi Gras ball of the season, had a reputation for being stingy. People would turn out for Comus just to yell at them.

Iris, the ladies' krewe; Zulu, the black krewe; and Thoth and Rex were known for putting on the most generous parades. A hand-painted gold coconut from Zulu was a coveted prize. The Zulu parade set out early on Mardi Gras Day. When folks heard the Zulu drums as early as eight a.m., they threw on their clothes and ran like crazy for the parade, yelling for a Zulu coconut.

More music sparkled down Canal. Two of the bands were from local high schools, and another was Pete Fountain's Half-Fast Walking Club, which played on the flatbed of a truck, so on that day, they weren't half-fast walking at all.

The other marching band was a rhythm section made up of triangles and wooden sticks. Cherie recognized them from Mardi Gras, and she loved their costumes. They wore black musketeer hats with white feathers, white, puffy shirts, and black pants with high boots. To Cherie, they looked like sassy Jean Lafitte pirates.

The caravan of convertibles in all different colors appeared. Cherie's heart leaped because Estelle was riding in one of those convertibles.

Cherie had never seen Estelle so dressed up, not even for Christmas. Estelle wore a long-sleeved, dark red dress with white lace at the cuffs and collar and a black velvet belt. Her long hair was half tied up in the back with a black velvet bow. She never wore it that way. And she had lipstick on. Cherie was shocked. Estelle hated make-up, ribbons, and bows.

Cherie ran up to the side of the car and trotted alongside.

"You look amazing. Who did your hair?"

"Tell you later."

"Did you meet him?"

Estelle nodded and looked away.

A lady in the front seat irritably shooed Cherie away so Estelle could resume her duties of properly waving to the crowd.

"Call me when you get home!" Cherie watched happily as the red Cadillac convertible with VIP Estelle trolled away. She watched her best friend wave at the applauding bystanders. *Wow*, Cherie thought, *she's so shy*. An older couple blew kisses to her, and Estelle blew a kiss back to them. *Katherine and Marlene should have been here to see this.*

Cherie couldn't wait to hear all about it, the luncheon, the award ceremony, the speeches, and best of all, almost as good as being in the parade, Estelle would get to meet a Broadway star. He flew down from New York to help raise money for TB research. His name was Bertie Murphy, and he was dubbed the new Prince of Broadway. Cherie knew about him because he was on all the night-time TV shows singing a song from his show.

It was dark when Cherie zoomed into Estelle's driveway on her bicycle and yelled through the screen door. Paulette told Cherie never to go to Estelle's house because of the TB. Cherie said she was off to Marlene's and went to Estelle's instead.

Estelle came out dressed in jeans, her hair loose, and all the make-up washed off. They sat on the front stairs and spoke in hushed tones.

"Oh, Cherie," Estelle slumped over as she exhaled.

"I'm going to sit here and completely shut up." She mimed zipped lips.

Estelle sighed deeply.

"Okay," Estelle began, "You saw the parade. Then, after that, we had the luncheon in the ballroom at the Royal Orleans Hotel."

"Is it beautiful?" Cherie interrupted.

"Wait, I'm getting to that." Estelle knew how to get Cherie to not interrupt.

"It's so beautiful," she continued. "But first, the Foundation man who was the King of Endymion last Mardi Gras welcomed everybody. They served us lunch. It wasn't a buffet. And the place was filled up."

"Oh wow, what did they serve?"

"Brunch stuff. Grillades with baked cheese grits and rolls, tomatoes, and lettuce on the side. Then we had little éclairs for dessert with coffee. Each one had a treble clef drawn on it in icing."

"Vanilla or chocolate?"

"Mocha."

"Mocha! I've never seen one like that."

"After lunch, I was introduced, and they said stuff and gave me a prize basket, but I didn't have to talk in the microphone."

"That was lucky," Cherie piped in.

"Yeah. I could never do that. I got like a citation in a frame for community service, even though it's just my family, a bath powder and hairbrush from K&B, a box of candy, and a gift certificate for $25.00 to Maison Blanche."

"That's a lot!"

"And then Mr. Murphy did his speech that TB could be like polio, that it wasn't impossible to find a cure, you know, so people would give money. He talks really fast and just gave his speech. He didn't even read anything."

"So you met him?" Estelle nodded yes and stared straight ahead.

"Is he as funny-looking in person as on TV?"

"I don't know. Looks the same as on TV. I met him the day

before at the hotel. He asked me to go with him to buy gifts for his family, and today, he sat next to me at lunch," she said blankly. "Everyone fussed over him. Oh, he's so cute," she imitated in a high, hussy whisper.

"Did he like the food?"

Estelle shrugged. "People kept talking to him, so he mostly pushed it around his plate."

"They should have let him eat," Cherie agreed. It was inhospitable for a New Orleans crowd not to let someone enjoy their meal, especially a guest from out of town.

Estelle continued. "When people lined up to thank him, he put his hands on my shoulders and said, No, don't thank me. I don't deserve any honors here. This young lady gets the entire honor."

"That's so nice."

"Then it was over, and I came home." Cherie saw Estelle's eyes glisten with tears and then fall down her face in a torrent. She moved closer to Estelle and took her hand. She felt scared.

"What's wrong?" she whispered.

"It was so great until... I hate it. And most of all that dancing pervert. He ruined everything for me."

Cherie gasped. She knew what was coming.

Murphy was a creep. After buying jewelry for his wife and kids, he coaxed Estelle to his hotel room with the promise of a necklace. He pushed her to sleep with him. He drooled, "Come on, tonight's the night. This is your chance, sweetheart. Your big chance." She bitterly told Cherie, "He was so surprised when I didn't want to, doop-dee-doo, as though being famous was a big gift."

Cherie stared straight ahead.

"Did you tell anybody?"

"Are you crazy? No, I can't. It means a lot to my family. Mama is so proud of me." She sighed deeply. "Maybe I will. But there's nothing she can do. I don't want my brothers to know."

"Pervy Bertie," Cherie rhymed.

"Pervy Bertie," Estelle repeated.

Cherie wanted to tell Estelle what had happened to her, but no words came out. They sat there silently. Then, "Let's go kill him right now!" Cherie spat through her teeth. "Make him pay for ruining everything. We can go to his hotel room like we want to go to bed with him, and we'll get him to drink a lot. I can sneak in some of my mother's sleeping pills, and then we can smother him with the pillow! They'll think he OD'ed."

Estelle smirked, "You're so bad. I wish, but he's gone. Flew out already."

Cherie let go of her friend. "See you tomorrow."

"Don't tell anyone! Not even Marlene or Katherine."

"I won't. Cross my heart." Cherie outlined the x over her heart as she said it because she meant it.

Cherie sped home on her bike in the dark. She was angry for Estelle and angry that her own dream of Estelle's magic day had been shattered.

Estelle went to bed early. As she lay in bed, her sisters asleep across the room, she clasped her hands in prayer even though she wasn't in church. She knew it wasn't a very Catholic thing to do, but she didn't care. She mouthed the words with barely a sound.

"Mother Mary, Queen of Heaven, please wash away these dirty feelings that I have on me. Please make Mama and Daddy well again. I promise I'll be good. *Benedicta excelsa Mater Christi, Maria sanctissima. Amen.*" She repeated her prayer for good measure.

Estelle punched her old, squished pillow. On the turntable

next to her bed, she played her favorite album on low and softly sang along, *"Ah, but I may as well try to catch the wind."*

Near midnight, unable to sleep, Cherie tossed with agitation. She got up and silently tip-toed to the kitchen, slipped a sharp knife out from the drawer, and returned to her room. Frenzied, Cherie stabbed and stabbed her pillow. Again and again, she stabbed it. She killed the slab of beef from Texas and shredded that New York celebrity rat until she was spent.

Moonbeams peeked through the windows. Cherie regarded the foam rubber mess strewed about from her pillow-letting. She figured out how she could get rid of it without Paulette seeing.

Cherie ferreted out her Wordless Diary, and she drew her numbers: 1–7–0–0. The one was a forked devil's tongue, the seven jagged teeth, and the zeros were crazy eyeballs.

As Cherie fell to sleep, she sensed briefly, for a moment, a slight movement from beneath the bed. She fretted that her tantrum may have disturbed the Monsters in the Floorboards. Would they punish her, invade her dreams until she woke from the nightmare hot and shaking? She whispered aloud to them, just in case, "Leave me alone."

It was three a.m. The reliable comfort of Missy Ruby Dawn's appearance was close at hand. It would be another beautiful day. She could ride her bike to Audubon Park and meet her friends at the lagoon. They could go visit the seals. At the end of the week, there was a party.

CHAPTER 7

The Swirly Dark

DEVIN LOOKED EVERYWHERE for their ride home, even in the far corner of the backyard, but he was nowhere to be found. He had dumped them at the party. He took off with a girl, and now Cherie and Devin were stranded. "Dammit!" he repeated five times.

They weren't stranded where they could jump on the streetcar or the Magazine Street bus. It was no man's land, one of the new suburbs northwest of New Orleans. There were no streetlamps or stores or restaurants around, just stretches of avenues within a housing development.

It was where the Crescent City mixed up with the other Louisiana. It produced an awkward blend between Cajun and Creole. "Good Lord in Heaven," Creole chefs fretted from Carrolton to Bywater; the Cajuns charred, fried, and peppered everything up so much you couldn't taste it. Then, they ate it accompanied by accordion music, not brass. *How the hell am I going to blend that into a proper Jazz Brunch?*

"I can't find him," Cherie reported.

"Me neither," Devin took a last sip and threw down his beer

bottle. *That pisses me off,* he thought. Devin was frustrated. At 14, two forever years short of a driver's permit, he had asked his brother's smiling, mad boy of a friend to drive them.

It had been, by teen standards, a great party worth the hassle to get there. Lots of kids, beer, soda, smoke, food, and a nice, dark make-out room. Maybe one parent somewhere. Perfect for late winter days after Mardi Gras.

Devin had found some guitars, all he needed to enjoy himself. Playing guitar was still touchy; he had broken his clavicle not eight weeks earlier when he hit a pothole and flew off his bike. He couldn't believe it. The other shocker was how painful it was to break bones and rip muscles. He tried to describe it to his friends, "Until you've broken something, you can't know."

He gave Cherie a determined nod, "Wait here. I'll find us a ride."

A few minutes later, Cherie watched him walk up with Anna Daniels, a pretty girl from school, and her date. Her parents were already waiting out front in their light blue Chevy with a beige interior. Anna was cheerful, happy to give them a lift back into town.

The four kids crawled into the back seat. Mrs. Daniels was driving, "Thanks for the lift, Mrs. Daniels," Devin said.

"Yes. Thank you, Mrs. Daniels," Cherie mimicked.

In short order, Anna pressed her folks for the traditional post-teen-party ride to Cafe Du Monde for coffee and beignets, but no sale. She whispered to the group, "We'll see."

Anna coughed, "It got cold out. I can feel it in my lungs. I need something hot to drink."

"Sorry, darling. The Quarter's too far," Anna's father responded.

"No, it's not," Anna tried again. "We can go down Airline Highway, and once we're in town, we can be there in 10 minutes.

It's closer than going home. It's on the way, in fact." It was not, but you'd never know that listening to Anna's persuasive tone.

"Don't insist," her father said quietly, "Mommy is very tired."

"Are you tired, Mommy?" Anna leaned in toward the driver's seat. "Then how about you drive us straight home, and Daddy will take us downtown. That will work, won't it?"

The parents stared straight ahead without answering.

She slunk back onto the seat and folded her arms in a huff. The whole car was quiet.

As they traversed the empty area, a frosty fog settled in. Cherie leaned forward from her seat and stared into it.

The headlights lit the mist as they crawled along. Tripping spirits. Cherie thought it looked beautiful. The spirits danced, raised from their graves into the fog. She could practically hear their macabre music.

Cherie saw Devin staring out the window, too, from his seat behind Mrs. Daniels. His face was pressed against the glass.

"It's so weird out," Cherie smiled, "The swirly dark."

"Yeah, it's the swirly dark," Devin muttered, mesmerized.

Anna's mother pulled up to a wide intersection. The lights cut shortly into the fog. It was empty in every direction. She waited at the stop sign, and then, very slowly, she inched the car into the intersection.

"Watch it!" Devin yelled. From the left, there was an explosion of white light and *ccrraasshh*, the car spun round and round. Its wheels and chassis screamed a loud crunching howl of metal and screeching tires. Devin heard his shoulder bone crack again, the sound ripping clear into his skull.

It stopped. All was pitch. Devin couldn't see anything. He wondered if he was blind or dead. His brain worked, but he couldn't move. *Am I dead?* Slowly, his night vision set it. He tried lifting his arm and moaned. The bone that had barely healed tore at his insides. He struggled to breathe. He gasped, "I'm alive."

One by one, they began to rouse. Daddy Daniels had been thrown into the windshield and was a horrific sight; thick streaks of blood ran down his face. Anna Daniels had been tossed into the front seats and was banged up but unbroken. Upon impact, Cherie managed to ball up between the back and front seats, braced and shielded. She was up within seconds.

As Devin crawled out of the car, he yelped in pain. The air smelled of burnt rubber. He sat on the curb, teeth clenched. His breath trolled through his teeth with rasping sounds. Anna's date sat quietly in the back seat, staring ahead.

Anna Daniels's mother was gravely injured, her very life in question. She had taken the brunt of the crash, and her insides were demolished. She sat sideways in the driver's seat, not moving or talking. Her eyes were glazed.

Anna Daniels fell to the ground and started to sob. Mr. Daniels tried to comfort her, mitigating his injuries — "It's nothing, it's just a scratch" — but it was hopeless. She couldn't stop sobbing, "Why did this happen to us?"

Cherie looked around, her night vision piqued, curious to know what had hit them. She ran across the intersection. It was a pickup truck, totaled. The driver was a young man. He was motionless on the pavement about fifteen feet from the truck in a large puddle of blood, strewed with broken beer bottles. Cherie saw a car approach and ran back.

A station wagon driven by a woman with her son's band in tow pulled up, thrusting the entire harsh scene into the beams of their headlights. The woman and three teenage boys in performance clothes filed out of the wagon with jaw-dropped horror.

"Get the first-aid kit! It's in the back," she ordered sharply. Once delivered into her capable hands, she wrapped up Mr. Daniels's head like a nurse.

She drove off to find a phone, leaving the boys. One of her

boys asked Cherie what happened, and when she tried to talk, she started to shake. He put his arms around her and held her tightly. She leaned into him with only one thought, *Tighter.*

A slew of savior black and white police cars, a fire truck, and two ambulances showed up. By then, gawkers were circling. The band boy gave Cherie a tight hug, kissed her, and disappeared. *Don't go,* she thought.

When they moved Mrs. Daniels onto a stretcher, she uttered her first noise since the crash. It was a pitiful wail that froze the crowd in their tracks. "Poor thing. Oh Lord have mercy, poor thing," was heard across the mist. Mr. Daniels accompanied his wife in the ambulance, and, at Anna's insistence, they allowed her in as well.

Behind their ambulance was another ambulance with the drunk driver in it.

"Look," Cherie alerted Devin, "He's not under a sheet. He's alive."

Devin held his body as though letting go would cause him to disintegrate. He was helped into a police car, followed by Cherie and Anna's date.

They were treated to a thrill ride back to New Orleans, far away from the weird new suburb and its deathly fog. They vroomed full throttle, red light flashing and sirens screaming. Cars and trucks pulled aside.

"I feel bad saying it, but this is really cool," Cherie whispered. The boys nodded yes.

They arrived at Touro Hospital and called their parents. Cherie knew Paulette was at a divorced professor's house for a party but couldn't remember his last name. Marlene, Katherine, and Cherie nicknamed him Profugly, a shortened version of Professor Ugly. She called Marlene to get his number since he taught at Tulane.

"I'm sorry I'm calling so late."

"That's okay. Katherine's here, and we're still up. What's the matter?"

Cherie told her. Marlene woke up her father, and he found the number. She gave it to Cherie and added,

"If you can't reach her, Daddy said we'll come and get you." It made Cherie want to cry. Cherie called Profugly's house. When the phone was handed to Paulette, before Cherie could explain, she said, "What now, already?"

Cherie and Devin sat in the Emergency Room hallway next to the treatment rooms. Beyond a closed door, they bristled, hearing Mrs. Daniels cry out in pain. , "No. Please stop."

Anna's extended family arrived to comfort them through the terrible night. Devin's mom walked in.

Cherie wished Paulette would show up. *Why is it taking so long? She's always late.*

In the turmoil, Cherie restlessly followed Devin and his mother to a treatment room at the end of the hallway. She sat across the hall.

She thanked her lucky stars it wasn't her. Cherie remembered the afternoon she swam into the barnacled seawall at Lake Ponchartrain. Her shin wouldn't stop bleeding, and the ER nurse dug out bits of shell in her leg with a metal instrument. It was painful, and it left scars. Whatever they would do to Devin, it was going to be terrible.

Devin spat out every curse word he could muster, "Shit, damn, piss, hell," until a nurse snapped at him, "We don't need to hear any of that, young man."

Cherie was indignant. *What a stupid nurse. Isn't that what swearing is for? To help you out when you're scared and really mad?*

The light in Devin's treatment room was dim. The doctor moved him from the exam table to a chair. Calmly, he began to play around with Devin's right arm.

Devin finally protested, "I told you, it's my left side."

Nevertheless, the doctor continued to joke with him. He gently encouraged Devin to put his arms out straight in front of him, and then bam! He yanked both arms over Devin's head and snapped the bone back into place! In the hallway, Cherie heard the loud pop and jumped when Devin screamed.

The doctor walked out. The nurses proceeded to bandage him up. By now, Devin was howling, "Mom, get me the hell out of here! Get me out of this goddam place! Moooooom!"

Cherie saw Paulette down the hallway and ran to her. She looked so different from everybody else in the Emergency Room. She wore a light green rayon blouse, a black straight skirt, and heels. Her dark brown hair was offset by freshly applied red lipstick. She looked glamorous. Standing behind her was her date, Profugly.

"Here she is," Paulette cooed. They all kissed. "It's good you called me yourself. Otherwise, I would have had a heart attack." Cherie recognized the sing-song voice reserved for others. "Let's go," Paulette added. She hated hospitals.

"Did they send Mrs. Daniels to surgery?" Cherie asked.

"It's horrible," Paulette emphasized the first syllable. Cherie learned from Paulette that Mrs. Daniels' spleen was busted, her lung had collapsed, and almost all her ribs were broken. They took her upstairs to operate on her.

"She will be okay. Don't worry about it." Paulette quipped.

"But..."

"She will be okay!"

Profugly added kindly, "The doctors here are first-rate. They'll take good care of her, darling."

Why is he calling me darling? Cherie thought.

They walked out. "Do you think she looks like me?" Paulette asked him with a smile. "Look, we have the same legs."

Cherie made a face. Paulette gave her the *don't you dare embarrass me* look. *Practice what you preach,* Cherie thought.

When they got to their place, Cherie heard her mother say to Profugly, "Wait here for me. I just want to get her into bed."

When they reached the front door, Cherie blurted, "You're not going to stay?"

Paulette whispered, "You're all right?

"Yes. I'm okay."

"Then I need to do my own thing, you understand?" Paulette pointed her finger at her. Paulette planted a big, lipsticky smooch on her cheek, waved at the man in the car, and pushed Cherie inside, following her.

Paulette seized upon Cherie. "He's waiting, so I'll make this quick. Monday, you have to miss school and go to the doctor. You tell him your back hurts. You understand me?"

Cherie shook her head *no*. "I don't have to. It doesn't hurt. And I'm helping in art class on Monday! I said I would help." Bruises were beginning to form on her legs, but her back was fine. Cherie hated doctors. Going to one when you didn't have to was stupid.

Paulette's voice went up an octave, her speech rapid-fire. "No! You're going on Monday and do like I said. What do you care? So he'll look at your back and give you some pills."

Cherie pleaded with Paulette, "No, I don't need to. I'm okay."

"He'll give you some pills! That's all. You have to go for insurance.

"Insurance? You mean car insurance?" Cherie asked.

Paulette looked over her shoulder, panicky. There were tears in her eyes. "He's waiting for me. I don't have time for this..."

"I don't want to do that." Cherie spat through her teeth.

"It's time you help around here!"

"Not like that!"

Paulette slapped her across the face and ran out. Cherie fell to the floor. She heard her mother apologize with a giggle and the car speeding away.

The heavy weight of the night bore down on her. Her tears burned her skin where she had been hit. She retreated to her room, acutely aware that her mother was desperate for money from the accident.

There was never any money for anything. They survived paltry paycheck to paycheck. Still, Cherie hated that getting through the crash unhurt wasn't good enough for her mother, that breaking a bone or two or ten would have been better for Paulette. *But I'm babysitting now,* Cherie reassured herself. *I can pay for all my own stuff myself. I can help that way.*

In the bathroom, she inspected the line of blood that ringed her nose. She stuck some tissue in it and took out her Wordless Diary from the bottom of the closet.

She drew the one as a broken beer bottle, the six as a car, with smoke swirling above it for the two, and the three as a cat, claws sticking out from its paws. She liked cats. She wished she had one.

Cherie knew what was coming. The Monsters in the Floorboards would rise up and attack Cherie in her sleep. Slither all over her. Poison her. Wrap around her throat. They would get her because she upset Paulette.

She stared at her Wordless Diary. 1-6-2-3. It felt like a million days to Cherie. She fretted, *What if I can't last this long? What if?*

Across town, Devin and his mother exited the St. Charles streetcar to walk home in the middle of the night. Every step hurt. His mother gave him the pill from the hospital, which he later described at school as voodoo.

Devin fell asleep and dreamt about a girl at school. She was half-Dutch Jewish and half-Mexican Catholic. She had large blue eyes and black hair and was beautiful. Her name was Adela.

In his dream, the misty spirits danced swirly to their jangly music. Adela appeared and beckoned Devin to dance with her. He put his arms around her. They danced slowly, and he kissed her, his tongue in her mouth. She kissed him back and hugged him. They spun around. It was so good. The music got louder and louder in his dream until there was a gigantic *screeeech* ... He woke up sweaty and in torturous pain. He crossed his good arm over his body to clutch back the good part of the dream.

Weeks later, Cherie ran into Devin and Garrett at school, away from everybody. Devin's arm was still in a sling, and his body was still bandaged.

"How's your back?" Garrett asked her. "Katherine said you had to go to the doctor."

"I'm fine." Cherie shrugged.

"It's so weird," Devin told her, "I'm nervous with cars now."

"Me, too." Cherie lowered her voice, "You know what?"

The boys stepped in closer.

"I keep thinking this evil thought," she confessed, "that Mrs. Daniels was a lousy driver, crawling into the intersection like she did. If she had gunned it like everyone else, the drunk pickup would have missed us. *We would have been out of the way!* Then I feel sad and guilty because she almost died and still might die, but another quarter-second, and Devin, it would have been you. You'd be even more broken up or dead. You were sitting right behind her!"

Devin shifted on his feet like a colt. "Yeah, no shit. I think about that, too." They stood silently as they contemplated the split second upon which his life had hinged.

Garrett snapped them out of their reverie. "Cherie, c'mon. He's alive. C'mon, y'all. You're alive. You're standing right here. It's what happened, and we can't let it drag us down."

"Yeah," Devin exhaled, "I'm alive. Okay. We just go with it. Move on."

Cherie nodded. "Yeah. You're here. Move on. No getting

dragged down." Cherie and the boys repeated it, "Alive," seriously at first, and then burst out laughing. Katherine, Marlene, and Estelle walked up, "What's so funny? What's so funny?"

Grandfather Clock and his big old pendulum tick-tocked on. The end of the 1966 school year finally appeared past Sissy Springtime's profusion of blossoms. All over town, vases and jars were filled with hand-picked flowers, and bowls were filled with camellias.

Devin's shoulder healed well thanks to the excellent doctor at Touro Hospital. He was back to normal, except his personality had changed. His temper was more explosive.

"And there it is," Devin's mama sighed as she gazed at her youngest. "All these years, I prayed that none of you got your father's temper. But there it is."

It was the traditional end-of-the-school-year assembly at McMain Secondary. The orchestra played "Ode to Joy" and the theme to *Bonanza*. The entire auditorium roared when the football team trotted out in tutus and did the Can Can. The boys were followed by the girls' gymnastics team. The audience oohed with appreciation as they formed a four-level pyramid with a little, short girl on top. Anna Daniels sang a sad folk song, "500 Miles." In a mournful wail that belied her youth, she hit every note like a star, "Not a shirt on my back, not a penny to my name. Lord, I can't go back home this a-way..."

"She's still sad about the crash," Cherie remarked.

"No shit, Sherlock," Devin deadpanned.

The assembly burst into appreciative applause when Anna finished the song. The band followed with a fanfare for the academic awards.

Mrs. Skillet took the microphone to announce the Social

Studies prize. "Every year, I put a lot of thought into who should get the Social Studies prize," Mrs. Skillet paused for emphasis, then continued, "Sometimes it's not always the A-plus student. Sometimes, it's the student who tries hard to understand why our blessed USA is the most advanced country in the world."

Mrs. Skillet's serious expression suddenly cracked into a big gleeful smile, "Devin Clarens, come up and accept your prize!"

Chortles of good-natured surprise and applause rippled across the auditorium as though to say, *Wasn't Mrs. Skillet wonderful?*

Still bruised from the lengthy whipping he had endured because of his *Das Kapital* book report, Devin ambled down the aisle and politely accepted it with an unhappy expression. Mrs. Skillet grinned at Devin with love as he received his certificate written in calligraphy and a pen in a box. Then, Mrs. Skillet planted a kiss on his cheek. Devin visibly cringed.

Cherie and her friends in the back row watched the proceedings in horror. They knew it was because Devin's father stepped in.

"Yuck!" Cherie spit through her teeth.

"More like vomit yuck," Marlene added.

"If I were him, I'd spit in her face," Katherine said.

Somebody let loose a loud one, followed by a burst of laughter.

"Cute! And I second that opinion," Garrett smirked.

When Devin returned to his seat, he writhed and dramatically rubbed Mrs. Skillet's kiss off his face as though it was poison.

"Here, use this," Marlene handed him a handkerchief. Devin spat on it and rubbed his face more.

"What a gross-out bitch," Cherie commented.

"Stop saying *bitch*," Estelle admonished, "I hate that word!" Feeling his eyes bore into them, Estelle looked over her shoulder to see one of the teachers, Mr. Verett, standing by the exit. He was very handsome, medium height, with black hair and brown eyes. He stood with his arms folded across his chest, expressionless.

Estelle nudged Cherie.

"What?"

"Mr. Verett. Right over there," she whispered, "Don't look."

"Is he going to yell at us for talking?"

"No. He's cool. He was my brother's favorite teacher."

"Can I look now?"

"Do it fast." Cherie glanced at him playfully. Both girls covered their mouths to repress their giggles.

Mr. Verett had heard tales waft through the smoke in the teacher's lounge about this foul-mouthed, insubordinate group of students and their immature, ignorant politics. He heard them say what obnoxious kids they were, the offspring of strays from broken homes and immigrants. A few of them were from good, old New Orleans families like Estelle, who were unduly influenced by the others. "What is the world coming to?" he heard them say.

Mr. Verett knew he was getting the whole bratty bunch for ninth-grade Advanced Civics. For the first time in a long time, he looked forward to September.

CHAPTER 8

Hatpin. August. 1966

IT WAS the last week of summer before school started, the last days to ride your bike to Audubon Park and hang around with friends, climb the low-hanging limbs of live oak trees, play with Spanish moss, watch the white herons return to their nests, read books, take naps, look at clouds, share a snack, and get popsicles from the snack stand.

Cherie could not have been more surprised when Katherine and Marlene showed up at the lagoon with their ears pierced.

When Cherie heard that Kaleb, Katherine's older brother, had pierced them, her interest went from fancy to obsession. Cherie grabbed at Katherine and begged.

"Ohhhhh, I want it done. Please, will he do mine, too? Please ask him."

"Okay. Okay," Katherine went along. They found a pay phone at the entrance of the Audubon Zoo, and Katherine worked it out. Cherie felt weak in the knees. The most beautiful boy she had ever seen would pierce her ears. Cherie memorized the instructions. *Katherine's house tomorrow afternoon. Bring gold posts or loops.*

"But I don't have any gold posts."

"I do," Katherine told her. "I have a pair I can give you." Katherine flicked her long, dangling earrings, I'm not using the posts anymore."

Katherine's mother was named Giselle. It was pronounced with a hard Teutonic **G** like in *goose*, not a soft one like in *genie*.

Mama Giselle was insular and misanthropic, a good-looking, demanding woman who studied architecture and art history. She gathered up piles of New Orleans' distinct stained and beveled window glass. No one knew why, and no one questioned it. She worked on projects at Tulane, translating historic New Orleans documents from French into English.

Like so many other war-bitten girls from around the world, Giselle nabbed an American GI right after WWII, and like ninety-nine percent of those marriages, it ended in divorce. Giselle met Katherine's father in a hospital in Brussels. He was serving as an orderly in the psychiatric ward, where she was a patient suffering from too much misery. Thus, he rescued her.

For European girls grieving the loss of boyfriends, brothers, and fathers, nothing harkened hope in war's aftermath like a handsome American GI with chocolate and cigarettes in one hand and a ticket to the glorious USA in the other. That was until the war brides arrived and discovered the streets were not paved in gold and a post-war recession was going on. *What the hell?* they thought.

Anybody looking in from the outside might assume that the mamas Paulette and Giselle were best friends just like their own Cherie and Katherine, but that assumption would be very wrong. Paulette and Giselle detested each other. It was a monumental clash from the minute they laid eyes on each other.

Giselle believed that Paulette spread lies about her, like how Katherine's little sister was the product of Giselle's affair with her lover and not Katherine and Kaleb's father. Paulette thought

Giselle flirted with her date at a party and henceforth used every opportunity to trash her. Giselle thought Paulette intellectually inferior, a simple secretary, whereas she, Giselle, had an art history degree and worked *with* professors, not *for* them. Giselle sneered in disgust when she saw Paulette.

By association, Giselle hated the sight of Cherie even though she was innocent. Once, Cherie heard her scream, "I don't want that girl here!"

"I'm sorry," Katherine said sadly, "but she hates your mother, not you."

Whenever Cherie argued with Paulette, her mother would assail her sarcastically, "Oh you poor thing, you are so mistreated. Be glad you don't have Giselle for your mother!"

Cherie pictured Katherine at home as Cinderella without the cheerful whistle and helpful mice. Katherine jumped when her mother yelled for her, "Where are you? Come here!" She'd make Giselle breakfast and coffee, do her laundry, iron her clothes, and find her keys. If something wasn't done right, and even if it was, Giselle would throw things and scream at her, "Get out!"

Katherine sometimes spent the night in the old family car in the driveway if she vexed Mama Giselle, even when she was as little as nine years old. Her brother Kaleb, a year older, would sneak out and bring her a blanket. Even though their father lived nearby, they knew not to call him, and he wouldn't have interfered anyway. They were all afraid of each other.

It's how Katherine got so close to Marlene, who lived down the street. Marlene's front door was always open for Katherine. The whole family welcomed Katherine as if they knew the truth. Marlene's parents, Dr. and Dr. Becker, taught anthropology at Tulane. They had lived in exotic places like the South Pacific to do their research. They were nationally famous in academia for one study in which they analyzed the social structure of a small

American town as objectively as if they were studying a tribe in a faraway place.

There was a lot of magic in the Becker home. Marlene and her older sister created nicknames for almost everybody. They nicknamed Katherine's mama *Gizzard*. The Becker refrigerator always had food in it, including pitchers of cold-drip coffee. This was much to the delight of their ever-hungry friends. The Becker home, modern in style, was piled with books and music. After raiding the fridge, the teens would often flop on the couch and leaf through the coffee table books. Katherine found sanctuary *chez* Marlene.

Being Katherine's best friend was one of Marlene's many roles in life, which she took very seriously. This included good daughter, great student, ballerina, and little sister. Little sister was tricky because Marlene's big sister was confident and creative. Marlene was equally gifted, but she didn't seem to know it. It was the one bit of knowledge she couldn't look up in a book. It eluded her, which sometimes caused a nagging self-doubt.

Together, Katherine and Marlene could be wicked. They concocted streams of deadpan commentary as they made fun of people, punctuated by facial expressions and gestures that put Cherie and Estelle in stitches every time they were together. Katherine, in particular, could mimic people with detailed perfection, contorting her pretty face and delicate fingers to grand effect.

Katherine, Marlene, and Cherie got off the Freret Street bus. Before leaving them, Marlene reassured Cherie, "It only hurts a little. You'll like it once it's over with."

They walked to Katherine's house, an uptown duplex near Tulane University. The girls entered through the back door, snuck past the kitchen, and slowly tip-toed up the creaking wooden stairs, careful not to knock over the scores of beveled glass panes that lined them. At the top of the stairs, Katherine gestured *shh* and pointed to the bedroom where Mama Giselle napped with the door open.

A noisy fan was whirring, which eased their nerves. They continued up another flight of stairs to the attic door. Katherine opened it. They filed in. She carefully shut the door, afraid of any telltale noise. Cherie knew there was no turning back. That would be wimpy.

Across the room stood 16-year-old Kaleb.

He hovered over all the accoutrements laid out on a dusty little table: some ice in a bowl, alcohol, matches, a sliced potato, a washcloth, and a long hatpin with an elaborate amber ornament. In the afternoon shadows under the harsh angles of the roof boards, he laid them out as ceremoniously as a surgeon. When he looked up, his mischievous almond-shaped green eyes caught a ray of light, and Cherie went weak in the knees.

Kaleb was tall and slim with perfect skin and features, his mother's sensuous mouth, and longish, light brown hair. Katherine adored her brother. They had been through a lot together. He looked at Cherie unsmilingly and said, "Okay, are you ready?"

Cherie was ready because getting her ears pierced meant that for ten minutes, maybe longer if she dawdled, she could be in the same room as Kaleb. Her stomach churned, and her heart beat like a bongo.

"Now don't play with them," Kaleb said, "Turn the earrings around in the hole in the morning and at night and dab them with alcohol. Don't mess with them, or they'll get infected."

Cherie nodded yes as she gazed at Kaleb, barely hearing a word. Protective of her brother, Katherine piped in, "And be quiet. He can't do it if you make noise."

Cherie held ice cubes to her ears. She sat straight and still, determined not to squeal. After a few minutes, Kaleb walked over and pinched her ear lobe, "Can you feel that?" he asked. Cherie smiled and nodded *no*. Kaleb smiled back at her. *Pain? What pain?* she thought.

He leaned in inches from her, studying one ear and then the other. He was so close. He placed his palm on her face as he dotted the spot with a pen. He waved the hatpin through a lit match to sterilize it and then dipped it in alcohol. As Cherie held a slice of potato behind her ear with one hand, she heard the hatpin push and pop through her flesh.

"Okay," he exhaled, "Now I have to put in the earring."

A deep breath, some laughter. The other ear. His hand on her face, the closeness. The rite. The sheer thrill of getting her ears pierced and not by some nurse, but this way, in a moody New Orleans attic at day's dying light, not by just any boy, but this one.

Katherine gave her a hand mirror so Cherie could see. She squealed soft voice, "Eeeeyah!" Two gold balls sparkled in her blood-tinged earlobes.

Paulette didn't notice Cherie's new earrings for a week, then suddenly, "Where did you get those earrings?" The pierced part went unmentioned.

"Katherine gave them to me," Cherie defended. She left the kitchen, Paulette's pumped voice trailing after her, "What is she doing giving you earrings?"

Cherie yelled back, "She didn't want them."

Cherie studied her reflection in her bedroom mirror. With her waist-long dark hair and hazel eyes, Cherie thought the look was perfect. She loved it. With a little more babysitting money, she'd buy silver hoops. She decided that silver would look better on her than gold.

Best of all, when her newly pierced ears were admired, Cherie threw back her head with bravado and said, "Oh yeah, it was Kaleb, you know, Katherine's brother? He did it with a hatpin. It was long and had a big amber jewel at the end."

If the other girl shuddered, Cherie would add with a

mischievous smile, "The only hard part was hearing my skin pop when he pushed it through."

Cherie never saw Kaleb after that. He was mysterious as if he had disappeared. Cherie heard things through the grapevine: who he kissed, who he petted, who he pranked, who he fought. Kaleb gossip reverberated at parties and pools in whispers like an underground radio show. She wished she was one of those girls so much, it hurt.

Nonetheless, she could proudly claim her own tender branch of the gossip, "Did you see Cherie? Kaleb pierced her ears in the attic."

In her Wordless Diary, she drew the one as a hatpin with drops of blood dripping off the end of it. The four and six were flowers with curvy stems, and the three a pair of lips.

CHAPTER 9

Advanced Civics

Ninth Grade Advanced Civics was the last class of the day. By then, Mr. Afternoon Sun was stretched out a little past his zenith, his golden coils penetrating rooftops for the rest of the day. In summer, afternoon storms washed down the streets and cooled his ardor. Still, by the time school started, he just hung around rich and dominant until Halloween's witches flew in on Northern breezes.

Unlike most of the United States, New Orleans knew mid-afternoon was time for a rest. Most restaurants and shops closed for a few hours, and banks closed by two p.m. Nobody ever kicked a door if it was closed in the afternoon. Afternoon rest time was respected.

Still, the school day lasted forever, all the way to three p.m. There was nothing to do last class except get through it. Heads plopped onto their desks last class were less disturbed by teachers than in the morning. If anything, a dozing boy was a great form of distraction. His friends would draw on his lips with pens or spread his drool onto his face and hair.

Cherie, Estelle, Marlene, and Katherine strolled into Mr.

Verett's class. Garrett and Devin followed them in, laughing and goofy. They took the last two seats in the back.

Cherie and her friends sat up front, ready for class discussion.

Earlier that day, at lunch, the four girls talked about him. They had heard said he was a political radical.

"His first name is Rudolph," Cherie said.

"That's a Russian name," Marlene added, "Like Rudolph Nureyev." Marlene knew all the famous ballet dancers of the world. She took ballet once a week, and sometimes Cherie took ballet with her. They loved it.

Katherine's eyes lit up, "Maybe he's a spy!"

"Yeah, he's a spy," they enthused.

Katherine was on to something, "I bet he's a Commie spy sent to infiltrate an American school and brainwash us!"

"I'm so scared," Cherie added with exaggerated fright.

"You know, if *we* were in Russia, we'd end up in Siberia because we couldn't stand all the rules," Marlene added.

"Yeah, we'd be in Siberia within twenty-four hours of landing," Cherie agreed.

"No, they'd just shoot us on the plane," was Katherine's straight-faced retort. In an accent like *Dracula,* Katherine assumed a severe expression and added, "Bad American girls don't respect rules!" Katherine banged the table with her fist, followed by hand-shooting everyone at the table, herself last.

Estelle stopped them, "Y'all, c'mon. Shut up. He's not Russian. My mother told me the Veretts are from Alabama. She went to school with a bunch of Veretts. They're from Mobile. She said they moved here because there were more jobs at the port."

The Port of New Orleans had long been bigger and busier than Mobile, but Mobile was modernizing. Port watchers wondered if Mobile could surpass New Orleans in volume. This was not good news for the Delta, which was reluctant to modernize anything.

People still complained bitterly about how the federal government, as it heralded modernization, ruined whole neighborhoods in New Orleans by building the projects in the early fifties. They groused angrily, "We didn't have ghettos here in New Orleans before those damn projects. Folks were poor, but they had their own houses passed down to them, not *buildings*. We had neighborhoods, not ghettos! That project business was an ugly northern thing, and they brought it down here."

"Those damn projects take people's own self away. Instead of your own porch to sit on, or even a little backyard with flowers or to grow vegetables in or have family over to grill, you are piled up one floor on top of another with no place to sit. It's crazy!"

Then, the finale, "The more that damn government stays away from New Orleans, the better!"

Devin and Garrett joined them and proceeded to gobble down lunch while they listened. Estelle leaned in, "A few years ago," she said softly, "Mr. Verett had to go before the school board. Mrs. Skillet, well, she turned him in for teaching socialized medicine."

Mrs. Skillet's handiwork had been to drag him before the school board in a flourish of local McCarthyism. There, Mr. Verett was interrogated and humiliated for teaching socialized medicine.

"What's socialized medicine?" Cherie asked Estelle.

Garrett jumped in with his mouth full, "It's the same as Medicare that President Johnson just got going. It means the government will help pay for your doctors when you're old.

"So what happened to him?" Cherie asked.

"He was officially... *censored*," Estelle replied. She paused before she said censored as if it was a scary word.

Garrett pushed back from the table and ranted, "That's so screwed up. It means he has to stick to that ancient textbook." The force of emotion in Garrett's words struck them. Poor Mr. Verett.

"Why doesn't he just quit?" Katherine asked.

Estelle responded with a frustrated hurt in her voice. "He can't quit! It's his job, and he has a family to support. Don't you know how horrible it is for somebody to lose their job?"

Estelle knew. Her father was fired because he got tuberculosis. Cherie did, too. Her mother got fired all the time, and she would get another secretary job. Cherie knew it was different for Estelle's father. He had a career, not just a job.

Katherine lowered her voice, "Kaleb told me Mr. Verett drinks a lot."

"So what?" Devin shrugged with a smirk. "All the teachers drink."

"And he said that Mr. Verett asks questions. It's called the *Socratic Method*. It's how he gets around the censorship."

The bell rang. Lunch was over.

"Turtle-lers." *Turtle-lers* was the girls' own version of *a tout a l'heure,* which meant *see you later.* Marlene had pointed out that it must have been the origin of toodle-oo in English.

"It's all right. Y'all can relax," Mr. Verett greeted his Ninth Grade Advanced Civics Class. "You see," he said as he buttoned his jacket, "I dressed up for you guys." The class applauded Mr. Verett, and he responded with a gentlemanly bow.

Near the end of class, Mr. Verett sat in an empty desk across the aisle from Devin. He leaned back into it and put his feet up on another seat.

"Congratulations on the Social Studies prize. I heard you had quite a time earning it."

Devin shrugged his shoulders.

"You read ... now, what book was that?" Mr. Verett smiled mischievously.

Devin bit the bait. "*Das Kapital* by Karl Marx," he drawled.

Cherie nudged Estelle to get her attention, but Estelle was off in another world as she gazed at Mr. Verett.

Then he asked Devin a question that *no one else had ever asked him* all those months, not Mrs. Skillet, not the vice principal, not his dad, not his mom, nor his brother.

"What did you think of it?" Mr. Verett asked cheerfully.

Devin looked up with surprise. He took a deep, fortifying breath and, when he exhaled, blathered out thoughts he'd been sitting on for a year.

"I could see that a lot of it was meant for countries or societies that are totally divided between really rich and poor, where people are trapped, and they can't move up from how they were born, that don't have a democracy or middle class and …"

Devin's voice trailed off, unsure about revealing this last thought, so Mr. Verett encouraged him, "And?"

"I also thought that there were some parts of it that weren't so bad."

Mr. Verett's playful expression darkened. "It's incredible, isn't it, what a little reading can do."

He stood up abruptly. "That's enough for today, class," he added, even though it was ten whole minutes before the bell.

Estelle smiled at Cherie and sighed, "He's so cool." Cherie knew it. Estelle had a giant, dreamy crush on the teacher.

Normally, Civics had a big fat B-for-Boring emblazoned on it, but Mr. Verett made it interesting. Week after week, past and current events merged as they worked through the need for government, the Enlightenment, and the genius of American democracy, its checks and balances.

By late winter, as they reviewed citizen responsibility, it was time to contend with the raptor of war that lurked over the room.

"Mrs. Skillet said that all wars are about money," Cherie complained.

"Well, she's absolutely right. They are," Mr. Verett countered.

What?! Cherie pressed on, "But she said that the Civil War had nothing to do with slavery and that the North couldn't have cared less whether or not there were slaves in the South. She said that it was economics."

"Mostly true," Mr. Verett said. The class was silent. Everyone was focused on him, a rare moment for a teacher, so he continued.

"Still, I wouldn't go so far as to say no one cared. There was a very vocal abolitionist movement, North and South, that wouldn't be silenced about the cruelty."

"Did you ever hear about the Grimke Sisters of South Carolina?" Everybody shook their heads, no, except for Garrett, who nodded yes.

Mr. Verett continued. "The Grimke Sisters fought tooth and nail to stop slavery. A lot of people cared very deeply. But the South had to secede to retain slave labor to run the cotton and tobacco plantations *profitably*. You get that? Profitably? And the North had to fight to save the Union."

Garrett raised his hand but didn't wait to be called on, "What about Vietnam?"

"What about it?" Mr. Verett responded.

"It's killed thousands of soldiers, and everybody hates us."

"It does cost us a lot," Mr. Verett explained, "but it makes a lot of people rich, too. For some people, the war in Vietnam is the best thing that ever happened to them."

"I don't believe it," Marlene said, "I don't believe anybody is happy about it."

"Oh really?" he said. "Okay. Who is getting rich off of the war in Vietnam? Anybody?"

The class fell silent, their faces registering that this was really scary stuff, people sending others to their deaths so they could get rich.

Garrett blurted out, "The people who make body bags." The class snickered.

Mr. Verett silenced his students by raising his voice a notch, "Y'all laugh like that's a joke, but it's actually a very good answer, thank you, Garrett, because, in times of war, body bags are good business. So, if you make body bags for the military, is it better for you and your family, and all the people you employ and their families and the town you live in for the war to end or continue?"

Estelle, who rarely spoke in class, broke in.

"If you're a peaceful person, you want war to end. And if you're greedy, you want it to go on and on," she answered.

"Good for you, Estelle, that's one right answer. But what if one of our allies begs us to rescue them from an enemy that's invaded them? What then? Do we turn our backs, or do we go to war to protect them?"

Estelle loved him. She loved him beyond teacher crush. She often stayed after class to talk to Mr. Verett, ask him about books or what she saw on the nightly news.

Mr. Verett let Estelle talk to him about her family's travails and this strange new phrase called *The System* as they sat separated by the old wooden teacher's desk. He listened to her with compassion and encouragement. He asked her what she thought and suggested magazine articles and books.

Estelle shared with Cherie during an overnight what she had learned about The System.

Cherie was happy that Estelle could stay over. Paulette had gone out for New Year's Eve to ring in 1967. Often, Cherie didn't mind being alone; she could watch anything she wanted on TV or play records with the volume up and dance and dream, her mind far away in a fantasy world. But Paulette was in a new crowd of friends, and being left alone so much was giving Cherie the creeps. She would hear scary noises or see shadows, prompting her to turn on all the lights and make sure everything was locked.

Cherie and Estelle were on the floor in makeshift sleeping

bags, staring at the ceiling. Cherie played with her flashlight. She held her fingers over it and created patterns in the light.

"You know what the system does to kids," Estelle explained to Cherie. "If you're born to parents that do blue-collar jobs, or you're poor, you're automatically B-tracked in school and kept out of advanced classes no matter how smart you are. Kids born to college-educated parents are automatically A-tracked for college, even if they're stupid. They're given the chance to stay in the middle or upper class, whereas poor kids aren't allowed to move up."

"But I'm born to an immigrant, well she's an American now, and she didn't go to college, and she works as a secretary, which might be considered blue collar, and I'm in advanced classes," Cherie argued.

"I'm talking about generally. There are always exceptions," Estelle replied.

"Well, that would be me," Cherie shrugged, the familiar feeling of not fitting in anywhere rose up in her guts. It made her feel angry and restless with Estelle. *Yeah,* Cherie thought, *the system this and the system that. Blah Blah.*

Cherie added with a huff, "And anyway if our system was so bad, people from around the world wouldn't be killing themselves to get here."

Estelle sighed deeply, feeling the weight of the world. "I saw a billboard today with an American flag on it. It said *Love It or Leave It.* Underneath, someone painted *Change It or Lose It.* That's all I'm trying to say."

Cherie turned on her side to face Estelle. "I get it. Okay? There's always stuff that needs to change. My mother yells about it all the time. I swear, the other night, I thought she was going to kick the TV in." Estelle smiled.

Cherie changed the subject, "Are you hungry? There might be

some cookies left. We could make toast, but I think the bread has mold on it."

~

Midyear in winter, Estelle broke down in Mr. Verett's class. Tears streamed down her face. She couldn't choke them back in. She began to sob.

Cherie jumped out of her seat and pulled Estelle out of class.

As they entered the large, third-floor girls' restroom with real marble sinks, dully observed by several hood girls as they smoked, Estelle slumped to the floor by the door. Cherie slumped down next to her and whispered catty things about the hood girls' teased hair until Estelle smiled and told her to shut up.

"My eyes are all red," Estelle fretted.

"Not too bad, more a dark pink," Cherie replied.

"I love him so much. I love him, but I know I can't get near him. I wish so much I could live with him and his family and learn everything they know. We're in high school next year, and I'll never see him again."

"You can come back and visit," Cherie consoled.

"It's not only that," Estelle wailed, and tears fell.

"What's wrong?"

"My father is better now, but no one will hire him. I went to talk to his boss, where he used to work, but he wouldn't even let me in. He called the guard to tell me to go home. It's not fair because my father is really good at what he does. It's not fair!"

"You went all by yourself?" Cherie was incredulous, "To the oil company offices downtown?"

Estelle nodded. She bit her lip. "They wouldn't even talk to me."

Marlene and Katherine came in. "Mr. Verett wants to know if you're okay."

Estelle nodded, "I'm okay." Marlene left to tell Mr. Verett. Katherine sat on the floor with them. She leaned on Estelle and took her hand.

Cherie kicked her friends playfully, "It's going to rain tomorrow. Bad."

Katherine lit up. "Oh really? You know what that means. Skip Day. Let's go see B'Lordy. We haven't bothered him in a long time."

Estelle sighed deeply. "I'd like to go see him."

"Let's do early-girly, so we can have coffee and beignets before we go see him," Cherie enthused.

"Yeah, let's do early-girly."

Late that night, the girls gathered at Marlene's house for a rare midweek sleepover. As they sat around the kitchen table dipping orange sections into a glass of vodka disguised as water, Cherie regaled them with a late-night, extra secret story. This one was about a girl at school. Cherie named her *Scaredy Girl*.

Marlene, Estelle, and Katherine frowned with vague recognition, unsure who Scaredy Girl was.

"Exactly. She's so quiet, nobody notices her."

"Who told you?"

"Anna Daniels. We were stuck in Phys. Ed. with nothing to do, and she told me. You're not going to believe it either."

"Then tell us, already!" Katherine yelled.

"Well, quit your yackin', and I will!" Cherie yelled back.

"Scaredy Girl is really shy, like a little stray dog. So, Anna Daniels took her under her wing to help her out. She doesn't live in uptown. She lives on the far side of Carrollton, like a mile up." This reference to the shy girl's home neighborhood was important. The *far side of Carrollton* gave Scaredy Girl a way over there, not here feel.

Cherie slurped on an orange slice and continued, "Anyway, Anna invited her to her house so they could play with makeup. Then and there, she spilled out her heart to Anna. She was *desperate* to have somebody to talk to."

"Poor thing," Marlene said. "Poor thing," they echoed.

"Poor thing for sure," Cherie nodded. "What happened was that after English class, which was her last class, Scaredy Girl started her period, and she felt like maybe she had bled on the chair, so she was frozen, totally afraid to move from the chair until everyone left the room.

"Ohmygod!" Estelle gasped.

"The teacher, Mrs. Taylor, you know, who's really pretty, too."

"Yeah, she's really cute. She wears cute clothes."

They all agreed, "Really cute."

"Was about to leave when she noticed that Scaredy was still there, all freaked out, so she asked her what was wrong. *Scaredy Girl started to cry.* Can you imagine? Sure enough, they saw that she had bled through her dress, but there was only a little dot on the chair. Mrs. Taylor offered to drive her home, but she started to cry because she was afraid to go home with her clothes messed up."

"Why was she afraid to go home?" Estelle asked.

"I don't know. Maybe it had happened before, and she forgot to bring stuff with her to school, and she didn't want her mom to yell at her?"

"You know," Marlene explained, "Some girls are so afraid of their periods, they feel like they'll die if somebody knows. It's totally ridiculous."

They echoed Marlene, "Ridiculous."

Katherine added, "like when that girl got out of the pool at that party in Audubon Park, and you could see it. She would never go back there again, and she switched schools."

"That's pretty bad." Marlene dipped another orange slice into the vodka and looked back at Cherie. "So, then what happened?"

"Mrs. Taylor brought Scaredy Girl home to her house and gave her this pretty lavender negligee to wear while she got her clothes washed, and even gave her a Midol. That's not all. Mrs. Taylor's husband, who teaches at Sacred Heart, got home. They ended up having a nice snack together. I think it was pecan pie and coffee, and they drove her home."

"Wow."

"But that's not the part of the story that's super-secret," Cherie leaned in and whispered, "And you can't tell anybody this because I'm sworn to secrecy."

"We promise," Marlene spoke for all. Together, they crossed their fingers on both hands and touched their hearts, the right hand over the left, in the Sworn-to-Secrecy salute.

Cherie whispered, "So Anna and Scaredy Girl were talking about using Tampax and stuff. Scaredy Girl told Anna that one time, when she first started using them, one got stuck up inside her!"

Marlene, Estelle, and Katherine stared at her, speechless.

"It was completely stuck! She tried so hard to get it out she was crying, and then finally, when she found the string and tugged on it, she screamed in pain. It hurt so bad. It was caught in her hymen."

A wave of discomfort seized the group, and they groaned. "Geez," Katherine cringed. "So, they took her to the doctor?"

Cherie shook her head no.

"They didn't take her to the doctor? Are you sure?" Marlene was shocked.

Cherie shook her head no again.

"What did they do?" Estelle looked pained.

"Swear you won't repeat this."

They nodded.

Cherie leaned in. "Scaredy Girl's father had been a medic in the army ..."

Estelle covered her face with her hands.

"No way!" Marlene gasped.

"No damn way!" Katherine repeated.

"*Her own father stuck his fingers up her and got it out.*"

"Aarrcckk!" they screamed. They covered their faces, stomped on the floor, banged on the table, and screamed some more. "Aarrcckk!" "Aarrcckk!" They didn't stop screaming for five minutes. Even after Marlene's sister appeared and yelled at them, "Shut your traps!" they couldn't stop screaming.

There wasn't a horror movie on *Morgus* that midnight or any other as frightening as the story about Scaredy Girl and the Lost Tampax.

Late that night, after her friends had fallen asleep, Cherie took her Wordless Diary from her book bag. She drew two tampons for the ones, a bat for the three, and an ice cream cone with sprinkles for the nine. 1-3-9-1. She closed the book, the fabric on the cover showing the slightest signs of wear and held it to her face. She whispered to it, *We're getting there.*

CHAPTER 10
Musettes

COME MORNING, it rained madly, ideal for truancy and a day in the French Quarter. Boots on (Marlene gave Estelle her extra pair), umbrellas in tow, they walked up to Carrollton to take the streetcar all the way downtown.

They had discovered Balladeer early in the school year during autumn's skip day. Balladeer wasn't his real name. It was his poetry name. Once said, people inevitably thought of music, not poetry, and they would ask him which instrument he played. It took Marlene all of one second to nickname him *B'Lordy*. Once declared, a Marlene nickname stuck like flypaper.

B'Lordy's real name was Michael, and he was from Boston. He was a wealthy young man whose father was a shipping magnate at the Port of Boston. But his daydreaming son left home and wended his way to New Orleans for one reason only, to suck up inspiration to write poetry. Typically, somebody like Michael would have headed for Greenwich Village or Cambridge in Yankee territory after college, but he didn't like those places; they were too close, too mean, and too icy, he felt for his sensitive soul.

No, he was in love with another port city. New Orleans. He

tried his best to explain it to his mother and father as he paced and waved his arms around in a rich boy's tantrum.

"It's where my soul lives, with the Delta Lady. She's my muse on the Mississippi River. Yes. The Mississippi! Not the Charles River and definitely not the Hudson. I need to breathe in her tropical flowers, and I will exhale poetry that's real to me. I'm tired of being fake, going through the motions."

They stared at him blankly, amiss with this human they had spawned. They looked at each other. They agreed, "Let him get it out of his system."

Cherie, Estelle, Marlene, and Katherine were in Cafe Banquette, splitting two hot chocolates and one hamburger four ways, when they noticed the appealing New Englander with long, dark, curly hair. He was writing in a composition book in the corner of the cafe. They buzzed and whispered among themselves.

"Is he looking at us?"

"I don't know."

"Smile at him."

"You smile at him."

"You do it. He's looking at you."

"He is not."

"Yes, he is. I can see him in my peripheral vision."

Katherine volunteered to smile at him. She turned her head slowly, just a bit, until her shy, playful gaze met his for a split second. He smiled back warmly, which provoked more buzz among the girls. He wrote in his notebook furiously.

As they counted their dimes, nickels, and pennies to pay for the check, he picked up the check, "Let me get this." Within seconds, he was swarmed. The girls walked him back to his upstairs apartment on St. Philip Street, off Royal.

"What are your names?"

They told him.

"What beautiful names you have. You skipped school? Really? Want to come up? Get out of the rain?"

Cherie, Katherine, Estelle, and Marlene traded looks to gauge each other. The rule was all in or nobody. They followed him up the stairs like he was the Pied Piper.

B'Lordy Michael welcomed their company, he wasn't used to living alone. Sure enough, they began to visit him on weekends or Skip Days.

They became his fan club. They enchanted him. He called them *my Musettes.*

They would hang around, talk, listen to his records, sleep on his couch, read his poetry books and magazines, watch him get stoned as they dramatically breathed in the secondary air, and raid the refrigerator. They would sing and dance freely to whatever he played. Katherine fell in love with his Odetta album and played it so much he gave it to her. He would speak French phrases with Cherie and Marlene.

He didn't object to them calling him B'Lordy. He liked it.

To Michael, they were the daughters of the Delta. They inspired him, these Delta babies.

He wrote in his notebooks as he watched them and sketched them with fine art pencils. Confident they would show up now and then as the weeks passed, he never asked for their phone numbers, nor did the girls ask for his.

Occasionally, there were playful attacks with couch pillows or a shaken soda bottle war in the courtyard. Once, it came up that Marlene had done an interpretive dance in modern jazz class to Robert Frost's *The Road Less Taken.* After her friends begged and stomped with encouragement, she replicated her performance as Michael read it from his personal copy. Then he grabbed her and kissed her on the mouth.

Sweet as sugar cane, most of the time, the girls learned quickly that B'Lordy was brittle when it came to his poetic idols. He hated it when the girls referred to Ferlinghetti as *Furry Spaghetti*. It turned into a big argument. They defended themselves. They told him that Ferlinghetti, above all people, would love it. B'Lordy would not accede.

The worst fight the girls had with him was the stormy afternoon when he insisted on reading Rimbaud's *The Drunken Boat* to them. Nobody was in the mood. Cherie and Marlene were in a corner reading a copy of Terry Sothern's *Candy*. Katherine was drawing pictures of angels, and Estelle was involved with memorizing the lyrics on Donovan's *Sunshine Superman* album. "*I'm just mad about fourteen*," she sang along.

"Don't you get it?" he emphasized as they traded looks among themselves. "It's from the boat's point of view. This ingenious French teenager from out of nowhere was doing something no one else had ever even considered." Once again, with dramatic fervor, Michael continued the poem,

> "Sweeter than the flesh of sour apples to
>   children
> The green water penetrated my pinewood hull
> And washed me clean of the bluish wine stains
>   and the splashes of vomit."

Katherine interrupted him, "You know what the New Orleans version of that poem is?" Michael patiently shook his head no, to which Katherine replied, "It's the Drunken Float, and it's going through a Mardi Gras parade."

Cherie staggered around the room as she paraphrased, "I'm the drunken Mardi Gras float. And the Rex Krewe just vomited on me from cheap wine, but I don't give a shit. Ohhh, ho ho, hose me down!"

Katherine, Marlene, and Estelle joined in. They spewed out vomit noises and yelled, "Throw me some barf, Mister!"

B'Lordy Michael had a fit and threw them out. A month later, they were back.

Estelle taught him how to make cheese grits. Marlene taught him cold brew coffee. They all walked over to the A&P on the corner of St. Peter's to get a cold brew dripper.

On the way back, they ran into Ruthie the Duck Lady. Ruthie was petite, frail-looking. She wore old ball gowns instead of dresses and rhinestone jewelry. Her long, dyed red hair was piled up atop her head. Her lipstick and eyeliner were smeared and ran afoul of her features. It was impossible to tell if she was young or old.

However, none of these things marked her as different, at least not in the French Quarter. Other ladies and gentlemen around town dressed up like that, too, often for the delight of tourists, as though they lived inside Mardi Gras all year long. Ruthie the Duck Lady got her name because she had a large, white pet duck that always walked with her, tethered by a dirty blue ribbon.

As they neared Ruthie, she stopped and said in a soprano sing-song, "Beautiful day today. Isn't it beautiful? Y'all got any cigarettes?" The girls politely told her it was indeed a beautiful day, and no, they didn't smoke. As soon as they passed her by, Michael sputtered and laughed. He couldn't muffle his laughter. Ruthie the Duck Lady looked back at him, hurt. She moved along as she muttered curses at him in a cry-baby voice.

The girls looked at each other, appalled. They whirled around and faced him. Eight young female eyes bore outrage and consternation. Estelle led the charge,

"Don't you laugh at her. That's rude!"

"Really rude," the others echoed like a Greek chorus.

"I'm sorry, but ..." Michael couldn't stop laughing.

"She can't help it," Estelle scolded, "Everybody knows she's crazy, but she doesn't hurt anybody. You don't know what happened to her. You don't have to be mean to her."

"Yeah, you don't have to be mean," the chorus echoed. In a

distinctly Southern tone reserved for outsiders, Estelle said to him, "Around here, no one's mean to her."

Michael caught the frosty tone, and it startled him.

"I'm sorry. Okay. I got it. No one laughs at the Duck Lady."

For the rest of the visit, they called him Ballard Duck and commented that Ruthie should walk him around on a ribbon.

Cherie felt a mix of alarm and jealousy when she saw Katherine snuggled up against Michael, his arm around her. Katherine was asleep while he read Sylvia Plath, a fellow Bostonian. He idly ran his fingers through her hair. Marlene and Estelle noticed it, too. On the streetcar home, no one brought it up.

One time, B'Lordy let them clamber up when he had friends over. "Hey! My fan club's here!" He introduced them to his girlfriend as his Musettes. She rolled her eyes and walked away, prompting giggles from the group.

They *were* his fan club. They bragged about where he was reading his poetry and who he partied with.

Cherie, Estelle, Marlene, and Katherine didn't realize how much he adored them back until Late Spring Skip Day when he handed each of them a copy of a book with a green cover of his printed poems and illustrations, signed personally, *Balladeer*. It was called *Love Too Far*.

"Don't read it until you are home," he ordered.

The St. Charles streetcar was crowded. Cherie and Estelle found seats facing each other while Katherine and Marlene stood with the conductor at the front of the car. Estelle started to read Michael's poems. As the streetcar trolled past Erato Street, Estelle gasped and held the book over her face with both hands.

"What?" Cherie felt alarm.

Estelle looked up, stunned. "This whole book is about Katherine. He's in love with Katherine. I'm not kidding. *In love!*"

Cherie grabbed the book from Estelle's hands, rapidly turning the pages. "You mean he didn't write anything about us?"

"There are a couple of poems about all of us and two about you. But it's almost all about Katherine."

Cherie found the two poems about her and raced through the lines, her eyes darting across the pages. One described her as a little French-speaking girl with a rag doll, and the other cited her emotions as twirling in the light like an Impressionist painting. The one with the doll embarrassed her. She thought it was babyish, and it made her cringe.

The rest were love poems about Katherine. The poems contained words like deep, darling, exquisite, time, grace, waiting, camellia petals, and love. And love. Love for Katherine. He wrote about a painful, unrequited longing and love for the fragile fawn he saw in Katherine. Cherie's mind spun around.

Huh?

The allegory made no sense to Cherie. Katherine could be funny, mean, and sarcastic like they all could be. Cherie never saw her as a fragile fawn. She hated it. She hated the whole book.

They were back together in Marlene's bedroom. They sat on the floor, a porcelain plate with homemade chocolate chip cookies between them, courtesy of Marlene's professor father, who liked to putter in the kitchen and whip up treats for his children and their friends.

The plate remained untouched. B'Lordy was on their minds. The artfulness of the poems, the extent to which they were moving and beautiful to read, and the delicate illustrations meant nothing to the girls. What Katherine felt, however, did mean something.

Katherine admitted, "Okay, I knew he liked me extra, more than y'all, but I didn't think it was anything like *that*."

"But you inspired his poems," Estelle pointed out. "Doesn't that make you happy?"

"I don't know," she whimpered. "I feel like I'm supposed to be happy, but I don't know." Indeed, she looked miserable.

Not yet fifteen, they agreed Katherine couldn't run away with him, even though running away sounded good.

Marlene asked her. "I know we all love him, but are you *in love* with him, too?"

"I don't know. Well, maybe a little. I did go see him by myself once, okay more than once, and we made out. "I'm sorry I didn't tell you," Katherine said to Marlene, "but I knew it would make you mad."

"Is he a good kisser?" Cherie asked. Normally, they would giggle over this, but they were dead serious. Cherie wanted to know how far Katherine went with him.

"I guess so," Katherine shrugged.

"Is that all? Just kiss?"

Katherine nodded. "And he had his arms around me tight," she hugged herself as she said it, "but he didn't feel me up. Well, yeah, a little. Mostly, we just kissed."

"Did you French?" Cherie pressed.

They stared at Katherine, wanting to know the answer. They had all French kissed boys at parties, but this was different. Katherine felt cornered, and instead of answering, she grabbed a cookie and threw it at Cherie.

"It's Eat-the-Cookie!" she yelled. The thought of a dirty-boy-contaminated cookie sent the four into hysteria as they tried to jam cookies through each other's clenched teeth until there was nothing but a crumbled mess over the floor.

Hysteria drained, they wiped crumbs off their faces and returned to the matter at hand.

"You know what will happen," Marlene told her, "If you have sex with him, he'll get rid of you. The poems are all about love that can never happen. He wouldn't love you anymore."

"He would still love me!" Katherine defended. She hung her

head in her hands and let out a pitiful, exasperated moan, "Oh, Michael."

Marlene's older sister yelled from the living room, "*Star Trek's* on, y'all!"

"I don't want to see him anymore. This is freaking me out."

"But do you *love him*?" Estelle asked again, "Because if you do, that means something."

"I love it when he hugs and kisses me. It feels so good ..." her voice trailed off. Katherine curled up on the floor like an embryo, knees drawn up, her hands on her head as though it hurt.

The image of Katherine and B'Lordy locked in embrace circled over them like a hungry hawk. Marlene reached over and tenderly pushed Katherine's hair off her face.

Marlene spoke as to lay down the law, "No. We can't see him anymore. None of us. Don't you remember? When we were hiding under the balcony? His girlfriend from Loyola yelling at him bloody murder about wasting her time. Don't you remember what she yelled? *'So when I'm in bed with you, that's who you're thinking about?!'* And we heard her hit him like five times, and we ran away when she came down the stairs? Don't you think it was because she saw the poems? We can't see him anymore. It's all ruined!"

Katherine sat up, feeling rescued by her best friend. She exhaled.

"Then it's over," Katherine said, looking relieved. The others responded, "It's over."

William Shatner's disembodied voice wafted into the room, *Space, the final frontier.*

They jumped up with Pavlovian ardor and knocked each other down to get out first. They raced to the TV, recited the opening in unison, and howled along with the theme song, vying for the loudest, most off-key howl. Estelle covered her ears. When Captain Kirk appeared, they made kissing noises, and when Mr.

Spock appeared, they raised their hands reverentially in the Vulcan sign. As they watched the episode, they entertained each other with exaggerated horror. Katherine's snorty imitation of Klingons sent them racing to the bathroom. They felt normal again; they felt everything would be alright.

His Musettes never thanked him for the books or albums, nor for all the food, coffee, and wine that disappeared during their visits, nor for his enthusiastic, affectionate tutelage about poetry, for his friendship, his affection, and all the fun. He was sanctuary until he committed a grave sin in their eyes. He gave his heart to Katherine, loving her beyond brother love, and ruined everything.

They walked down Chartres instead of Royal, and if they saw him, they avoided him, hustling into doorways and shops as though they avoided a disease. They ceased all talk about him. His poetry book ended up in the trash, except for Katherine, who buried her copy under the house lest she risk Mama Giselle's wrath.

It wasn't long before a For Rent sign marked Michael's balcony.

Late at night, when she couldn't sleep, Cherie thought about Michael and secretly missed him, even though she was jealous that he fell for Katherine and not her. Unlike Katherine, she would run away. She wouldn't chicken out. She dreamt about running away with him when she turned sixteen in another year, and they could get married. She could even, she figured, run away right now and marry him at fifteen. Some girls in Louisiana got married as young as thirteen.

Mama wouldn't even come after me. She'd have to make a big fuss so everybody would think what a terrible daughter I am for hurting her so much, but she'd like it so she could finally be free. Especially because Michael was rich. He could give Mama money.

Cherie's elated dream of leaving home gave way to tears. Underneath it all, she knew that her mother loved her in her own crazy way, even though she never said it. Cherie believed her mother couldn't help herself. She acted like she did because of war trauma. Cherie believed she had made her mother's life worse by being born.

She found her Wordless Diary where it was hidden in the closet under a coat. She counted ahead from her last drawing a few weeks earlier. She drew carefully, first a one like a flying arrow, the two was a boat with her in it, hair in the wind, sailing away, the five was the water with rippling waves, and the zero a heart circle at the tip of the arrow. 1-2-5-0 days left.

CHAPTER 11

What Devin Saw

It wasn't even midnight, but Devin and his older-by-two-years brother, Chris, had already broken curfew, and their father had locked them out. They headed to the back of the house and quietly discussed getting in. Banging on the door wasn't an option. It was far better to let their old man sleep.

When Devin and his brother lived at their mom's house on weekends, they were on their own. This lack of supervision rankled their father to no end.

Mr. Clarens felt his ex-wife let his sons run loose like wild animals. *He knew* they were too much for her. The boys, however, relished the freedom their delicate mother gave them and took hearty advantage of it. They passionately defended this independence to their father as self-reliance, character building, and the value of street smarts.

Mr. Clarens considered it blarney. He had a thing or two to teach them; top of the list, obedience. When the boys were at his house, there were rules to follow.

"Rules. You know what rules are?" he barked at his boys, "And there are consequences for breaking them. Do you know what consequences are?" Devin nodded yes with a blank face, all the while thinking, *I hate this stupid shit.*

Devin and his brother didn't feel they could be themselves at their dad's house. Their father's fiancée was an interior designer and had been working all her prissy skills on the house. She had even convinced their dad to install a chandelier in the entryway. It felt unnatural like they had to walk on tippy-toes over there.

Devin couldn't help but feel how much easier it was living with his mom. Despite the mess, the garbage and piled up dishes, the broken gas stove that only lit one burner, and the occasional dried-up fur balls barfed up by the cat named Mr. Green Jeans, living with her was so much better.

When they lived with their mother, Garrett and all their friends would hang out with them to play music and smoke, even when it was hot and there was no air conditioning. Nobody would hang out with them at their dad's.

Staring up at the back of the house, the boys analyzed the situation. They decided they could climb up the adjacent live oak tree, grab onto the bottom of the iron grillwork that graced the window of their room like a Juliette balcony, and get in. That window was always unlocked. In the morning, they could beg for mercy from their dad.

"Okay, you first," Chris decided, "Don't kick over the garbage can."

Devin, his heartbeat quickening, climbed on the metal garbage can. The top dented under his weight, emitting a loud ping.

"Don't blow it!" Chris snapped in a low voice.

"Shut up, man."

Devin lightly jumped from the garbage can, grabbed the branch, agile as a bobcat, and pulled himself onto it. The plan was working. Devin edged up the tree until he was level with the bottom of the decorative grille.

Devin reached for it, but it was a couple of inches beyond his fingertips. He almost fell. He grabbed the branch and clung to it, catching his breath. He braced himself, tried again, and grabbed the curlicue iron bars. He got both feet on it and climbed up, almost through the window. Then he froze.

Chris whispered from below, "What's the matter?"

Devin looked down at his brother, a stream of sweat running down the side of his face that glistened in the street lights, "Daddy hung himself."

"What!"

"Daddy hung himself," he hyperventilated, "he's in the stairwell."

"Get outta here. You're stoned."

Devin grit his teeth, "No, I am not. I swear I am not. I swear it."

"Are you sure?"

"I can see him through the curtains and the door." Devin started to shake.

"C'mon down, man. Shit. Just drop down."

Devin plummeted to the ground. He babbled, teeth chattering,

"Wh... wh... what do we do? It's our fault. We p... p... pushed him over the edge."

"Shut up! I gotta think." They headed to Myrtle Bouilley's house next door. Myrtle Bouilley was the mean secretary at Fortier High School. All the students disliked her, but it seemed like the best plan.

They banged on the door and moaned pitiably, "Our Daddy hung himself."

She called the police. Within minutes, a bunch of police cars, lights flashing, filled the street. Neighbors materialized by the dozens, taking in the excitement. One to the next, they shook their heads in sympathy, "Oh, those poor, poor boys."

Suddenly, Myrtle Bouilley screamed so loud everybody

jumped. Standing beside her was Mr. Clarens, holding a large pizza box over his head like a waiter and a six-pack of beer.

"Didn't mean to startle you, Myrtle. What's goin' on?" he asked.

Devin and his brother ran to him. They threw themselves on their old man, "Dad, you're alive! You're alive!"

Mr. Clarens, his brow knitted in confusion, responded in kind. He put down the beer and pizza and patted them lovingly.

Murmurs trickled through the crowd. "You mean that's their daddy? Was this some kind of joke?" Sympathy turned to condemnation in a heartbeat. "Those damn boys woke up the whole neighborhood for nothing? Good God-o-mighty. Those kids need to sober up. Yeah, and I know what else they need!"

The police cars disappeared one by one, and everybody went back home.

Devin and Chris stuffed themselves with pizza and, thoroughly exhausted, threw themselves on their beds.

Downstairs, Mr. Clarens said goodnight to the detective, "Even if it was new, how could he confuse the chandelier for a body and think it was me?"

"We checked him out. He wasn't drunk or high," the detective reassured. "That's a good thing."

"Yes, it is," Mr. Clarens sighed.

"We're just glad this one had a happy ending."

"See you at the club. Thanks again." Mr. Clarens gently closed the door.

He leaned against the door and stared up at the boys' room. He wondered, *How in the world could my boys think I would do something so crazy? I play golf. I'm getting married. Oh no. This nutty-as-a-fruitcake crap is from their mother! Better to put an end to this bullshit once and for all.*

Devin was almost asleep when the door flung open. Light

streamed in, framing Mr. Clarens, who set upon Devin, whacking him with one of his son's most beloved possessions.

"Not my cornet! Ow, stop, ow!" Devin wailed, covering his head. "Not with my cornet, Dad! Ow! Stop, you'll hurt it! It won't play right. Stop! Ow! Oooooowww!"

A few days later, as the friends idly watched the snowy egrets in Audubon Park, Cherie offered an explanation, "You saw a ghost. Somebody hung themselves in that very stairwell one hundred years ago, and you saw his ghost."

"There are ghosts all over town. They're everywhere," Katherine added breathlessly, "Sometimes, when I wake up at night, I see one all shimmery at the foot of my bed. She looks like an angel, like Mother Mary. There's one in our attic, too. Kaleb saw him. You saw a ghost."

"Yeah, maybe it was a ghost," Garrett pondered without a bit of sarcasm.

"Wow," Devin piped in, "my first ghost sighting. Holy shit. But I could have sworn it was." He frowned and left it at that.

With one thousand and one hundred days to go, Cherie drew ghosts into her Wordless Diary that night because it was all so amazing, two flying ones and two zeros.

CHAPTER 12
The Giddy Gadget

AMONG THE ANTIQUE stores and boutiques that lined narrow Royal Street in the French Quarter, the girls noticed a curious store that opened catty-corner from the grand Monteleone Hotel.

It was a psychedelic head shop called The Giddy Gadget. Wondrous, funny things lined its display cases. There were bongs and roll-your-own papers, lava lamps and strobe lights, posters of rock stars, melted glass Pepsi bottles you could use for vases, patchouli and musk colognes, big plastic daisies and sunflowers, baseball caps with peace symbols, fake draft cards, and license plates with irreverent letter and number combinations such as F69GR8.

Back at high school, around the lunch table, Garrett summarized The Giddy Gadget. "It's just more materialism," he sniffed.

Devin nodded, "Yeah. The revolution is being co-opted and diluted into the mainstream. Like buying all this shit is all you have to do, and you're cool."

Cherie felt stupid. She loved The Giddy Gadget. It was the most fantastic store she had ever seen.

Tired of babysitting and sick of drunk and stoned daddies trying to kiss her when they drove her home, dubbed Daddy Leeches by Marlene, Cherie dressed up as cute as she could in a black miniskirt, boots, and a fake silk purple shirt with her hair half-up in a tooled leather hair clip. She took the bus downtown instead of the streetcar since she and Paulette now lived on Willow Street. She took a deep breath and walked into The Giddy Gadget to ask for a job.

Cherie met with an older lady who managed the store for her son, Berley. Cherie told her she hadn't worked in a shop before but was a quick learner. Berley's mama looked her over. "You're cute, and my son wants cute girls working here for tourists and conventioneers. The other weekend girl was just fired, so why don't you be here at nine a.m. on Saturday, and we'll see how it works out."

"Thank you so much!"

Cherie couldn't believe her good luck. It was a real part-time job. It would pay a quarter more than the dollar an hour she earned babysitting, plus it freed up Saturday nights! She eagerly related all this to Estelle, with a promise to see about getting Estelle a job, too.

Berley's mother and the other Giddy Gadget girl showed her how to work the cash register, roll posters without paper cuts, hide the large bills, do inventory, set out products, and watch for thieves. Cherie loved working in the store, particularly when someone from school walked in and she could point out her favorite merchandise.

Berley usually showed up near the end of the afternoon. Like his mother, he was short but made up for it with muscles bulging beneath his T-shirts. He'd come in and yell at his mother because she baked cookies for the girls and yell about how the merchandise was poorly displayed or how the glass cases should be cleaned more often. Berley would often lock himself in the storeroom at the back of the shop. If his mother knocked on the door, he would yell, "Leave me alone. I'm doing the accounting."

Sometimes, Berley came in with his boyfriends and would give them gifts.

He particularly loved Paul McCartney and Donovan. He'd run his hand down the Donovan poster permanently affixed to the storeroom wall, thrust his hips, and say, "Ohhh, Donovan. I love him."

As Cherie swept the storeroom, she found a syringe with a needle in it. She gingerly picked it up and brought it to Berley's mother, who jumped at the sight of it. "Oh, my Lord, that must be Berley's. Uh ... he's diabetic," she sputtered. Cherie looked away and bit her lip. Needles.

One Sunday afternoon, Berley called for Cherie. He handed her a stuffed brown paper lunch bag that was stapled shut. A big X in red marker was drawn on the fold. "You bring this to Victor at Lafitte's. You know where that is?"

Lafitte's was one of the gay bars. Cherie felt she shouldn't be going into a place like that. She was too young, and she'd be invading their territory. It was the early afternoon, though, maybe that would be okay. Despite the fear that seized her, Cherie nodded yes.

Berley snorted at her, "Oh yeah? How would you know where it is?"

"It's on Bourbon. It's famous," Cherie said.

The bar's full name, Lafitte in Exile, referred to a sad footnote in history when the handsome Creole pirate, Jean Lafitte, beloved in New Orleans, helped Andrew Jackson defeat the British in the War of 1812. Andrew Jackson thanked Lafitte by betraying him. Jackson exiled Pirate Lafitte from the city, and thus, he was wrenched forever from the loving arms of the Delta Lady. Lafitte and his brother went to the southern coast of Texas, where it is believed he perished in a storm. Right into modern times, some

New Orleanians sorely resented Jackson Square being named after that backstabber. "Andrew Jackson was a rat. It should be Lafitte Square, not Jackson!" The small building was originally a blacksmith shop belonging to Jean Lafitte's brother.

The bar named after this debacle frequently hosted Tennessee Williams and many famed writers and actors who visited the great playwright before he retired to Key West.

"Look at me!" Berley snapped his fingers in her face. "You walk in, ask for Victor at the bar, give it to him, and then walk out. And then you take your lunch break."

"What if he's not there?"

"He's there. I just talked to him. If he's not, bring it back here. You don't leave it with anybody. You got that?"

Cherie dutifully wended her way to Lafitte's. She stopped at the door and looked in. *It was empty.* Like most New Orleans bars before the perfumed partiers arrived, it smelled thickly beery and sweaty. Cherie went straight to the bar, and before she could say a word, the lean bartender, whose face was boney and angular, confronted her in a cold, flat tone of voice full of disapproval.

"What are you doing here, little girl?"

"Is Victor here?" She cleared her throat.

"Maybe," he replied.

"I have a lunch bag here for Victor from Berley Ganderson," Cherie said. She looked back at the exit in case she had to run for it.

Bartender burst out laughing and yelled toward the back room, "Hey, Vic, get a load of who Berley has running for him."

Victor appeared dressed in a beige suit with matching beige socks and loafers, a white shirt, and a red tie. He was tall and had curly blond hair.

"Pathetic or what?" Bartender smirked.

Victor gave him a look, "Makes me shudder to think what made you so mean."

"Like it doesn't thrill you."

"I'd say smart move," Victor countered, "Who would ever suspect this little innocent?"

Victor towered over her. She handed him the package. He checked the X carefully.

"Thank you, honey child. Now get lost."

Cherie ran out as fast as she could, but that afternoon wasn't the end of it. Almost every Sunday she worked, Berley would call her over and secretly hand her brown paper bags to run over to Victor or other people around the Quarter. Bartender got sweeter. He gave her a bottle of ice-cold Coke when she showed up. Cherie no longer felt scared and soon welcomed the chance to get out of the store and away from the cash register.

Cherie knew it was weed or worse but figured that if the bags were taped and X'ed, she could play *dumb girl* if anybody stopped her.

Out of the blue, Berley surprised her with a bonus of three crisp twenties.

Jimi Hendrix showed up in New Orleans on tour. The mayor gave him the key to the city in Louis Armstrong Park off of Municipal Auditorium. The local TV reporter said the event wasn't well-attended, particularly by local musicians. It was reported that some of them didn't like what Hendrix was doing with music and that he was vulgar on stage, not elegant like they were. He humped his guitar and lit it on fire. Even so, the concert was sold out.

At the Giddy Gadget, the other shop girl yelled for Cherie, who was in the storeroom rolling posters, their biggest seller. She ran back to get her.

Her eyes were afire, and she spoke in a panic, "You gotta come up front and cover for me. A reporter here is having lunch with

Jimi Hendrix at the Monteleone. He wants a girl to go with him, so I'm going! I'll be back later."

Cherie was burned up at the missed opportunity. "Damn. Jimi Hendrix!" She would have been able to tell everybody, and now she had nothing to tell.

Three hours later, the other Giddy Gadget girl returned. She looked bad. Her eyes were half-shut, and her hair was a mess. She stood behind the counter and put her head down on the glass case. She drooled on it, smudging it up.

"What happened?" Cherie asked, grabbing a paper towel and the glass cleaner.

She barely lifted her head and slurred her words, "It was great. Oh, wow. I can't believe it. He wore a yellow flowery shirt with ruffles and maroon pants. He had a glass of milk for lunch. And then we went up ... I gotta go throw up."

Walking as though drunk, she staggered to the bathroom. Cherie felt sorry for her. The closed door didn't muffle her retching. Customers smirked at the sounds. She was in there forever. It was crowded up front. Berley's mother was gone, and Cherie needed help.

Berley appeared. He yelled holy hell at Cherie. She defended herself, told him about the Hendrix lunch, and that the other girl got food poisoning. She thought Berley would let them off the hook. *It was Hendrix,* Cherie thought, *That's huge. He's got to understand.*

"How long was she gone?" he asked.

"I don't know," Cherie shrugged.

"Don't you give me that? How long?"

"I don't know. It was busy."

Berley snorted. When the bathroom door finally opened, Berley stood there staring at her. "You're fired!"

"You can't fire me because I got sick!"

Up front, Cherie winced as she listened in.

"Look at your eyes. Look at them! You think I'm stupid?" Berley yelled at her. Customers looked over their shoulders.

He ranted at her, "Like you got food poisoning at the Monteleone? You're going to insult my friend who cooks at the Monteleone and the fine people that cook there and say you got food poisoning there? Get out of here, you drugged-up slut whore! Doing that on my time!"

"Give me my pay, you junkie pig," she croaked. "You owe me two weeks."

Berley threw a few bills on the floor. She had to crouch down to gather them up.

She ran out in tears.

Cherie was stunned. It never occurred to her there was more to it. Jealously turned to relief. *Thank goodness I was in the storeroom.*

A new clerk was hired, a lady who had experience working in the Quarter. Cherie didn't like her because she was bossy, and Cherie felt like she couldn't do anything right.

A couple of weeks later, Berley accused Cherie of stealing money, "$246 is missing! So where is it?" The false accusation terrified her.

Cherie didn't want to tell her mother, but Paulette coaxed it out of her.

Paulette was sympathetic. "Tell him to go to hell. You can go work someplace else. How much does he owe you?"

"Not much. I was just paid."

"Then quit. Tell him if he bothers you again, you'll throw a rock through the window."

"I'm not going to say that!"

"Tell him I'll throw a Molotov cocktail through the window."

Cherie started to laugh.

"There, I made you laugh," Paulette smiled. "You don't have

to cry over that stupid SOB." Paulette pushed the last piece of pizza on the table towards Cherie.

"You don't want it?" Cherie asked.

"You take it. I'm getting fat."

Near midnight, Berley phoned Cherie to tell her he had found the money.

Cherie held the phone but couldn't reply. It was all too awful for her. The Giddy Gadget had become an evil, sinister place. Babysitting and fending off Daddy Leeches didn't seem so bad anymore.

Berley cheerfully continued, "So there's nothing for you to worry about."

Cherie croaked, "I have to quit. My grades are bad," she lied.

Berley yelled into the phone, and Cherie held the receiver away from her ear. "Are you kidding me? You're quitting? Not give me even three days' notice? You stupid little bitch, of course, your grades are bad!"

Cherie knew he was angry because she left him in the lurch with his paper bag deliveries. As he continued to yell, Paulette grabbed the phone.

"Go fuck yourself!" Paulette yelled into the phone. She slammed it down and went back to watching *Late Night*.

Cherie stood there, feeling her heart bang around her insides, amazed that Paulette cursed at Berley. She leaned over to hug Paulette, who responded, "Oh, what's this all of a sudden?" Paulette grabbed Cherie and hugged her tightly until Cherie pushed back. Paulette held her tighter and started to laugh, "Now what are you going to do?" forcing Cherie to struggle until she could free herself from her mother's unyielding grip.

⁓

A year earlier, Cherie and Estelle looked alike. They both wore their dark hair long, almost down to their waists. They were about the same height and weight and didn't wear makeup, but now, as they approached sixteen, they looked different.

Cherie loved makeup. She wore frosted lipstick and lined her eyes in black. She played with her hair more, sometimes braiding it in one braid down her back and cut her bangs. She divided her wardrobe into two looks that she called dayglo and death-warmed-over. Death-warmed-over was winning; it made her feel cool and different.

"Why do you wear all black?" people asked her.

"I was born too late," Cherie replied with a rehearsed sigh. "I'm a bad hippie. I was supposed to be a beatnik and hang with Furry ... uh, Ferlinghetti, but I missed my reincarnation slot by a couple of years."

Estelle's rock idol, Donovan from Scotland, was set to appear at the Loyola University Field House in uptown. The quartet of friends all dressed in black dresses and tights and wore their hair parted in the middle. They could not have looked more separate from the colorful, beaded, and tie-dyed concert crowd than if they had worn nun's habits.

It disturbed people in the audience. They were questioned, "What's wrong with you? Why are you wearing black?" and one lady called them *devil girls*.

"We're Quakers and mourning because of the Vietnam War," Katherine shrewdly retorted. They sat seriously until they could no longer repress their laughter.

"I don't even know what Quakers look like," Cherie said.

"We're missing the white collars," Marlene answered, "We need big white collars with lace on the edges."

"My papa is the man on the Quaker Oats box," Katherine added, "That's my Dada. Drooly fat face."

At the end of the concert, Estelle gasped to see her younger sisters and baby brother at the side of the stage. Instantly, she was out of her seat and raced down the aisle toward them. No one stopped her when she took the stairs onto the stage to hug them and stand with them. Cherie followed her, thrilled to get closer.

"How'd they get in?" she asked.

Estelle smiled, "The ticket man saw them dancing outside by the door and let them in."

As the crowd roared after the encore of "Universal Soldier," Cherie and Estelle looked up to see Donovan walking toward them, only a few yards away, as the crowd spilled from their seats and onto the stage. They would be close enough to see the color of his eyes.

Cherie could hear Estelle squeal behind her. As Donovan looked ahead, Cherie swore that he smiled at her. The next thing, like an ugly, fast-moving cloud that blocked the sun, she saw Berley as he held onto Donovan's arm to lead him offstage past the crowd.

As Berley passed by Cherie, he thrust out his muscular arm, slamming her in the chest. The force knocked her to the ground, past Estelle, who struggled to keep her little brother perched on her hip and break Cherie's fall. The entire crowd of girls behind them shuffled backward.

Cherie pulled herself up to her knees, her breath knocked out of her. Marlene appeared and rubbed her back until she took a deep breath. Her three friends and Estelle's siblings were gathered around. They hadn't seen Berley punch her, just that Cherie hit the ground.

The blow hurt and embarrassed her, but she wouldn't admit it. Everybody was so happy, she didn't want to rain on them. She bit her lip, determined to be tough. Nevertheless, her mind churned, *I hate that pig Berley! I hope he overdoses. I hope he rots from the inside out and dies!*

Estelle leaned in. "Are you okay? You got knocked down. Did you see him? I almost touched him!"

Cherie stood up and brushed off. She tried to speak as she caught her breath, but her voice sounded like a whisper, "I'm okay. Yeah." They helped her to her feet.

As they walked away from the auditorium, "Devin's party is still going on," Marlene offered,

Katherine piped in, "Yeah, let's go to Devin's, then play Scrabble."

"I can't," Estelle said, "I gotta get them home, and I'm going to see my boyfriend."

"We'll walk with you," Marlene said.

Estelle's boyfriend was one of Garrett's new friends, a fellow revolutionary. He was cute with sandy hair, blue eyes, glasses, and opinionated. He read everything Garrett read. Estelle had a big crush on him, and they started dating.

"But it's against our pact," Cherie confronted her.

Cherie, Estelle, Marlene, and Katherine had a pact never to break plans with each other because of boys. It was a given among girls that a boy's invitation instantly canceled plans with a girlfriend. Marlene and Katherine thought that was stupid and initiated the radical pact.

"You're not going to break the pact, are you?" Katherine asked her.

"You can't break the pact," Marlene insisted, her moral sense ruffled.

Katherine weighed in, her tone full of indignation, "It's a pact. It's sacred. It means our friendship is just as important as going out with boys. You said that you're for women's liberation. That's what this is."

Cherie defended Estelle, "But we didn't have exact plans for after the concert, so Estelle's not breaking the pact."

"It's half-broken," Katherine concluded.

Nothing else was said. Katherine and Marlene walked ahead of them. Katherine draped her arm over Marlene's shoulders.

Estelle felt badly, but her crush overwhelmed it. She whispered to Cherie, "Thanks."

~

Late that night, Cherie pulled out her Wordless Diary and counted down her numbers.

It was nearing the end of 1967, and a great turning point flickered on the horizon – one thousand days left. She could practically taste it. She could imagine one thousand days as divine nectar the gods would bestow upon her, a great reward.

For her numbers, she drew three detailed flowers laden with petals and a peace symbol. She felt as though the three flowers were Marlene, Katherine, and her, and the peace symbol was Estelle, ready to roll away. Cherie's tears fell and smeared the whole thing. She ripped the page from her notebook, crumpled it, and threw it down. *No!* she told herself. Then she drew it again, but differently. She drew three snakes hanging from a stick for 9-9-6, which would be true in a few more days. *Not mean snakes,* Cherie thought. *Pretty green garden snakes with smiles.*

CHAPTER 13

Danger. Flammable

MISS BREAUX STOOD up in front of her 10th grade American History class at Alcée Fortier High School tall, slim, and purposeful before thirty restless kids. Her brown hair bobbed down to her jawline, and she had pretty blue eyes and high cheekbones. She wore a matching skirt and sweater and penny loafers. Her voice had a harsh pitch to its tone, her Southern accent deep, as she rehashed the reasons for the Spanish-American war. Even though she was twenty-eight, she still was a "Miss" and wore her boyfriend's fraternity pin on her sweater as if she was still in college.

Cherie and Katherine thought that was pathetic. Cherie leaned over to Katherine and whispered, "She's too old to wear her boyfriend's pin."

"She just wears it because she doesn't want people to think she's an old maid," Katherine responded with a sneer.

By the windows next to them, Garrett glared at Miss Breaux and drummed the desk with both hands. He raised his hand extra high to get noticed. As soon as Miss Breaux looked at him before she could even say, "Yes, Garrett," he shook his long, sandy hair out of his face and forged ahead full throttle.

"Why don't you tell everybody the truth about the Spanish-American War? That it was a totally invented war that didn't have to happen, and it was about America showing off and setting the stage for exploitation of the world's resources ... that it's exactly the same thing as Vietnam, a fabricated conflict!"

A collective groan tittered across the class. *Here he goes again.* Others woke up.

Miss Breaux pursed her lips. "Vietnam again. Garrett, no matter what we talk about, you always bring that up. Do you want *all* of Asia to be communist? Why are you so against the war if we are fighting communists to protect their freedom and ours?"

"Because it has nothing to do with communism. It's the military-industrial complex that President Eisenhower warned about, and we're nothing but slaves to it!" Garrett raved in one breath.

Miss Breaux stayed calm. She sensitively offered, "Is it because of the numbers we're losing that you're so upset?" It was a good question. Recently released numbers of Americans killed had crested at 12,000, and American wounded or missing was 58,000. A lot of people were shaken by the reports.

"No!" he shot back, "It's because of the numbers we're killing."

Miss Breaux wasn't dumb but seemed dumbfounded. Garrett had hit a nerve.

She turned away from his glare and sighed, "Class, let's get back to President Theodore Roosevelt."

"Why do you do that?" Garrett protested as his voice rose in volume, "Why are you so afraid of the truth that we can't even talk about it. Isn't this whole building here for education? Then let's get educated!"

By now, everybody in the class was awake. Devin, Cherie, Estelle, and Katherine greeted the exchange with smiles and thumbs up, a mini-Greek chorus that echoed, "Yeah."

Miss Breaux countered him with force, "You be quiet right now! *I will not* let you dominate my class, Garrett. You sit there quietly and listen or get out!"

"Listen to what," Garrett snapped, "More lies about American history?" He grabbed his books and stormed out. Devin followed him.

Garrett may not have been doing his homework, but he was doing a lot of reading. He formed a study group with like-minded souls. He begged every kid he knew to read *Who Rules America* by Domhoff, Alex Haley's *The Autobiography of Malcolm X*, Heinlein's *Stranger in a Strange Land,* and *Compulsory Miseducation* by Paul Goodman, one of his favorites. His mother encouraged him. They would pass the same book back and forth and talk about it.

While Garrett's oldest brother read Buckminster Fuller and dreamt about building his own geodesic dome, and his artistic second brother sped around on his motorcycle, Garrett read about the cultural shifts gripping America and took every word to heart.

Within days of the latest confrontation with Miss Breaux, he was expelled from Fortier for insubordination.

"I just can't deal with him anymore," she complained to the principal. "That boy insists on disrupting my class!"

Garrett was reassigned to Booker T. Washington High School in Mid-City, an all-black high school in which Garrett would be the only white kid in the student body of 1,200.

Those in charge figured, *That'll teach him a lesson about shootin' off at the mouth, once the Booker T. kids kick his teeth in, maybe then he'll learn some respect.*

Garrett was unrepentant. If anything, it energized him. *They,* the omnipotent *They,* were repressing his freedom of speech and rights of civil disobedience. *Good*, he thought, as he cleared his locker and marched out of Fortier, *Better than good. I can organize at Booker T. as well as anywhere else.*

The potent brew that smoldered inside Garrett burst into flame. His spirit, mixed with brains, spiced by books, and seared by the counter-culture, sparked into radical youth action the likes of which New Orleans had never witnessed. No adult, not his parents, the police, nor the juvenile judicial system, could figure out how to cool his fire.

Alcée Fortier High School imposed itself upon the low-lying residential neighborhoods at Freret Street and Nashville Avenue, one mile from Tulane and Loyola Universities. Built during the Great Depression of the 1930s, the massive red-brick building loomed four stories high and lined three sides of the block, sheltering an inner courtyard. Beyond the courtyard was the gym that doubled as an auditorium, followed by the football field.

Its most elegant hallmarks were the grand marble stairs and curvy banisters at the entrance that led to the second-floor administrative offices. Like the antiquities of Rome, the marble stairs were worn from usage.

Tenth grade for the McMain Secondary kids heralded the great divide. After hours of tests, some got into the extra smart school, Benjamin Franklin on Carrolton, and those who would go down two blocks to Fortier. Marlene glided right into Franklin.

"It doesn't make that much difference," she reassured her friends. "Fortier has lots of advanced classes."

After Ben Franklin High School, Fortier was considered the second-best public high school in the city. It was named after a professor.

Alcée Fortier, who lived from 1856 to 1914, was a French

Creole who became a Tulane language professor and folklorist. He researched and wrote about Louisiana's unique dialects and folktales.

In addition to a beautiful uptown location, Fortier's principal, Joseph Schwertz, was the other reason the school maintained such an excellent reputation. He had built his career as a creative and forward-thinking education reformer. Early in life, he gained national prominence after *Time Magazine* in 1949 wrote about his successful educational reforms at Beauregard Elementary on Upper Canal, a depressed little muddle of a school before he walked in. He promoted shocking programs that included doing away with report cards and letting children progress at their own speed from one grade to the next.

In the fall of 1967, the Federal Government tired of the Crescent City's litany of excuses. The Feds ordered the city to complete the school integration process. Seven whole years after six-year-old Ruby Nell Bridges walked into Frantz Elementary during the officially declared New Orleans desegregation crisis, Fortier High School would be integrated.

All of a sudden, hundreds of black kids and hundreds of white kids were in school together at Fortier for the first time. The atmosphere in the school was unruly and chaotic. Fights broke out more than usual. There was a huge fight between two white high school fraternities that put one boy in the hospital when his head was split open by a brick, and another fight between a large group of black girls that put a girl in the hospital for stitches when she was shoved into a glass-paned classroom door.

Then, there was an interracial attack. Two white boys, introverted art student Alan and extroverted Matthew, who led the band, were jumped by a dozen black students on the stairs. It sent both boys to the emergency room and kept Alan in the hospital for a week. The attack made the *Times-Picayune* newspaper.

A few weeks later, the boys received recruitment packages from the American Nazi Party. This was particularly mind-bending for their families because they were Jewish. Their parents didn't know whether to laugh or cry.

Threats to the black students in Fortier increased. A popular black guy named Edmond, whose musician uncle toured with famed entertainer Fats Domino, was beaten up by white boys in a counterattack. Afterward, students never traveled alone in school or even in twos. They traveled in groups.

Tires were slashed, windows were broken, teachers' cars vandalized, and ugly words appeared on Fortier's blank gray walls. Fire alarms went off almost daily, and there were bomb scares several times a week. This forced everybody to drag out to the field and stand miserably in the hot sun.

The kids retreated into their respective groups.

Socks were a problem for the girls. None of the girls, black or white, from uptown's checkerboard neighborhoods wore socks with shoes anymore. But black girls from neighborhoods farther away near Mid-City came to school wearing white cotton socks folded down at the cuffs. It provoked alienation. Uptown girls were embarrassed by it; they felt it was so old-fashioned. Mid-City girls didn't know whether to stand up proud and be themselves or conform to pressure from the uptown girls.

Unfortunately, Fortier's students knew nothing about Principal Schwertz's radical leadership in education reform. If they had, they might have been more respectful to him. They saw him only as a stout, humorless old man who was out of touch.

Principal Schwertz felt himself besieged. The brutal teachers' strike had barely been settled, and now this. He walked about the school with a slightly bent posture as though the world was on his shoulders. This added even more shadows to his droopy face, the lower half of which seemed to melt into his neck.

In his molasses baritone, Principal Schwertz typically

addressed the student body over the PA system after the morning pledge to the flag,

"It has come to my attention that some young ladies are not wearing anything on their feet under their shoes and then take off their shoes during class or lunch. This is not allowed. You may not take off your shoes. Furthermore, sandals or open-toed shoes are not allowed. The boys must wear socks, and girls must wear stockings, socks, tights, or footies." A burst of laughter was heard from classroom to classroom when Principal Schwertz said, "Footies."

When complaints from black students and parents about racist incidents thrust upon them by teachers crossed his desk, Schwertz responded according to the recommended protocol. "I will look into it, but you must anticipate an adjustment period." Under the circumstances, this line smelled like a tray of rotten crawfish to angry and hurt students and their families.

When teachers confronted Schwertz with complaints of student insubordination and outrage over racist behavior by other teachers, he'd reassure them that the appropriate inquiries and action would be taken. The vice principal, the man with the paddle, would tell these teachers, "The coaches are happy. Go talk to them and see what they're doing."

The high school coaches of New Orleans were indeed happy. More important to them than a school self-immolating was that New Orleans finally had its own NFL football team called the Saints. Not a whole lot could ruin their good mood. Their talk was more about whether or not *Saints* was a ferocious enough name for the team.

Principal Schwertz stayed strong and maintained his cool as he faced the volatile winds that threatened to tear off the roof. Instead of leadership, it looked like inertia to those surrounding him. He called for patience. It was the worst thing he could have asked for.

"Period of adjustment, my butt!" was the outcry. Fortier needed decisive action, not investigative committees. The students hated him. They thought he was too damn slow, another useless old person.

Crushing incidents happened to the first black kids that ever went to Fortier. This included being ignored in class and never called upon, assigned broken lockers or desks, given old, torn-up textbooks, and unfair grading.

The request for a Black Student Union was flatly denied.

Frustrations spilled over in hot-headed ways.

Fragile new friendships between black and white fell by the wayside with few exceptions like the gay black student warmly accepted into the Drama Club. "He's so cute and good at make-up!" the drama queens gushed.

Other students didn't bother with fighting or confrontation. Leading the charge for love and peace were the smokers and stoners.

The smokers and stoners were the most integrated group at school. They quickly found each other, blended, and shared their cigarettes and weed before school and in the bathrooms. They were true models of civilized grace, maturity, and tolerance. They joked amongst themselves that Fortier High School could be a joyful place if only people would act like them.

The other integrated group, the politicos, was tiny compared to the smokers and stoners. This group included a handful of Black Power students and the revolutionary "Peace Now" kids, whose names were Cherie, Estelle, her new boyfriend, Devin, and Garrett before he was expelled, Katherine sometimes if she wasn't too scared, and others.

Devin traversed easily among the smokers, stoners, and politicos. It wasn't long before the black kids knew Devin to be the coolest white kid in Fortier, much to the chagrin of white high school frat boys, in particular, a boy named Spratt.

Spratt wanted to kill Devin. Whenever he saw Devin, he would mutter, "Damn, he pisses me off."

In the courtyard during lunch, Spratt observed Devin's anti-Vietnam black armband featuring a leg cast with a gun stuck in it. He grabbed Devin's arm.

"Take it off, you piece of shit," Spratt greeted him. Devin found himself surrounded by frat boys itching to beat him up, but he would rather die than cower.

"I can wear what I want, you lame loser," Devin growled.

In a second, Devin was on the ground getting kicked around. He fought like hell to hold on to the armband even with his broke-twice shoulder.

Some black girls who liked Devin ran and got Hercules, the football team's star, and the toughest black kid in Fortier. Hercules risked suspension to rescue Devin. He jettisoned the frat behinds off the skinny white kid on the ground, and they didn't dare fight back. Spratt retreated, swearing, "It ain't over yet!"

"Yeah, it is," Devin croaked as he gasped for breath. He held his sides as he stood up, "You're over with! You were over with the day you were born!"

Devin turned to Hercules. "Thanks, man."

"Good luck, man," Hercules replied and walked away.

By Christmas, the words *black student walkout* were being whispered, one to the next, followed by *Oh, sweet Jesus. You think?* Cherie's stomach twisted as she listened.

The black high school organizer, Jeanette, spoke passionately to everyone she could, every chance she got. Cherie and a group gathered outside of school to listen to Jeanette and other organizers make the case for the Black Student Walkout.

"We won't be alone. Teachers and students from Xavier, Loyola, Tulane, and all the colleges will march with us. Now is the time to stop being helpless and express our power. A walkout will force Principal Schwertz to take action and meet our demands. We need a Black Student Union to address all the racism. We need black teachers. There are no black teachers, no black coaches, and *not even one* black guidance counselor. We need, we demand, better education. We need an African history elective more than the Egypt unit. C'mon, it's happening all over the country!" she encouraged.

"Yeah, but New Orleans isn't the rest of the country. New Orleans does things its own way," a voice in the crowd interrupted. Nervous laughter erupted across the crowd. "They'll send a hundred police to bash in our heads and throw us in Central Lockup to get gang raped. They'll say, Oh, we didn't think you were students. We thought you were them outside agitators."

Other adult organizers weighed in to support Jeanette, "No, no," they reassured the gathering, "All you have to do is stand together and tell your grievances, what's been happening to you, to the TV stations and newspapers. It will be alright. It will be a peaceful student walkout in front of the school, up and down Freret. It's going to make things better."

After a few more weeks of meetings, the morning came. It was a sunny winter day in early 1968.

Estelle looked at Cherie when the morning bell rang. "What do you want to do?" she asked. Her expression was full of tension.

Cherie was just as scared as Estelle but replied bravely, "Let's stay out and join the march. It can't be just black students, it's got to be white, too. I mean, we want fairness, too." Cherie was happy to see Estelle. It had been a long time. Estelle went to a lot of political meetings with her boyfriend. To Cherie, everything with Estelle had become so serious, so life and death. There was no longer room for fun and friendship.

As students poured into school, a large group of black students mobilized on the front sidewalk with placards that read

Fortier Unfair, Black Student Union Now, and Integration, Not Persecution, among others.

They saw Katherine as she headed into school. She stopped and yelled, "I want to stay out here with you, but I can't. I just can't."

Devin and his brother showed up next to them with big smiles. Seeing them made Cherie and Estelle feel a whole lot better.

"Wow. This is really cool!" the boys observed approvingly.

"Is this it? Just the four of us?" Devin said, referring to white student support. They looked around and saw that it was. "C'mon, let's join the end of the line."

Cherie and Estelle followed Devin and Chris to the end of the line. Cherie counted almost two hundred students, parents, and adult organizers. Estelle found her boyfriend, and they found Garrett there with his friends from Booker T. "I wouldn't miss this for anything! We're part of history," Garrett gushed.

As the organizers had predicted, the local TV cameras and reporters soon arrived, and black civil rights leaders from Xavier and Dillard Universities joined the march. More adult sympathizers joined by the second day, including Jewish New Orleanians. They weren't allowed to join Mardi Gras Krewes either, even if their families had been in New Orleans for more than a hundred years.

One family for which Cherie babysat lived a block away from Fortier. Cherie was on the march when she saw the mom wearing a sign that read Support These Students as she pushed the baby in his stroller up and down the block in front of Fortier. She also opened her house to protesters. Cherie yelled and waved to her.

Devin's father drove up to the marching line and gestured his boys into the car. "I want to talk to you." They got in, and he drove away.

"I forbid you to be part of this," Mr. Clarens ordered.

"No," they argued. "We gotta do this. Things at school are fucked up. Stop the car. Stop the car, Dad!"

He kept driving, but at the next red light, Chris jumped out with Devin behind him. Mr. Clarens grabbed at Devin to stop him, but Devin was too quick.

"Devin, get in the car!"

"No!"

The boys high-tailed it back to Fortier and rejoined the line.

By the third day, folks from across town drove by to gape and yell nasty slurs at anyone participating in the walkout. Men across the street took photographs of them.

The Fortier Walkout made the front page of the *Times-Picayune* five days in a row. From the Mississippi River to Lake Ponchartrain, New Orleans peed in its collective bloomers from the shock.

After a week, it ended. Principal Schwertz conceded to look into the students' demands, primarily to start teacher sensitivity training, to resolve complaints of discrimination more quickly, and to hire black teachers and guidance counselors.

The black student leaders of the march were permanently expelled from Fortier, some from public school altogether. Other student marchers, including Cherie, Estelle, Devin, and his brother, were suspended for six weeks and required to sign a pledge that they wouldn't cause any more trouble. Cherie was grateful that Paulette didn't make a big deal out of it. If anything, Paulette seemed to enjoy the excitement. She bragged to her friends about Cherie's suspension. Cherie and Estelle tried to find student-leader Jeanette, but she had disappeared, and no one knew where she went.

Come June, Cherie arrived at school to see black girls crying again, slumped in each other's arms in the hallways. Taking Martin Luther King, Jr. wasn't enough heartbreak for Mr. Devil. Now Bobby Kennedy, who was going to be the next president of the United States, was dead, too, assassinated by gunshot far away in California.

~

Cherie and Estelle dragged blankets and pillows to the floor in Cherie's room. Side by side, they stared at the ceiling and talked.

Estelle waxed on about her boyfriend and told Cherie all the things he said and how devoted he was to a better America through revolution.

"We were walking along Audubon Park, and I was saying how beautiful all the houses off the park were, and then he said, 'Wouldn't it be great if everybody in America could have a house this nice?'"

"That could never happen. It's crazy," Cherie said.

"But that's just it. It's *not* crazy. He told me that only seven percent of American families own about sixty percent of the wealth. If only even one or two percent could be redistributed to the working class, it would eliminate tons of suffering. It would make us stronger as a nation."

"I don't know," Cherie replied. "It sounds good, but people always mess things up. Like if they did that, it would be great for a while, and then go right back to the way it was."

Estelle hmphed, "I guess then he's right about you."

"Oh no, now what?" Cherie sighed. She knew Estelle's boyfriend didn't like it when she was around. He made fun of her, even her frosted lipstick.

"That you're a cynic, and cynics are the enemy of the revolution because they can't accept a vision of a better world," she told her. "You're a drag on the future."

"What?" Cherie exclaimed. She stared into the darkness. Her friendship with Estelle flashed before her eyes and died—chatter, secrets, games, school, joy, sadness. Bang! Dead and gone. Cherie had no idea how it happened or why. *Bad what? Huh? Drag? Are you kidding?* Her mind whirled, but she didn't reply. Instead, she said,

"Let's go to sleep."

Within days, angry notes were exchanged between Cherie and Estelle, filled with accusations. Cherie wrote harshly, "How dare you blame me for anything!"

Estelle reached out, she even apologized, but Cherie never called back. It was all ruined. Like her mother, Cherie knew only one way to deal with people when it went wrong, counterattack and run. It hurt her, though. Cherie sat in the kitchen in tears when Paulette walked in. She made a terrible mistake and told her mother what happened.

Instantly, Paulette dismissed the whole scenario. "Oh, what do you care?" She gestured as though to wipe her hands off, one against the other, "Enough with that little bitch and her sick family already! Get rid of her."

Cherie slammed her fist on the table, "Don't say that!" Paulette laughed, her summary response to Cherie's anger. Cherie ran to her room, Paulette's voice trailing behind her, "She'll be pregnant before she's eighteen."

Cherie shut the door and slid to the floor with her back against it. In a voice too low for Paulette to hear, Cherie spat through her teeth, "You're the sick bitch! I hate you!"

Paulette hounded her through the door, not to be swayed, "Believe me. She is doing you a big favor. To hell with her! Better you stay friends with Katherine and Marlene."

Cherie covered her ears and banged her head on the floor. Paulette tapped on the door with her fingernails. Ratta-tap-tap. "Do you hear me? I swear you need your hearing checked."

On the other side, Cherie curled up on the floor, *Why won't you ever shut up? Shut up. Shut up. Shut up,* Cherie cried to herself until she was spent, and she lay there motionless, staring ahead at nothing.

A few hours later, the phone rang, and Paulette picked it up.

"It is for yoooou," Paulette called to Cherie in a sing-song voice reserved for her own dates.

Cherie's heart leapt. *Maybe it's that boy from art class.* She got up, wiped the tears off her face, and ran for the phone.

CHAPTER 14
Boyfriend

THORNTON, the boy from art class, was quiet except when he had an opinion. Even though he was artistic and creative like his mother, he only mentioned his father, an FBI agent. New Orleans was a hub for FBI, but you rarely knew who they were among your neighbors.

On two separate occasions, he proudly told Cherie the story about how his father had changed rank and rule in his college fraternity in Wyoming when he brought in a friend who was a Shoshone Native American. He described how his father toughed out all the fights that ensued with his frat brothers to protect his pal. Thornton was proud that his father thought for himself and turned his back on racism way back when.

True to these egalitarian beliefs, Thornton hated racism, war, and the divisions between people. In particular, any notion of Divine Right disgusted him. If the subject came up, he raged.

"That was the lame excuse our government coughed up to slaughter Indians all over the country," Thorn said. "Violence in the name of God is bullshit. It's better to be real and say, 'We want your land, so we're going to kill you.'"

Cherie readily agreed. She loved being with Thornton, her first real boyfriend. Besides all the delicious mouthy petting, she truly loved the night they went to see Antonioni's *Blow-Up*. To celebrate the occasion, Thornton dressed up like the main character in the film, sporting a blue checked shirt, white jeans, and a navy sports jacket.

She gripped his arm during the sequence when the two girls plunged laughing and screaming into an unspooled roll of purple paper and ripped off each other's clothes. "I want to jump in and do that," she whispered to him. "Me too," he whispered back.

The Zephyrs accompanied Evening's entrance with warm, soft breezes across the French Quarter. As Cherie and Thorn wandered down Royal Street towards Esplanade Avenue, they were stopped by a young lady in a doorway. In a clipped English accent full of urgency, "Please come in, come in, join us. Come, learn the truth about your beautiful, infinite souls. The workshop is starting right now, and it won't cost you a penny. Come in! Right now, it's starting. We'll teach you to open your mind. Don't you want to know how limitless you are?"

As if heeding the Pied Piper, Cherie and her boyfriend smiled at each other and rolled their eyes as if to say, "Okay, this is stupid but weird, so we've got to check it out." They walked through the doorway down the damp, stone corridor into the courtyard. It was filled with several dozen seekers in fold-out chairs.

The workshop leaders were hippies from Great Britain, followers of the new Process Church of the Final Judgment. They had stringy hair cascading down their shoulders and wore long, purple capes even though it was hot. Their skin was pasty white, and the men and women wore amulets on leather cords. Cherie nudged Thornton as they sat in the crowded, darkened courtyard, "Hey! It's the Purple People Eaters," she whispered.

The purple caped, self-dubbed Processears introduced themselves as part of a new, alternative religion. "We exist, we were born, truly, to help you reach your own cosmic potential," the leader announced with a courtly flourish.

The workshop began. The first exercise was to develop mind-reading for psychic development. Everybody was paired up with a stranger. As instructed, they gave the stranger one of their belongings to hold and meditate over. "We want you to tune in to the power of the object, feel its vibration, and read what it is telling you about its owner."

Cherie was paired up with a cheerful woman whose face looked weather-beaten to Cherie. The cheerful woman took a tooled leather ponytail holder from her shaggy mane and gave it to Cherie. Cherie gave her the necklace she was wearing, a turquoise stone on a silver chain from the Giddy Gadget.

The hippie woman closed her eyes and held Cherie's necklace aloft as if it were sacred. She opened her eyes, smiled sweetly at Cherie, and proceeded in a low voice, "Your necklace, beautiful Cherie, tells me that your dream of dreams is to get married and have lots of children and chickens and goats on your own little farm far away in the mountains."

"No way!" Cherie protested. Cherie waved the tooled leather barrette that had some strands of graying hair in it and protested, "No way, not in a million years that's me you're talking about. That's your prayer to get married and have kids because no doubt men have been really awful to you, and I don't know, you like chickens or something." She handed back the barrette and grabbed her own necklace out of the woman's hands.

At the words "or something," Cheerful turned into Miserable and started to blubber. Two of the Purple People Eaters came over to comfort her, and she proceeded to sob in their arms.

Their angular young leader, shoulder-length hair flying and eyes ablaze, descended on Cherie angrily as if he was reciting Shakespearean, "What did you say to her? Do you know nothing of kindness? How could you be so cold-hearted?! This! This is the origin of evil. Look at what you've done!"

Cherie had no idea. She was being honest, yet she froze in the onslaught of condemnation. Magically, Thornton appeared and grabbed her hand, "Leave her alone!" he yelled at the Purple People Eater. They ran out, knocking over chairs. Back in the street, they kept running as Cherie yelled, "I hate chickens! I'd never own a chicken!"

A few minutes and a few blocks later, wrapped in the fragrant warmth of Cafe Du Monde, Cherie accidentally inhaled some powdered sugar off her beignet, which turned into a big coughing mess. Even the always-serious Thornton started to laugh. It got gut-busting worse when some Swedish tourists asked them if they would share their weed.

Happily, Cherie had the apartment to her latchkey self. At night, Paulette went out so she and Thornton could make out as much as they wished to the brink of desire and back.

The few times she was over at Thornton's house, she thought his father was ridiculously strict. One time at dinner, Thornton's father would not let the younger sister come to the table because she'd been in her room sick all day, even though she felt better by nightfall. "If you're too sick to do your chores," he yelled up the stairs at her, "then you're too sick to have dinner with us." Thornton's mom pouted when he rendered his decision and said, "Oh Daddy." Cherie thought *Yuck. No wonder Thorn never laughs.*

Cherie felt defiant, and it emboldened her. She goaded Thornton's father over dinner. She mouthed off about the war's stupidity and lied about wanting to visit Russia.

Thornton's parents visibly bristled and exchanged looks. Cherie worried them, different as she was from girls they liked. They wished their son would break it off, and they wouldn't have to wish for long.

Paulette would strike the death knell on Cherie and Thornton's relationship.

Paulette was out. Cherie and Thornton had the music on high, and they were on the floor, hugging and kissing. Thornton's hand was under Cherie's shirt, and her jeans were unzipped. Cherie's hand ran up and down Thornton's leg as they embraced.

They didn't hear Paulette and her date come in. On pure instinct, Cherie opened her eyes to see Paulette staring at them. Standing beside her was her new boyfriend, a businessman from Amarillo, Texas. The look on his face was all dirty smirks. Cherie knew the look. She had seen dirty smirks on men's faces a thousand times. She hated that look so much.

More embarrassed in front of her new boyfriend from Amarillo than anything else, Paulette shrieked with horror, "What is going on here?" and to Thornton in an accusatory tone, "You leave my little girl alone!"

As they sat up, zipped up, and buttoned up, Cherie glanced at Thornton, who whispered back, "Talk later." As he left, Paulette yelled, "I'm calling your parents!"

Cherie yelled at Paulette, "Leave him alone, and me, too!" She shut the door to her room and locked it. She could hear Paulette's date comfort her through the door, and she knew that she, Cherie, was no longer the focus of her mother's attention.

Cherie felt that Paulette honestly didn't give a damn about her making out with Thorn. She knew they were doing it, and her entire outburst was nothing but a performance of chaste motherhood to impress her date. As it was, Cherie had barely seen Paulette for several months. Her mother often went out at night, even during the week, and Cherie spent weekends at her friends' houses.

The next day, "I'm sorry, Mama. We didn't hear you come in."

"That's it!" Paulette yelled. "You get rid of that boy with his crazy FBI father. There's something wrong with them!"

"Don't say that! There's nothing wrong with Thornton or anybody in his family."

Cherie yelled at her mother inside her head, *If anything, you should be kissing his feet for being such a good boyfriend to me! He stays late with me so I'm not here alone...*

When Thornton came to pick her up, he had a big, ugly bruise on his face, and his hair was strictly shorn in a military cut.

"Ohmygod, what happened?"

"My father and I got in a fight." He said it blankly as though he was telling the time.

"Why?"

"I refused to get my hair cut."

"So he punched you in the face?"

"I started it. He said I looked like a piece of garbage, and I told him to fuck off."

"Jesus." She ran her fingertips lightly across his face, "Does it hurt?"

"Doesn't matter. I deserved it."

Over the following week, Cherie endured Paulette's snare drum-like yelling as she absorbed the high-pitched bang, bang, bang of her voice.

"How could you do this to me? I thought you were too old for a babysitter. Is that what I need to do now? You know what I'm going to do? I will call his father and tell him to keep his son away from you. Let's see how he likes that!"

Mirror to her mother, Cherie responded, high-pitched and panicky, "Mama, I'm sorry! The Amarillo guy still calls you, doesn't he? He didn't break up with you because of me? He thought it was funny. He was smiling. It turned him on!"

"You get rid of that boy, you hear me!" Paulette hammered, "And then maybe it's time to get rid of you around here. You know, he said he would pay for boarding school for you. That you are heading for trouble. There's one in Texas. Not Amarillo, in Dallas. I called them. They are sending me the papers!"

Cherie's stomach knotted up. Cherie knew that if Paulette forced her into a boarding school, it wouldn't last long. It would end as soon as her mother and Amarillo Man broke up, and as Cherie knew, *They always break up. It would just be another big mess for nothing.* Still, Cherie knew her mother wouldn't shut up until she got her way.

Later, in her room in the closet in the dark with a flashlight, as she clutched the Wordless Diary, Cherie wondered if the FBI-father thing made Paulette paranoid, maybe because it triggered her mother's deep and ingrained fear of secret police. *Secret police picked up her father, Henri, in Paris and murdered him. That's why Mama hates Thornton. Walking in on us is just the excuse. What do I do? Please, God, and gods and goddesses and angels, help me.*

The answer came quickly, *Stay out of her way. Break up. If you don't, she'll hammer you to a pulp. She'll send you to Texas.* Cherie tried to draw her numbers, but she couldn't. All she could do was draw nails sticking into a head until the face was covered entirely with nails.

CHAPTER 15

Monsters in the Floorboards

PAULETTE'S LEFTOVER WWII misery that came out anywhere from clowning to yelling to headaches and depression was shit-real for Cherie. It never went away. It never stopped. It created monsters that Cherie lived with, corporeal, reptilian creatures that followed them wherever they went.

Cherie called them the Monsters in the Floorboards. That's where they slept, and they were extremely sensitive. The slightest infraction might awaken them, these slimy, sharp-toothed war-trauma monsters. Cherie learned early never to upset her mother because the Monsters in the Floorboards would exact revenge. As soon as she fell asleep, they would rise to bite Cherie's ankles. Their stinging tentacles would crawl up her arms and neck and legs while she slept, and she would wake up from thrashing. When they attacked, she would struggle to scream but never could. She could only fight them off.

They were sneaky, too. If the monsters were awakened during the day by Paulette yelling at her, they would wait and get her in the middle of the night. They invaded her dreams and turned them into nightmares. Cherie had lived with their fearsome punishment as far back as she could remember. She hated going to sleep.

She wondered if her very first infraction was being born.

She knew Paulette loved her but felt her life itself put a ball and chain around her mother's restless ankle. If Paulette hadn't become a mother, as Cherie was frequently reminded, she may have gone to college or got married.

Cherie felt bad about that, too, Paulette's sacrifice.

She lived keenly aware of two big deals about her mother and her. The first was that her mother's suffering in the war so overshadowed her infantile American travails as to render them ridiculous, and that Cherie was, in fact, the result of Paulette's failed efforts to abort.

"Oh, and when I realized I was pregnant," Paulette had told her, "I did everything to get rid of you. I jumped off the roof. I took these pills some woman gave me. But when I realized you wouldn't go, I said 'okay,' and I drank milk and took care of myself. And then when I saw how beautiful you came out ..." Lipstick smooch. Rub it off.

Cherie knew it was only her mama jabbering over a glass of wine. Yet, each time she heard it anew, the words bore into her guts, another prick, and a drop of poison. Drop by drop, the poison was adding up.

Cherie also knew she hadn't been her mother's first pregnancy. When she was ten, her grandmother told her the story during one of her rare visits from St. Petersburg, Florida. The visit didn't last long because Paulette and Grandma loathed each other and fought like hornets. Grandma looked like an older version of Paulette but had different coloring. Her gray hair was tinged with dark blond, not brown like Paulette's, though her eyes were hazel, the same as Cherie's.

In the story her grandmother told her, it happened after Paulette and Grandma fled Paris during WWII after Grandpa Henri was arrested by the Gestapo and sent away, never to be seen again. Paulette was in danger, too. Henri had taken her with him on resistance missions. When Paulette was fifteen, she went out in the dead of night with her father to post anti-Nazi notices on kiosks in Paris. Caught, she would have been shot on sight.

"But why did he do that if Mama could have been killed?" Cherie interrupted, thinking, *What kind of daddy would endanger his own daughter's life that way? It was creepy.*

Like Paulette, Grandma ignored the question as if it hadn't been spoken at all.

"*Il etait si beau,* so handsome," Grandma said as she evoked Henri's memory. "*Mon Dieu,* how he loved your mother."

She was lost, for a moment, in the past. Cherie waited.

"We left Paris. We were staying in Brittany. Paulette was too nervous. She couldn't stay inside. She went off somewhere. I don't know where. She was gone. She was so difficult." Grandma then pointed her finger and tapped the table to emphasize every word, "*She would not do what you were supposed to do!* And just like that," she snapped her fingers, "she broke the curfew and was arrested and sent to one of the Guernsey Islands. You know they are in between France and England. The Nazis put her in a labor camp."

"Your mother, she started a love affair with one of the young men in the camp from Spain, but he was married, or there was another woman, and there was trouble. He helped her escape the island on a Swedish boat. You know what they could have done to her on that boat, a young girl? And then throw her overboard and drown her?"

Even though she was only ten at the time, Cherie sort of knew, but that wasn't part of the story.

"The Swedish sailors brought Paulette safely back to France. Then, can you imagine? Paulette, oh my God, she finds out she is pregnant by the Spaniard. There was no money, no food, no anything. On top of that, we had bombs falling on our heads."

Grandma continued, "I didn't know. How could I know, and what could I have done? I didn't know anything until she came into the basement where we were. And in the middle of the room, she screams with pain and holding her stomach. She is bent over, and I see she is bleeding. Blood is running down her legs, right on the carpet!"

Cherie nodded. She understood that Grandma was the type of person who would be very concerned about the carpet.

Grandma helped Paulette into the bathroom, where she miscarried into the toilet. Then it got worse. Paulette didn't stop bleeding, and Grandma had to take her to the hospital that was crawling with Nazis.

As Paulette lay in the hospital ward, the French police questioned her to make sure she hadn't had an abortion, which was punishable by getting your head chopped off in a modern guillotine, even if you had other children.

"Very smart girl, your mother. She made up a story to shut them up, and they left her alone."

Grandma squinted, looked at little Cherie, and lowered her voice. "She had gone, your mother, to some lady somewhere, who knows, who did something to her, put something up inside of her, to make her have the cramps and get rid of it. But your mother was smarter than those stupid pigs in the hospital. They did not find out." She shook her head and let out a long, drawn-out sigh. "She was so thin, so pale."

Grandma repeated the refrain that Cherie had heard every

time they were together, "Such beautiful furniture we had. We lost everything."

Cherie had a lot of questions, but Grandma was done talking about it. She turned her attention to the TV and *Green Acres*. She loved all of the Gabor sisters, Eva most of all.

Cherie felt sorry for Paulette. As Paulette described it herself, her life was nothing but bad luck. "With my lousy luck" was one of Paulette's oft-repeated phrases.

The extent to which she, Cherie, was a part of her mother's lousy luck was something she tried to compensate as best she could. She went along with Paulette's erratic demands and fits, took care of herself, and kept to herself unless Paulette wanted company or wanted to go out.

Cherie believed these were the good things about being Paulette's daughter. First and foremost, Cherie loved the freedom. Paulette rarely noticed or questioned her, except for the involved-mother-show she displayed when other people were around.

The other good thing Cherie loved about being Paulette's daughter was worldliness. Paulette read books and watched the news. She was smart. Cherie appreciated that her mother had taken her to the ballet, puppet shows, and movies with subtitles when she was little. And being pretty and having a French background. That was good, too.

Sadness for her mother's lost youth, lost father, and unwanted motherhood weighed on Cherie. When things went wrong between them, Cherie cried alone in her room with feelings of guilt. Her feelings of self-recrimination gave way to panic. She feared the Monsters in the Floorboards would punish her for such transgression. Her throat tightened with the thought, and she struggled to take a deep breath.

Cherie got out of bed and stared into the darkness. She turned to the blank wall over the headboard. It was still blank. Cherie felt the familiar, sickening burn in her stomach, as though one of the Monsters had slithered down her throat and was boxing in her guts.

A few months earlier, this part of her bedroom wall hadn't been blank at all. It was covered with the only poster she had from the Giddy Gadget. It was the last one of its kind and torn in the corner, so Berley's mother gave it to her.

It was a brightly colored poster of the Greek god, Zeus. In it, Zeus was atop Mt. Olympus. As his long, golden locks caressed his shoulders, he drew down great lightning bolts from the stormy clouds above him with his powerful arms. Z E U S was printed in bold, Greek-style letters across the bottom.

Cherie adored that poster; it touched a sense of devotion in her, this poster of a beautiful, all-powerful father god. Sometimes, she imagined he would step down and battle with the Monsters in the Floorboards. He would vanquish them. She loved him so much that she would stand on the bed and kiss him until the day she came home, and he was gone, ripped down. All that was left was an empty space and four thumbtacks.

"What did you do with my poster of Zeus?" she yelled at Paulette.

Paulette looked up from the couch where she was watching TV, an empty pan of tacos on her lap, her glass of wine and pill bottle on the coffee table. She shifted on the couch and pouted in a whiny voice, "I didn't like it, the way it looked. It reminded me ... Sit down and watch this with me. It's so funny."

"But it was in the corner. You couldn't see it. It wasn't even facing the door!"

"I didn't like it ... it reminded me ... so blond like that."

"So now I'm supposed to hate blond, too, along with everybody else I'm supposed to hate!"

Paulette let loose the loud cackle she used to turn things into a joke.

Cherie ran to the garbage can outside. *Maybe I can just tape it back,* she hoped, but it was ripped to bits.

Later, alone, Cherie cried with frustration. Tears streamed down her face as she raged to herself. *It was in the corner! It didn't face the door. She couldn't see it. Why did she do that! Why!*

Cherie began to doubt Paulette. Cherie began to think that maybe Paulette evoked war trauma just to push her around, as though Cherie wasn't her own self but her mother's puppet to mess with. She stared ahead, not seeing anything, and clenched her teeth, barely breathing. Her fists were so tight her nails dug into her palms.

These were daunting thoughts for Cherie, fraught with blood heresy, *She just uses the whole war thing to beat me down. She knew I loved my Zeus picture. It's her lying, rotten excuse to beat me down and get her way no matter what.* Cherie was filled with frightening thoughts. *What if I can't keep it in anymore? What if I start screaming? What then? Will the Monsters in the Floorboards eat me alive? What if I can't wake up when they get me? Will I go crazy and die? Or kill ...*

Cherie stayed up all night. She didn't know what to do. She didn't want to lose Thornton. It wouldn't work to see him in secret for long. She couldn't run away, nor could he, not yet, not that he even wanted to, but Paulette would never shut up, not ever, until she got her way.

Break up. Just get it over with, and the monsters would slink back into the floorboards.

Deep in her closet, where she hid babysitting money and little things away from Paulette's busy fingers, she had a card Thorn had drawn in pen and ink for her. It featured a heart-shaped kite. Cherie modeled her Wordless Diary numbers into heart kites for what was left, 8-6-2, two years, four months, and 12 days.

Across town, deep in the French Quarter on Chartres Street, Katherine, Marlene, and Katherine's new friend, Lila, looked through the wrought iron gate at the dilapidated courtyard of the abandoned Ursuline Convent. It was a beautiful evening. The breezes were soft, and faint traces of hops from the Jackson Brewery off the Mississippi River twitched their noses.

The courtyard was large, about an entire block, grassy and overgrown. It was crisscrossed by brick walkways and formed a maze-like impression. It was barely visible beneath the strands of moonbeams that appeared through the thick, slow-moving clouds.

"My mother is translating a document about this place," Katherine whispered as though betraying a secret. "I saw it on the kitchen table. The Ursuline nuns came here from France in 1726, and after a while, they started a boarding school for orphan girls, and it didn't matter if they were black or white. The nuns freaked everybody out because they were on their own with no priests to rule them. They were so radical."

"That is *so* cool," Marlene nodded.

Lila stood on tiptoe and looked in. She was thinner and taller than both Katherine and Marlene, her lean figure topped by silky blond hair in a pixie cut.

"I feel like the courtyard is calling me," Lila broke the silence.

"Lila, Lila," Katherine taunted in ghostly tones, "I'm calling you," followed by Marlene's "Katherine, Katherine," followed by Lila's "Marlene, Marlene, I'm calling you," a siren's choir.

"We have to go in there," Lila declared with urgency. "I'm not kidding! I feel like it wants me to visit. It's lonely, it wants us to be in there. It needs us. It really does."

"Let's climb in," Katherine proposed. She looked at Marlene for approval.

Marlene was game, but true to her nature, she could see all sides of the situation at once, the heaven of sneaking in and the hell of getting caught. "Okay, but only for a minute. I don't want anybody to yell at us or call the police."

They helped each other climb over the gate and into the empty courtyard.

Katherine whispered, "I love it in here. I can see all the Ursuline sisters walk around. They're holding their rosaries." She clasped her hands together in prayer.

"I don't care about nuns," Lila laughed as she dropped to the ground. "Ooohhh, it's so cool in here. Look at the moon. Mr. Moon, I am your July child, your moonchild. Hug me, kiss me with your rays!"

"C'mon, get up," Marlene said, but when she tried to pull Lila to her feet, Lila pulled her down and tickled her. Katherine fell on top. Suddenly, Katherine pulled Lila's T-shirt off and took off at a run. She waved Lila's T-shirt over her head.

Lila was left topless since she didn't wear a bra. She chased after Katherine. "Take your top off," Lila yelled ahead to Katherine. "It feels so good."

In seconds, Marlene looked to one end of the courtyard to discern Lila and Katherine's bare derrieres at a run over the walkways, up and down and back and forth.

Oh no, she thought.

"C'mon, c'mon," they entreated her, "It feels so good. You have to do it. You have to. Do it before you think about it!" and "If you don't do it, you'll hate yourself."

Too late to stop them, Marlene joined in, tossing off her clothes. She took off after Lila and Katherine, choreographing her sky-clad run in the deserted convent garden with grand ballet leaps of joy.

They didn't get caught. By the time they were dressed and back out on the sidewalk, they were starving. Arm in arm, Lila,

Katherine in the middle, and Marlene headed toward a busy Italian diner on Bourbon Street. They walked in zigzags and chanted, "Spaghetti and tomato sauce. Spaghetti and tomato sauce."

"Let's call Cherie," Katherine said.

"Yeah, maybe she's better by now," Marlene agreed, "Yeah, let's call her. Let's play Scrabble tonight." Then, to Lila, "Do you play Scrabble?"

Lila gasped, her eyes widened, and a half-smile crossed her face as she stopped dead and faced Marlene and Katherine, "You're joking, right?"

"Okay, okay. Whose house?"

"Let's go to mine." Lila offered, "We can pick up Cherie on the way. She's only like eight blocks from me on Willow, right? I've got all this new, incredible music. I just got three new albums. I got Aretha Franklin.

"I love her!" Katherine chimed in. "Yay," Marlene added, "We can dance. Dance off the spaghetti."

"Yeah," Lila trilled, "and I think really late tonight, *Zorba the Greek* is on TV. That movie just kills me. I'm so hungry. I love their salads. Let's get salad, too, with oil and vinegar. Did you hear? Andy Warhol's coming to New Orleans. He's hosting an exhibit of his favorite *objets d'art* at the museum in City Park. I can't wait to meet him. Ohmygod, look at the clouds moving across the mooooon!"

CHAPTER 16
Misfit

IT WAS the 1968-69 school year, and 11th grade chugged along. Cherie accepted the hard, cold fact that she was a misfit and outsider. She felt as though every rotten thing Estelle's boyfriend, Thornton, and everybody else had ever said about her was true.

In thought, word, and deed, Cherie wore her alienation like a badge of honor. She was vocally anti-war, wore black most all the time (black boots, tights, skirt, and turtleneck, T-shirt when it was really hot), decorated herself with sarcastic and profane political buttons, and wore a black glazed African tiki around her neck. She lined her eyes with black eyeliner and wore silver frosted lipstick, which gave her a ghoulish look, far from the bright colors of popular fashion. She loved the look, and she liked that others hated it. At home, Paulette assailed her every day for how ugly she looked, repeating, "Sweet 16 doesn't apply to you!"

Going to school was torment for Cherie. *You just have to last this year and next year,* she told herself. She hated all the cheerleaders, the high school sorority girls, football games, pep rallies (*It's just brainwashing everybody into robots,* she thought), assemblies, and dragging out to the field to stand under the hot sun during bomb scares. She often snapped at classmates even when they were nice to her. "Leave me alone!"

After the black student walkout, an integrated choir formed. It was led by a loud, upbeat, guitar-playing girl. They performed at all the outreach assemblies. Principal Schwertz was a different man. He smiled more and was friendlier in a concerted effort to be more available to students. The hideous words on the industrial grey walls of Fortier High School had been painted over in grey, but there was talk about repainting the school in prettier hues such as mauve and cream.

Cherie dully watched the assembly proceedings from the back row of the bleachers. She turned her attention to her copy of Hugo's *Les Miserables*. She was right at the part when Fantine sells her front teeth. Cherie felt sick that a beautiful French girl would be so poor that she would sell her teeth. It felt surreal to Cherie, set against the assembly songs about friendship, peace, and rainbows. *It would make a good poem,* she thought, *I Go to High School and Hugo to the French Revolution.*

She looked for Katherine but couldn't find her. *Probably sick again*, Cherie considered.

Cherie looked over to where Estelle sat with her new girlfriends. Cherie hated how they followed Estelle around like worshipful puppy dogs. She and Cherie barely acknowledged each other in the halls. Her lungs tightened up when she saw Estelle. Cherie stopped herself, *It doesn't matter anymore. I have Lila now,* she lied to herself, smashing down the hurt.

On top of that, Cherie missed Thorn, his tall frame, different way of thinking, his creativity, his hands, and his mouth. It made her ache with sadness.

Cherie recalled the unbearable break-up.

Wearing an expression that belonged to the dead, Cherie had told Thorn it was over. She had no choice, she explained.

He slumped as though his breath had been knocked out of

him. He stared unmoving, finally nodded, and left. He would never talk to her or look at her again. Cherie did what her mother insisted she do, cut and run. She had done it to Estelle. Cherie grimaced, thinking about it.

Neither Thorn nor any of his friends would talk to her either. They wouldn't even look at her like she was poison. They turned their heads away.

Cherie's new black girlfriends had been expelled after the student walkout, and the rest retreated from interaction. Garrett was expelled, and Devin rarely showed up for school at all. *Maybe he's expelled, too,* she figured. Lila and Marlene were at Ben Franklin High School. Everybody was gone.

Cherie sat down at a lunch table with Anna Daniels and her best friend, who, like Anna, had parents who survived the WWII Holocaust in Europe. Cherie had noticed that those kids whose parents had lost so much in the genocide always found each other as though magnetized by the shadow of death that hung over them.

In one long breath, Anna caught Cherie up on the conversation.

"Hi, we're talking about the book *House of Dolls*. It's from a maybe diary, but I think it's real, from Auschwitz, and it's about the section of Auschwitz where they force Jewish and other prisoners to be sex slaves for Nazi soldiers, and if they refuse, or if they don't act like they're happy and a soldier complains, or if they get venereal disease, they're instantly killed." Anna then turned back to her rapt best friend and continued,

"So, there's this boy named Moni. He's about twelve, and he has beautiful eyes," Anna related, widening her own beautiful eyes. "And they give him to the Block Chief, who's a pervert. And a lot of the boys who ended up that way, the Nazis when they got tired of them would break their necks."

Cherie pushed her tray away, but stayed and listened, repulsed by the story as she was fascinated with Anna and her friend's way of talking about it. They continued the conversation with a straight-forward, cool approach like that were reporting the nightly news: *More Nazi horrors revealed in mysterious diary.*

"Is that what happens to him?" Anna's friend asked.

"No, he can't eat because being raped like that makes him nauseous, and the Nazis don't want their kid prostitutes to be bony. They like them chubby, so he's beaten. He can barely move but still manages to throw himself on the electric fence and commits suicide." Anna took a breath, ate a bite of her sandwich, and continued, "That's what happens to the main character, Daniella, too. She commits suicide in the end because her brother sees her at a soldier orgy, and she's too ashamed to stay alive."

"May I borrow it when you're done?" her friend asked.

Anna nodded yes. "But don't you still have my copy of *The Boston Strangler*?"

"I thought I lost it but found it in my sister's room. She's always taking my stuff, but I got her back. I hid her copy of *Mila 18* before she finished it."

"Good one," Anna laughed, and her best friend did the same.

Anna turned to Cherie, "Do you ever see Kaleb, Katherine's older brother? Did he really run away?"

Cherie picked at the butterscotch brownie on her school lunch tray. It was one of the best things the lunch ladies made. Estelle loved them and wanted to get the recipe.

"Yeah. Katherine got a letter from him at Marlene's like six months ago from Colorado, but nothing since, and no return address."

"I think Kaleb was the sexiest boy in New Orleans," Anna's friend added.

"Not as good-looking as Garrett's brother," Anna countered, "Black hair and light blue eyes are so cool."

"And Fielding and Warren and Eric," her friend added.

"And Mark and David over at Neumann," Anna replied, and they laughed together.

The beautiful boys of New Orleans made for endless conversation, but Anna and her friend's joy made Cherie feel miserable. She stood up to leave.

"Do you still see Thornton?" Anna asked, "I heard y'all broke up."

"Yeah. We broke up."

"You know, he liked me before he liked you, but I didn't want to go out with him."

Anna's best friend added, "Yeah, if Anna had gone out with him, he never would have called you. Not in a million years."

Cherie took her tray and left, their whispers and giggles behind her, "God, the way she dresses. Thornton hates her. Stupid bitch. Freak."

School didn't matter one bit to Cherie. *Just go and make good enough grades to get out.* She forced herself up after a few hours of sleep, donned her black rags and paint, and made it through the school week without screaming, at least not on the outside.

On Friday night, she would move into Lila's house and live there all weekend with Lila, her mama Faylene, and her little sister.

CHAPTER 17
Sanctuary

CHERIE HAD NEVER KNOWN anyone like Lila. She was a hurricane of imagination, opinions, and emotions. Like a growing toddler with a sky-high metabolism, Lila couldn't get enough to satisfy her voracious curiosity.

Lila bucked convention without effort. Early in the school year, Lila unwittingly turned Ben Franklin High School upside down by wearing a floor-length skirt to school so she'd have to hold it up when she walked up the stairs. It riled the school's administrators, and Lila's long skirt turned into a big rigmarole, resulting in *Lila Takes on Ben Franklin High School.*

Lila, more than anything else, loved being free — free to do whatever she wanted for as long as she wanted. She felt entitled to it. Anything less would trigger tearful hysterics and emotional, manipulative litigation to obtain her desires. This part of her personality rattled her friends, especially when it seeped into blatant lying. Cherie hated the lies but forgave her for it. When Cherie brought it up, Lila would shrug,

"That's what we have to do! You have to make excuses. You

can't go around hurting people's feelings all the time. Being mean is against my values."

At school, several teachers, the vice principal, and the principal himself confronted her as a group about her long skirt as though they were afraid to confront her alone.

Lila countered them. She derided useless administrative obsessions, such as student wardrobes, when so many, much more important things were happening in the world, like starving people and the Vietnam War. At that, Lila would wipe away voluminous tears and blow her nose.

Ben Franklin's principal and the rest of the committee discussed it until the following afternoon. Victory for Lila. They declared it would henceforth be acceptable for female students to wear long skirts as long as they didn't drag on the floor for safety reasons.

Besides freedom, Lila's engine was fueled by *joie de vivre*. She loved New Orleans' subtropical days of warmth, sun, and blue skies and greeted every day, bursting through the front door and yelling, "Oh, it's so beautiful out!" She loved blue and lavender, restaurants, having sex with her boyfriend, books, playing Scrabble, being the center of attention, art, and movie stars.

And Cherie. She loved Cherie. Lila had never had a friend like her, who would listen and defend her even to her parents, watch forbidden adult films with her, laugh for no reason until tears rolled down their faces, and indulge her adventurous spirit. Lila typed up poems about their friendship and gave them to Cherie.

Lila invited Cherie to go with her to the opening of the Andy Warhol exhibit at the New Orleans Museum of Art. It wasn't an exhibit of his paintings, however. Warhol had put together a display of favorite objects that influenced his art, and he would be there himself to present them to New Orleans' elite.

The New Orleans Museum of Art was gorgeous by anybody's standards. It was a 25,000-square-foot neo-classical temple in City Park. It was originally named after sugar baron Isaac Delgado, who gave the city $150,000 to build "a temple of art for rich and poor alike." Sadly, Mr. Delgado didn't live to see its grand opening in 1911 because he died a few weeks earlier. His love for New Orleans didn't stop there. In his will, he left his family's art collection to the new museum.

The museum's greeter, who always caught the fancy of the young and immature, was a large bronze of a muscular archer, legs apart, generous genitals on display, ready to launch a mighty arrow from his great bow.

Marlene named him Captain Beau Scrotie, so the quartet called him that.

It was impossible for Cherie, Marlene, Katherine, and Lila to walk past Captain Beau Scrotie without a giggle, tickle (if no one was looking), and then run up the museum stairs to the entrance. They never entered the museum without playful grins on their faces.

Lila dressed engagingly for the Warhol event. She wore a rust-colored, shiny velvet mini-dress with long sleeves and a high collar. It had pleats down the front and hugged her slim shape. The hem settled slightly above mid-thigh. With it, Lila wore bare legs and soft leather boots with leather ribbons that crisscrossed up from the ankle. She had barely entered the grand foyer when a *Times-Picayune* photographer stopped her for photos. He called her "Sweetheart."

There he was, the real Andy Warhol. Next to him was Jane Forth, a young woman from his Factory crowd. She wore a slinky black dress, and her hair was pulled tightly back in a chignon.

Andy was chatting with folks and signing soup cans they had brought with them.

Although Cherie held back, Lila grabbed her hand and pulled her forward to meet them.

Lila effortlessly talked to Andy Warhol and Jane Forth. She asked them what they had seen of the city and where they had eaten. She cracked jokes about the cuisine and made them laugh.

When Lila disappeared to get Jane a drink, Cherie overheard Jane Forth say, "She's funny. She should come to our party later." Andy smiled and nodded at her.

Cherie stared at him as he signed an autograph for her. He looked exactly like his photos except for one thing the cameras missed. His eyes. She had never seen eyes like that. They were strange, dark blue and glassy. Still, they weren't a wild man's eyes. His expression was relaxed and sweet, his platinum hair and skin so white it was almost translucent. He evidently avoided daylight. Cherie liked that; *seizing the night* was something she aspired to. They didn't stay long. Lila was suddenly anxious to get home.

Cherie couldn't wait to get to Lila's house after school. Indeed, there were two big surprises. The first was the morning paper, which featured a photo of Lila on the marble stairs of the museum at the Warhol event. The second was the elaborate basket of fruit, flowers, and candy on the dining room table. The card read, "Mr. Warhol, Welcome to the Monteleone Hotel." *Ohmygod*, Cherie thought, *she really did go to their party*. Lila had gone to their hotel room, and they gave her the gift basket.

"What did you do there?" Cherie eagerly asked.

"Not much," Lila shrugged like it was no big deal, "People were standing around, and it was crowded, and they were all stoned and drunk, so I stayed for a while and then left. I talked to Jane about films, and she told me I should call her if I visit New York. Then, as I was leaving, she gave me the basket to take home. They had at least a dozen piled up in the corner."

Cherie was humbled and grateful for Lila's best friendship and hospitality. She could barely stand being home on weekends anymore when Paulette brought home George, her portly, old lawyer boyfriend. George would make dirty comments about Cherie growing up, which made Paulette laugh. Paulette thought he was funny.

Cherie loathed him. She wished he would get hit by a bus. She especially hated the birthday card he gave her when she turned sixteen. It depicted an ugly, goofy cartoon of a Playboy bunny with a big behind and a joke about bunny tails. Cherie cringed when Paulette bid her to thank him with a kiss for the twenty dollars stuck in it. She tried to get away with an air kiss, but he put his heavy arm around her and pulled her close into his repellent wool jacket.

"You're mighty welcome, honey."

It made Cherie sick, but she knew it wouldn't stop until she left home. She threw some stuff in her backpack, rode her bike to Lila's on Friday afternoon, and stayed away until after school on Monday. It wasn't long before Lila's mother, Faylene, called Cherie My Weekend Daughter.

Lila's pretty mama, Faylene, was a complicated person. When Cherie first met her, Faylene was in bed in her well-appointed bedroom wearing a white silk and lace nightgown and a matching white silky robe. A tray of picked-at toast and coffee was on the night stand, and she was surrounded by books, *Life* and *Time* magazines, and stationery strewn about the white sheets and pink chenille bedspread.

Meals, household chores, and childcare were left to the housekeeper. Nevertheless, Mama Faylene was always there for her girls and their friends. It was not unusual to find Lila, her younger sister, and their friends stretched out on Mama's bed, deep in conversation, lapping up her comfort and advice.

One night at a party, Garrett drank too much and started coming apart about poverty in the country. He had just returned from central Louisiana on behalf of Students for a Democratic Society, and the sight of a baby with rat bites haunted him.

"It's wrong. It's just so wrong. We shouldn't have that here!" Garrett yelled at Cherie, "There's so much wealth," his voice cracking as he ran his hands through his hair. Cherie ran and got Lila, who grabbed him by the hand and ushered him to Faylene's bedroom.

"Talk to my mama. You need to talk to my mama," she said, and at the door, "Mama, will you talk to Garrett?"

"Sure, darlin'," Cherie heard Faylene's thick Alabama accent through the door. "Garrett, honey, hand me that remote for the TV. Let's get this thing turned off. I don't even know why I was looking at it. It's so dumb. I usually just watch the news. There. Now sit here and tell me what the matter is. Lila, keep it down out there, will you darlin'? It's late! I don't want a migraine."

Cherie observed that the door to Faylene's clothes closet was ajar. Taped to the inside of the door were photos of horrors perpetrated in war. One photo showed a soldier comforting another as the latter wept in his arms. She also spotted a photo of civil rights protesters being attacked by police dogs, one of Angela Davis, and one of Martin Luther King, Jr.

Cherie and Lila closed the bedroom door and listened on the other side as Garrett ranted about the world, and Mama Faylene talked to him until he calmed down.

Faylene was from Birmingham, Alabama. She was raised in the hills outside the city riding horses English style. Her daddy adored and doted upon her, much to her mother's jealous and unforgiving sorrow. Her family was both Catholic and Jewish, but she subscribed to neither. Blond, petite, and beautiful, her manners and dress were perfect. Recently divorced and unable to separate from the fine upbringing that trained her to be a dependent woman, she did the only thing she could do. She took to her bed.

There, all by herself, Faylene supported progressive causes. She sent part of her alimony to Julian Bond and Morris Dees, who founded the Southern Poverty Law Center, to NAACP, and the newly founded Vietnam Vets Against the War. She wrote letters to the President and to Congress. In addition, as part of the divorce, she had it put on paper that housekeeper Carmella's healthcare bills would be paid for, along with her salary.

Sometimes at night, when she left her bed to dress and leave the house to attend an art gallery opening, a school function, or an event at Tulane, Faylene looked like a movie star, often sporting sunglasses, pearls, a silk scarf, and gloves to match her suit. Her fancy exterior belied a free-thinking interior, which few people recognized. One person who did see Faylene's soul beyond the glamour was Flooky, a young, black organizer at Tulane University. Faylene and Flooky became friends.

Faylene opened the doors of her townhouse on Vincennes Place for secret, invitation-only meetings that Flooky arranged. The guest list included Black Panthers, Students for a Democratic Society known as SDS, anti-war student activists, and others.

Lila's little sister, barely in her teens, carried out tradition as hostess. Her thick, brunette curls spilling over her shoulders, she would greet attendees upon arrival with a bright smile and a cheerful, "Good evening. Please leave your guns at the door. Right there. Thank you so much. There's lemonade and cookies in the dining room."

Although Faylene's ex-husband fancied himself an open-minded man, he was still one of New Orleans' good old boys who followed a self-serving, hard line of well-polished protocol. Lila and her little sister never told their daddy about Faylene's secret meetings at the townhouse he paid for. With panic in her voice, Lila told her little sister, "Daddy can't know. If Daddy knows, he'll shit a brick, a whole mess of them. He'll kill Mama and us, too!"

As Cherie and Lila hung out in Lila's room, Lila shared a story about her mother. Faylene went to a movie theater in a black neighborhood to see a film about a black and white love affair called ONE POTATO, TWO POTATO. As Lila related it, Faylene was the only white person in the theater.

"How do you know?"

"I was up when she got home, and it looked like she was crying, so I made her tell me."

"I can't believe she went all alone," Cherie whispered.

"No kidding. She dressed up for it. She was wearing her light blue Davidow suit." Lila smiled at the wonder of her mother's style. "You know, the film was at Cannes, and they all loved it, but it was banned here, and somehow that theater got it anyway, and Mama wanted to see it. She had to cross some stupid picket line to get in, and the crackers yelled at her. It really upset her."

"My mother once went to a Klan meeting," Cherie confided. "Well, she didn't go to it, she *observed* it," Cherie offered as though it was a weirdest-mother contest.

"What? Paulette did what?"

"I'm not kidding," Cherie added. "It was a long time ago when she was a secretary at Tulane. One of the grad students found out where it was going to be because he was studying Indian mounds west of Baton Rouge, so my mother and him and somebody else, I don't know who, drove there. They watched it from a hillside, and there was a bonfire, and whole families were there, some of them in white sheets and hoods. Then they thought they were spotted, so they ran like crazy back to the car and hightailed it out of there."

"God knows, Klanners are gonna burn in hell," Lila hmphed.

Cherie nodded. "Anyway, the only men I like in masks and

hoods are Mardi Gras Krewes on floats and horses, targeting *me* for Mardi Gras beads."

Lila shook her legs and arms straight up, chanting, "Mardi Gras! Mardi Gras!"

Cherie did the same, "Over here. Over here. Me! Me! Mardi Gras! We love Mardi Gras!"

Lila fell asleep singing Mardi Gras Mambo. *It takes a cool cat to blow a horn.* Cherie grabbed the Wordless Diary and marveled at the numbers 5-5-5. Pencil in hand, she stylized the fives into a Zeus Mardi Gras float.

CHAPTER 18
Elaine in Chains

COLD DRIZZLE WET THE CITY, an insult on a Saturday morning, especially in April.

Cherie, Lila, Marlene, and Katherine headed into the Quarter for coffee and hot chocolate at a popular cafe called the Fatted Calf. Cherie looked to the sky, "It's all drizzly, but it's like little kisses when it hits my face."

They walked down Chartres Street, bypassing Royal, and as always, they avoided Bourbon Street altogether. After Friday night partying by the frats, drizzle seemed to amplify the odors of liquor, vomit, and urine on Bourbon rather than wash it away. By afternoon, the noxious smells would be gone. Pails filled with soap and water would be thrown onto the sidewalks and swept away.

As they light-footed down Chartres off of Canal, they filed into the Tiki Shop, an obligatory stop on the block. There, they could smell the black Spanish soaps, play with the jewelry, and dawdle over pretty things from around the world. They compared the African incense sticks they had purchased.

Two blocks from the cafe, they also discussed whether or not they should order croissants, too, and if they did that, was there enough money left between them or just stick to hot chocolate and coffee.

Lila pointed out, "If Francesco's there, he'll give us a baguette and butter for free. He's my favorite waiter. Daddy and I always sit at his tables."

Ensconced in the little café on the corner of Bienville Street, surrounded by French Quarter locals reading their newspapers and a wall of seasonal glass panels that sheltered them from the cold, they ordered their hot drinks.

Two of the girls would get coffee, and two of them would get hot chocolate. They could get hot milk in a separate pitcher if they asked nicely. Then they would make a rollicking mess dribbling the hot mixtures back and forth across the table into each other's cups, sputtering, laughing, and sipping, until everybody had what they really wanted, hot mocha. The thick white porcelain cups used for coffee complicated the happy ritual as they were the worst cups to pour out of, though this never discouraged them.

With each sip, they purred with happiness until they were interrupted. It was a girl their age. She clanked her rings on the cafe's glass and waved at them. Patrons were beginning to frown and object.

"Ohmygod! It's Elaine." Lila jumped up to get her.

Lila pulled her into the cafe. The girls grabbed another chair and scooted aside to fit her in. Cherie, Katherine, and Marlene didn't know Elaine well, but Lila did. Elaine ran in a different crowd.

Elaine turned heads wherever she went. She wore tight jeans with a green plaid flannel shirt topped by a denim jacket and a hunter green wool scarf, which offset the mop of auburn curls that fell past her shoulders.

As she sat down, she peeled off her jacket and stretched backward, letting out a growl of relief. She stretched as though *even* the confinement of a jacket was too much for her. It brought an approving smile to the face of the husband a table over, matched by chagrin from his observing wife.

Elaine's eyes were rimmed with red from crying.

"What's going on? What are you doing down here all by yourself?" Marlene asked.

Elaine started to blubber. She pushed her tears away with her palms, "I had to get out and walk. I just had to get out and walk. I wrecked my room." She blew her nose into a paper napkin and continued, "I'm not kidding. Somebody's going to die in my house. I hate my parents so much. Either I will kill myself, them, or somebody because I can't take it anymore!"

She ranted on with bitterness in her voice, "I was just sitting there, and my mom started ragging on me, and when I finally ran out, I slammed the door so hard the antique mirror over the couch fell and cracked, and she started yelling even more, 'Is this what you're going to do now? You're going to destroy our house?' So, I yelled back, Yes! And I went in and wrecked my room, and now I'm here." More tears fell.

They all nodded at Elaine sympathetically. They knew exactly what she was saying.

Elaine went on. "What do they want? What do they fucking want? I don't do weed, I don't screw boys, well, not right now, for me to be like my robot sister and stay at home every minute and wash the bathroom toilet for them and study every second like a jerk?" Tears streamed down her face. They handed her more paper napkins.

"You're so thin," Marlene noticed. "Are you hungry?"

Elaine shook her head no, her curls moving in tow. "No, thank you. I can't eat anymore."

Lila cut in. "Are you going to a shrink?"

"Yes, but I hate him, too. He makes me sick. I'm not going back. Do you know him? Dr. Janks?"

Marlene and Lila gasped in unison, "Oh God, not him. He's such a creep. Don't go back to him!"

Marlene leaned in, "My parents sent me to him last year because I was completely depressed. I went like four times. During the session, he put his hand on my knee and told me that he had dreams that he loved me."

Lila cut in. "When I went to him, he used to wear shorts and put his fat legs up on the table so you could see his underwear." Frowns and "Eeww" twittered across the table.

Marlene cut in, "He's such a perve. I heard from my neighbor whose mother is a shrink that Cecil Janks got a formal reprimand because even though he's a psychiatrist, he gave a woman patient a gyno exam."

That did it. The collective squeals of horror drew another round of impatient huffs across the cafe. People shushed them.

"He's not a psychotherapist," Cherie declared mischievously, "He's a psycho-the-rapist. That's what it spells, you know."

"Janks...Stank," Marlene rhymed.

"Janks, the jinx shrink stinks," Lila added.

"Janks the jinx shrink wanks and stinks," Katherine joined in.

All earnest sympathy for Elaine ceased. Once the laughter began, it took on a life of its own, building to a snorting, rib-clutching crescendo until it dribbled down to its nose-blowing conclusion.

Elaine didn't laugh. "Thanks, y'all, but I don't feel like anything's funny. I have to walk." Elaine left. Marlene stood to run after her, but Katherine stopped her, "Let her go." Katherine covered her face with her hands, head down on the table. She gasped for breath.

~

"You just need approbation," Elaine's father had said to her, over and again, without giving her any. *Approbation.* The very word threw Elaine into another rage.

On top of that, a girl Elaine idolized at school had a nervous breakdown, and she rushed to visit her fallen teen hero.

Elaine tip-toed into her friend's hospital room and felt as though she walked into an 18th-century British novel. Tears filled her eyes as she observed the 16-year-old patient in bed wearing a pink ruffled nightgown with her long black hair asunder against the white sheets. Elaine thought she looked frail and beautiful yet heroic in her fight for life against the ravages of torment and bulimia. Elaine loved her; she wanted to be her.

Elaine proceeded to starve herself down to 85 pounds. A few months later, she had fully embraced a weak constitution, harking every Bronte and Austen novel she had treasured. She felt herself to be tragic, given to fits of feminine hysteria. She wanted desperately to be saved.

Elaine met some boys at Tulane and got stoned as she walked about. When she told them she was crazy, they talked up the new hip mental hospital.

"It's all the latest, really cool, not scary like the old DePaul Mental Hospital where they did electroshock, and God knows what else."

Elaine learned that the new place was founded by a charismatic shrink with long hair who had been to California. The Tulane boys told her more that he lectured in their classes about catharsis, whereby a patient releases suppressed feelings like an exorcism, and they're better afterward. *Catharsis.* To Elaine, they made it sound as good as *orgasmic.*

Elaine walked toward the new, hip place. She walked for miles until she got there. She stared at the entrance and the modern, two-story building behind it. She felt happier at once. She felt a glimmer of hope.

She walked in, past the sign that read Iris Gardens Center for Mental Health. Elaine wondered if it wasn't a Monet tribute, and she was right. Behind the front desk was a large, framed print of Monet's irises.

The people behind the desk were so sweet. They walked her around, and Elaine saw other teenagers there. She learned their main protocols were based on "Regression Therapy," pioneered at the Chestnut Lodge near Washington, DC, and California methods.

The Chestnut Lodge was famous. It was where the CIA experimented with LSD. There was even a book written about the Chestnut Lodge. It was called *I Never Promised You a Rose Garden*, about a schizophrenic girl who was cured there.

Elaine also learned that they mixed in healing protocols from California. *Those guys were right. This is so cool,* she thought.

The admitting doctor at Iris Gardens explained kindly in slow, hushed tones that with the guidance of the caring and friendly psychiatrist assigned to her case, Elaine would break, scream, and burn through all the mental garbage that destroyed her life until she was clear and ready to face the world fresh as a newborn babe. *Rebirthed* was the word he used.

Elaine thought *They* were brilliant. They made her feel as though They could really help her. And once They had reassured her that there was no connection with that pervert, Dr. Janks, right then and there, Elaine checked herself in. Her surprised but beleaguered parents didn't protest. When the accounting department saw that Elaine was a CHAMPUS kid, they nodded yes without hesitation.

CHAMPUS stood for Civilian Health and Medical Program Uniform Service, a program of the Department of Defense that provided medical coverage for eligible veteran families. It meant that the Veterans Administration would pay for her treatment for as long as They deemed necessary, and the government would pick up the tab.

Elaine felt excited. There was hope in the air at Iris Gardens. Most of the patients were young, teens, and twenty-somethings. A communal atmosphere was vigorously promoted. The patients ate together and did all their own cleaning, dishes, and mopping, although they did have good local cooks. There were even people there who had been in the news, like the teen who killed two people at Redemption Lounge.

Just as the boys at Tulane said, her therapy began with, yes, catharsis. Her pleasant, young shrink, Dr. Welder, encouraged Elaine to unravel emotionally ("We need to get at what's underneath") in biweekly sessions, supplemented by group therapy, exercise, arts and crafts, and her homework so she could graduate.

Pictures out of magazines and posters appeared on the walls of her room. A few treasures from childhood made their way into her little hospital dorm room. She began to refer to Iris Gardens as *home.*

Elaine was a compliant patient. She poured her heart out about feeling not good enough and her true failing – being born a daughter instead of a son, not even one bit a tomboy. Dr. Welder took notes and later looked it up in his Freud references – was it penis envy? If *she* had been a *he*, all would be well at home, full of love and approbation?

Week after week, every last corpuscle of emotion Elaine ever felt, every hurt, remark, or look she had ever hated, every frustration was prompted and pulled "into the open." Dr. Welder exhorted her to let it out until her knuckles were raw from pounding the rough upholstery in the treatment room, her nose sore from sobbing, and her throat hoarse from howling. Then he would hand her Kleenex or a stuffed animal and put his arm around her thin, trembling frame.

Elaine felt dazed with exhaustion. At night, she crawled into bed and coiled up.

Several months in, Dr. Welder called her in. He announced that he was very proud of her and noted excellent progress. Then he told Elaine that she could go no further without a change in treatment because she had indeed reached that mysterious turning point, her *empty place*. To rebirth herself, he gently explained, it was best to start small, with baby steps, so to speak, and build up from there.

They wheeled it in.

Elaine looked at it blankly as though she wasn't sure what she was looking at. It was a wheelchair with leather and chain restraints: two restraints for her wrists, two for her ankles, and one that went across her middle.

They, with little protest from their newly emptied and dazed young patient, put Elaine into her new little world, in which she was chained around the clock.

She was Elaine in Chains.

Daytime, Elaine was confined to the restraining chair bound up for sixteen hours a day. She was only let go during supervised showers and bathroom breaks. At night she was tied to her bed all night until morning. No one disputed or protested what was being done to her. It was for her own good. They knew what They were doing.

Nobody was allowed to touch Elaine or talk to her. This was the symbolic equivalent of entering her world without her permission. They explained how this would raise her self-esteem, except for when she begged to be relieved of the restraints, plus the cringing mortification of supervision in the bathroom. These indignities dulled Elaine's efforts to grasp the cosmic joy of building a new self.

Side effects from the restraining chair included aching muscles from lack of use and jammed-up guts from holding "it." The wrist restraints were just long enough for her to lean over to eat, draw, read, or turn the wheels to get around. She was allowed to stretch when she was released to "go potty," she could stretch in bed at night. Despite her pleas for an aspirin to relieve her PMS, no medication was allowed. "I swear to you, it's not Freud. It's cramps!" she implored. But to no avail.

The only affection she received was from a little stuffed bear named Neat-O that Dr. Welder had given her. They kept Elaine in chains for six whole months.

Finally, the day came when the restraints were unbuckled. She stood up, sighed oh so deeply, and smiled. She felt light and clear. *And dammit,* she thought, *I'll never go through that again.*

Now, she would cherish her freedom, understand her choices, and be a respectful girl, nonviolent and in control. They claimed the chair-chaining treatment was a success.

As for Elaine, her sense of humor, goodwill, and brains served her through the time warp.

Unbuckled, but not released. Iris Gardens continued to keep her.

Cherie noticed that Elaine had disappeared. They wondered if she had been sent to live with relatives out of state or hustled into boarding school. Lila then heard through the grapevine that a girl just like them from uptown was in the loony bin, and that girl was Elaine.

"Oh, no," Cherie replied.

"Gives me the shivers," Lila shook as she said it and wrapped her arms around herself.

"Why?"

"Because sometimes I feel so crazy, it could be me."

Cherie nodded because she knew it could also be her, although she couldn't admit it.

~

"What the hell is this?" Paulette stood in the middle of Cherie's bedroom holding her Wordless Diary.

Cherie's insides knotted. She felt flush but answered coolly, "Nothing. A drawing book I like to scribble in."

Paulette continued to stare at it, turning the pages. "What is this bullshit?"

"I like to draw. It's nothing. Give it to me." Cherie stepped closer and held her hand out, but Paulette continued her inspection, one page after another.

"Please, give it to me," Cherie repeated, forcing her voice to be soft.

"If you think you're going to be an artist, you can forget it."

After a few more seconds, not finding anything she could pinpoint, Paulette stared at Cherie with a searching look, "I don't know what is going on with you. Maybe you need to go talk to somebody. Something's wrong with you. Are you listening to me?"

Cherie didn't move. She couldn't meet Paulette's eyes and played with a torn fingernail instead. Finally, Paulette threw the Wordless Diary on the bed and walked out. Cherie ran over, scooped it up, and held it close. It was a close call. She curled up in bed and looked around her room, anxious to find another place to hide it. Now that Paulette had found it, she might quickly become obsessed with it and harangue Cherie about the drawings or steal it again, show it to people and ask their opinions.

Cherie scoured her room for a place where her little notebook, her lifeline, her countdown, would be safe. She settled on her math textbook. She carved out the pages in the middle. Her

Wordless Diary could live inside it, comforted by fellow numbers. Paulette would never open one of her textbooks. Cherie decided if she asked, *I'll tell her I threw it away.* That way, her room wouldn't get torn apart if Paulette decided to mess with her again.

Cherie biked to Lila's house. She could hear Mama Faylene crying and wailing behind her bedroom door.

"What happened?" Cherie asked.

"We have to leave Mama alone ... she's freaked out about the fire on Iberville. The gay guys."

"What fire?"

"You don't know? It happened yesterday."

"No, I don't know! Stop giving me grief."

"Some asshole threw a firebomb inside the door of the gay lounge up on the second floor, and a bunch of guys couldn't get out because of the bars on the windows, and they burned to death. The picture of it was so gross. They were all fried. They can't even identify some of them."

"How many guys?"

Twenty-nine dead, and about the same got out alive.

Cherie ran for the phone. She called The Giddy Gadget.

"What are you ... ?"

"Shh!" Cherie held the phone so Lila could listen in. They stood close together.

A weak, shaky lady voice answered the phone, "Giddy Gadget. We're closed."

"Don't hang up!" Cherie interrupted. "This is Cherie. I heard about the fire, and I was wondering ..."

Berley's mother replied very slowly, and she slurred her words, "Oh, Cherie. I remember you. Berley was very fond of you, very upset when you left us. But he's gone now. He died in the fire. I don't know what I'm going to do. Do you think you could come down here and help me ..."

"Take care, Mrs. Ganderson!" Cherie slammed down the phone and fell to the floor.

"My boss from the Giddy Gadget. I hated him so much, and I wanted him to die. I prayed he would die a terrible death. And he did. I feel really weird. All the time, I wish people I hate would die, but they never do, and now it really happened."

Cherie crossed her arms over her body. She could feel Berley punching her as if it had just happened. She curled up on the floor. "Burned alive! It's so horrible."

Lila sat on the floor beside Cherie and hugged her.

"Cherie, listen to me. What happened had *nothing* to do with you. Don't think that way! We'll wish peace upon those who died, okay? Let's have a glass of sherry and toast that their souls are in heaven. That's all we can do."

Cherie let Lila pull her to her feet.

"Your poor mama," Cherie said.

Lila nodded, "Poor Mama. Lord knows who she knew in there. I don't know how much more she can take."

CHAPTER 19

Hot Nuts

THE ORIGINAL NAME was Congo Square. Before the Civil War, it was the only place in the United States where free and enslaved black people were allowed to gather and practice their native religions from Africa and the Caribbean.

Once a week on Sundays, folks would converge on Congo Square to chant, pray, and drum for their freedom and curse their enemies. They traded goods and information and conducted business. Marie Laveau, the most famous of all voodoo queens, held court there.

Congo Square sat near one end of Basin Street in the Treme neighborhood near the French Quarter, with no distinct features, just a big ol' square.

In the late nineteenth century post-Reconstruction, the name was changed to Beauregard Square after the Confederate general, P.G.T. Beauregard, and a statue of him was added.

Municipal Auditorium was built next to it. Nearly all of the city's grand events happened at Municipal Auditorium, from ballets and operas to rock concerts and Mardi Gras Balls. Comus and Rex, the two Mardi Gras Krewes whose parades concluded

Mardi Gras season, always convened at Municipal Auditorium on the night of Fat Tuesday, sharing the ballroom for the grandest of Mardi Gras galas.

On this day, however, in Beauregard Square, which would soon be changed back to Congo Square due to an urban renewal project, a lively crew of war protesters needled the Legionnaires gathered for their annual convention.

The protest didn't last very long because the Legionnaires called the police. Before the cops screeched in, a photographer managed to snap a few. The best photo, the one of Devin, would appear in the next issue of *Jet Magazine*. In it, a scraggly Devin with a big toothy smile holds his protest sign, surrounded by old Legionnaires in little white waiter hats, holding their noses.

Within minutes, the cops descended, and the brothers ran for it. They escaped, but Garrett was cornered and nabbed by the cops. He knew the routine. He would be held in lock-up, roughed up, and released to his father because he was a minor and hadn't hurt anyone. The charge would be Public Nuisance.

Devin and Chris stopped at Canal and Loyola Place to catch their breath and share a leftover butt of wild-grown weed. That's how it grew in New Orleans. Wild.

"Mom's going to kill us," Devin exhaled.

"If Dad doesn't kill us first," his brother replied.

They sat beneath a statue of a noble military woman titled Molly Marine. It was sculpted by the modèrne artist Enrique Alferez, whose extraordinary legacy to New Orleans rested on the elegant statues he created for City Park.

Chris pointed at the statue and asked Devin, "You know who that is, don't you?"

"Your girlfriend?" Devin countered.

"Shut up, man. It's Garrett's mom. It's Miz Bettina."

"Get out."

"Yeah. She modeled for it. There were a couple of models, and she was one of them. I can't believe you don't know that."

"How come you know it?"

"Mark told me."

"Garrett's brother, Mark?"

"No, Mark Twain. Who do you think?"

Devin looked up at the Alferez statue with new appreciation.

Garrett's mother, Miz Bettina, was not, as people liked to say, "Run of the mill." She was a slim, blue-eyed beauty from Covington, Louisiana, across Lake Ponchartrain. As a girl, she painted watercolors and dreamed she would someday join the ranks of great painters. Bettina was a smart young lady, the valedictorian of her high school.

At eighteen, she fled across Lake Ponchartrain for the French Quarter. There, she fell in love with the famed folklorist Owen Francis. Owen left his wife for her, and his close friend, William Faulkner, attended their wedding. They moved to Hollywood and straight into a lofty crowd of famous writers, filmmakers, and actors.

Then, disaster for beautiful Bettina. Owen dropped dead of a heart attack a few years over 40. His young wife became inconsolable, and her folks were worried. "Uncle Bill" Faulkner, as he was known to her family, was dispatched to rescue Bettina. William Faulkner, the great Nobel Prize novelist and screenplay writer for movies, traveled to California and brought her home to recover from her broken heart.

Not for long.

Restless at home and horrified by the news coming out of Europe, Bettina joined the WACs, or Women's Army Corps. She wanted to be part of the valiant WWII effort. After a year in the military, she met a handsome soldier who dazzled her with his sharp intellect, humor, and political bent. Together, they decided they would change the world. Within weeks of their first date, she married him.

Post-war, they started life together as Tulane graduate students. Bettina's oil paintings and watercolors helped pay for their tuition. Then came the family, five children all neatly spaced at two and a half years apart. She nursed them all herself, an unpopular activity at the time.

"Honey," the nurses pleaded with her, "Do you know what you're going to look like after nursing all the babies? You're going be thin and saggy, that's what. Darlin', you gotta look after yourself."

Bettina paid them no mind. She regarded the boxes of manufactured, fake baby formula with disgust. No, her children would flower in a wild garden of nonconformity outside the manufactured mainstream. They would think for themselves.

The middle child, Garrett, was sandwiched between two older brothers and two younger sisters. Thin and on the short side, he made up for it with a fearlessness that stunned his southern family. If it hadn't been for Garrett's good manners and sunny personality, he could have been mistaken for an angst-driven Yankee instigator.

Beginning at fifteen, Garrett hung around campus radicals at Tulane, attending discussion groups and late-night lectures. He felt on fire, knowing he could be part of something world-altering and just. His "brothers and sisters in revolution" embraced him in a way that made the black sheep of his family feel like the Golden Fleece.

Garrett was recruited by the Southern Student Organizing Committee as the south-wide high school organizer. In this role, Garrett would introduce fellow teens to underground newspapers, tell them how to protest the war and create action committees.

They gave him a VW bus and a credit card for gas. He celebrated his sixteenth birthday on the road, traveling to a conference in Atlanta with revolutionary pals Estelle and her boyfriend.

In Atlanta, Garrett met everybody: the Weathermen, the soon-to-be Chicago Seven, and even a bunch of people whose faces were on "Wanted by the FBI" posters on post office walls for vandalism and inciting riots.

Back home, Garrett returned to Booker T. Washington High School, where he was immensely popular. The more he learned about his new black friends' struggles in life, the more it radicalized him.

As Garrett increased his local activism at protest marches and strikes, the NOPD stepped up their harassment. He was arrested and smacked around, thrown into traffic, and burned with cigarettes eighteen times between the ages of fifteen and seventeen. Every cop in New Orleans knew the boy named Garrett. No matter what they did to him, he refused to curtail his protests.

Garrett's suffering only increased his resolve to sacrifice for the greater good. As Jesus made his way to Calvary, Garrett bore a heavy cross of the world's ills on his shoulders. The centurions drew blood with every stroke of the whip. They hated all this revolution talk. It was bad for business and terrible for tourism.

At the latest Vietnam protest, Garrett was arrested, and Devin and Chris failed to escape. They ended up in lock-up, too.

Their mother appealed woefully to her boss's boss, who worked for the city police superintendent, to help her boys.

"I'm so sorry to ask you this," she explained. "I've tried so hard to keep my boys away from politics and all that screaming music. You can't know how hard I've tried." Her boss's boss nodded with kindness and made the necessary call. Devin and Chris were released immediately, but she could do nothing for Garrett. His record was too long.

Garrett was transferred to Juvenile Hall with the highest bail ever, so he was told, set on a teenager. Plus, he was betrayed by his brothers and sisters in revolution. The New Orleans SDS chapter would not put up the money to bail him out. They broke their promise.

Garrett stared at the wall in his cell in Juvy. He was angry and hurt but not surprised that they had betrayed him. The whole atmosphere had started to change for the worse. He and Devin talked about it. The war in Vietnam was being built up instead of disengaged. There was talk that the CIA and Harlem drug dealers worked together to get folks addicted to quell the black uprising and progress. Increasingly vicious and soulless, the revolution had become as ugly as the establishment. And now he was locked up. His hands coiled into tight fists, and his body was rigid. *I've got to get out of here,* was his only thought.

Miles up the Mississippi River at Marlene's house, the clock struck two a.m., and the last game of their Scrabble marathon had been played. Cherie, Katherine, Marlene, and Lila mixed martinis.

"You know what a baby Martian is called? Lila asked, to which they responded in chorus and clinked their glasses, "A martini!" That would be my Warhol Factory name," Lila continued, "Olive Martini."

"Mine would be Zizi Sazerac," Marlene responded, "In honor of Zizi Jeanmaire. She's a jazz ballerina."

"I'd be Ginny Fizz," Katherine piped in, "or Abby Sinth or Biddy Bitters."

"You're not going to believe what I heard," Cherie said, offering one of her late-night stories with a sly smile. She turned off one of the lamps. The friends leaned in as they sipped their drinks.

"I was at a party, and you know that cool boy, he plays music, and he wears cool clothes, he's real thin and hangs out with Devin's brother? His hair is straight black, and his eyes are grey, all weird?"

"Oh yeah, they live by Audubon Park," said Lila. "They've got a real Miro and a real Picasso in their house. I know he's got a total crush on me, but I don't care."

"Well, I got him to spill the beans."

"About what?" the girls said in unison.

Cherie took a breath and smiled. "Initiation for high school fraternities."

The girls stared at Cherie in disbelief. They knew the girl side of it. Initiation into high school sororities was public, stupid idiot stuff, but what boys did to other boys for frat hazing was strictly secret.

"It's so scary," Cherie began. "He told me about fifteen guys met at his house, and then they walked over to the park to Monkey Hill for nine-at-night pick-up. They had to wait and wait. They could hear the peacock screams from the zoo, which made them nervous.

"Finally, about eleven o'clock, a couple of pick-up trucks pulled up with some frat brothers in the back. They all had hoods on with holes for their eyes, so no one could tell who was who. The leader told them that this was it, and if anybody was too much of a chicken to go forward, now was the time to go home crying to Mama. He said it all formally and pointed his finger at them. He said, 'Let it be known that if you go home now, your name is henceforth excrement to us.'"

Katherine sputtered out her sip.

"That's the word he used, *excrement*! So, they climbed into the trucks. They drove them out to Bayou St. John. It was totally deserted where they got out."

Cherie took a sip of her cocktail and continued.

"They made them strip off *all* their clothes, and the boys in hoods put blindfolds on them."

"So, they're naked and blind?" Lila summed up.

Cherie nodded.

The girls shuddered.

"Get walking! The leader yelled at them. They smacked them with paddles until they were about butt-deep in the water. Not only did the paddle smacks sting, but the mosquitoes were also eating them alive, and there were things in the bayou that brushed up against their legs."

"That's horrible!" Marlene made a face. "So stupid."

"There's more," Cherie interrupted. "They pelted them with eggs, which caused huge welts, and since they were blindfolded, they couldn't even dodge them. He said the hooded guys laughed, hahaha, when they got hit and jumped around. Finally, they told them to get out, and they all kind of limped and moaned out of the water.

"So that was it?" Marlene interjected. "That *has* to be it."

Again, Cherie shook her head *no*.

"What happened next?"

"The leader told them to take off their blindfolds. He told them how proud he was of them, his new brothers, and how tough they were, blah blah bullshit like that, and ... are you ready? There was still one more test."

"Oh no," Katherine exclaimed.

"They made them get down on their hands and knees, so he thought it would be just one more paddling. But that wasn't it." Cherie stopped to pour another.

"If they didn't paddle them, what did they do? Ohmygod," Lila said nervously.

"He told me, and I swear this is *exactly* what he told me, the frat leader called out, 'Anybody here got a good recipe? Cause I'm in the mood to marinate! I think it's time for some hot peppered nuts!'

And the other hooded frats around yelled back, 'Yeah, me, too!'"

Lila and Marlene paused for a second, their eyes wide. Their eyes met, and they began to yowl.

"I don't understand," Katherine looked at the others.

"They basted their balls with Tabasco sauce!" Cherie revealed.

"You mean like ... basting a turkey?" Katherine asked.

"Don't you get it?"

"Like ... with a brush or with the squirter thing?"

Cherie, Marlene, and Lila laughed so hard they couldn't speak. Cherie mimed pumping a basting bulb and liquid squirting out of it.

"Oh my God! That's torture. They were tortured!"

As she wiped back her tears from laughing, Cherie nodded and concluded the story, "He said they cried and groaned the whole way back. And when they got back to his house, there was a boy in every sink, bathtub, and toilet they had all night long. There was even one boy sitting on a frying pan full of ice cream!"

Later, Cherie heard that the Cool Guy with Grey Eyes, who passed his frat initiation, flunked his draft induction for the Army. He fell asleep on the floor at the induction center. When the Sergeant came out to get him, all he found was a bony guy with long stringy hair snoring under the bench. The Sergeant had to kick him to wake him up. He crawled out, sat up, looked at the Sergeant, and said, "Huh?"

The Sergeant kicked him again, disgusted to the core. "Get out of here, you pathetic piece of shit." Mr. Cool Guy wavered out, truly hurt that the Army didn't want him. Unfortunately, the Sergeant didn't know how strong, and grit-your-teeth tough this young man was and how he had survived *Hot Peppered Nuts a la Bayou St. John.*

A boat with sails and a big anchor hanging off the bottom. Four sad faces through the portholes. As her friends slept, Cherie drew that in her Wordless Diary for the days she had left. 4-4-1. One year, two months, two weeks, and a day, maybe two. Junior year was almost over, and she turned 17. They all turned 17 except for Katherine, who was 16 until the end of summer. She carefully inspected the Wordless Diary. The fabric on the cover was well-worn, and the binding was starting to give. A few pages that had fallen out were taped back in. She said to her book, the repository of her soul, *We can't fall apart. We have to last. I'll get you more glue. I promise.*

CHAPTER 20
Pink Camellia

GISELLE, Katherine's mother, was taking forever getting ready for a gallery opening, carefully choosing her dress, and she hovered over Katherine as she ironed it. "Don't burn it, dumbbell! The fabric is delicate."

Katherine ironed it meticulously and handed over the silky black shift on a hanger. Katherine wondered what was happening. She hadn't seen her mother so excited since she couldn't remember when. Katherine knew she wasn't getting ready for her old, long-time boyfriend.

Her mother stood in the bathroom in her slip, plucking her eyebrows and putting on makeup. She snapped at Katherine,

"Hang it over there. Go make coffee. Make sure there are no dishes in the sink," Giselle ordered as she wiped off her violet lipstick with an agitated gesture and started to reapply it.

"Who's coming over?" Katherine asked.

"A man. A painter. You don't know him."

"Roland De Veers?" Katherine blurted out.

Giselle stopped and stared at her tensely, "What do you know?"

"Lila was talking about him. She said he was so good the Valencia Gallery was arranging better studio space for him. Isn't he from Holland?"

"Lila, Lila. All the time, Lila! What is it with that girl?" Giselle went back to her mascara. "Go make the coffee, and don't bother me. I need to get ready."

Roland De Veers was born to a family in Europe with a long royalty adjacent history. As was typical, when the twentieth century rolled in, and WWI ended, his family didn't have servants anymore, so Roland had to work to support himself.

He split for the New World, first heading for cowboy country, where he started playing around with paint, and then, hearing the sirens of the Mississippi Delta in his dreams, he went to New Orleans to find his true soul. The romance was too hard to resist. *La Nouvelle Orlèans.* He said it aloud, and it rolled off his tongue like lingual liquor. It wasn't long before Roland dumped the high desert's yellow prickly pear blossoms for the Delta Lady's pink camellias.

Roland quickly became besotted with New Orleans, and the Delta Lady didn't disappoint. He painted obsessively. Before long, his oils clung to the canvas, and his stylized portraits exalted their subjects.

It didn't take long for Giselle, Katherine's mother, to find him. She tingled with excitement to make the acquaintance of an artist schooled in Europe and who spoke five languages.

For Katherine's mother, it was love. With easy familiarity, Giselle and Roland chatted about art nouveau in Brussels, architecture, and design. Not only that, he wasn't that much younger than Giselle's forty-two, maybe ten years, she guessed. He wasn't particularly handsome, but he was attractive enough. He was medium height and had a strong build. He wore his brown hair long, down to his shoulders. His clothes rumpled. No matter, his talent and forthcoming manner compounded his appeal to everyone who met him. Giselle flirted with Roland as though her life depended on it.

Roland liked Giselle. He thought she was infinitely charming, attractive, and intelligent. Her knowledge of art history and her collection of beveled stained glass window panes impressed him.

Her teenage daughter, Katherine, who served them coffee so quietly in the living room, really caught his eye.

As Katherine leaned over and poured milk into his cup, Roland nodded at her, "Thank you." Katherine met his eyes for barely a second as she glanced at him through locks of silky hair that had fallen in her face. It was a shy glance so full of innocence and promise it made his guts lurch, and he shifted in his seat. Katherine disappeared back into the kitchen, dutifully leaving her mother and her guest alone.

When Giselle left the room to get her purse and sweater before heading out, Roland stood in the entryway to the kitchen and asked Katherine if she liked music. She nodded yes. Then he asked if she had a favorite. Again, she nodded yes, then spoke, "I love Otis Redding."

"Redding?"

"He's a soul singer. But he's not from here. He's from Georgia."

"Maybe then, you'll let me borrow one of your albums? I like to listen to music when I work."

Giselle reentered the kitchen, and Katherine didn't dare reply, staring down at her magazine. As Roland opened the door for Giselle, he looked back at Katherine over his shoulder.

Katherine felt his look and the blush of heat that came with it. She ran to the window to watch them drive away to the party in his dented station wagon that had paintings and frames piled in the back. She prayed he wouldn't tell her mother he had talked to her. She prayed he wouldn't mention anything about her at all. She feared that if he did, if he said something to her mother like,

"What a sweet daughter you have. How old is she?" she'd be in for a river of grief. She could hear Mama Giselle already, "What were you doing? Flirting with him like a little whore!"

But if he didn't say anything, if he understood it was a secret, then all she would need to do was find out where his studio was, and that wouldn't be hard at all. Lila would know.

Albums tucked under her arm, Katherine hesitated, then knocked on the door of Roland's studio on the second floor of a ramshackle building near the river.

When he opened the door, myriad scents tickled her nose – paint, cigarettes, coffee, dust, and wine. He eagerly greeted her. He beckoned her in and kissed her lightly on one cheek and then the other. He took the albums from her and looked them over, one by one. He selected the Wilson Pickett to play, but Katherine stopped him.

"Wait. First, before anything else, before even one more second, you have to promise me, swear to me an unbreakable oath that *my being here* is a complete secret, and you cannot tell one person ever. Promise me, or I have to leave right now."

Roland was taken aback by Katherine's intensity, *uncomely in such a young girl,* he thought, but he went along. He raised his hand and repeated after her with a flourish, "I swear a sacred vow of silence and secrecy." Then he bowed theatrically and looked up to see her smile.

He was revved to have her in his studio in her jeans and little white cotton blouse, and he didn't want her to go. He wanted much more but contented himself this first visit with conversation. He wanted to get her to relax and share a glass of wine.

When he idly picked up a sketchbook and began to outline

her face, she jumped up and grabbed it out of his hands. She tore the page into shreds and yelled at him, "You promised. You took a sacred oath!"

He was shocked that she would dare tear his sketchbook out of his hands. A wave of pain and anger streaked through his head. He was used to candor and friendship, but he felt, despite all his worldly experience, he was out of his element with Katherine. He wanted to yell at her but held himself back. *What was she so frightened of? Not Giselle. No, Giselle would welcome me to paint her daughter. Her father, maybe?* Roland backed off, downing some tabs from a medicine bottle, and washing them down with red wine. He turned back to Katherine, "I'm sorry. I wasn't thinking. Please forgive me," he said to her softly. He held out his hand to her, and she took it. He pulled her to him. As he gently enveloped her in his arms, he heard her exhale with a shudder, and he felt her melt against him.

That's all he did for the next hour that Katherine stayed. He held her in his arms, and they listened to her favorite Otis Redding and Wilson Pickett albums. As she stood at the door to leave, he kissed her. He kissed her again, pushing his tongue past her lips and teeth. Katherine let him.

Katherine pranced down the creaky stairs, feeling light and happy that maybe he liked her. Loath to return home, she took the streetcar to Marlene's house. On the way, she stood outside a liquor store near the Tulane frat houses. She handed a few dollars to the next frat boy who showed up and asked him to buy a bottle of sloe gin for her.

"Sure thing, sweet thing," he said as she handed him the money. A few minutes later, he stepped out of the store, handed her a brown paper bag, winked, and walked away. She saw that he treated her to the gin, her money still in the bag. Katherine smiled to herself, *Oh, happy day. Someone amazing likes me, and now this.*

She arrived at Marlene's house tipsy and giddy. Katherine

flopped down on the couch, and she replayed her time in Roland's studio in her head. She giggled and applauded Marlene as she danced the entire second act of the *Nutcracker*, the furniture in the living room pushed aside.

Marlene was high, too. She had just seen Edward Villella dance his famed *Prodigal Son* at Municipal Auditorium. She described to Katherine how he executed his astounding grand jeté in the opening, and everyone in the audience gasped. Marlene related that she had been invited through her ballet school to dance as one of the court maidens in the upcoming production of the opera *Boris Godunov*. Marlene capped the sentence with several turns, spinning like a top.

Unable to hold back, Katherine told Marlene that she gave Roland some records.

"You better be careful," Marlene chided her. "And not just because your mother will kill you."

A week later, toting more R&B left behind by her brother Kaleb when he ran away, Katherine knocked on Roland's door. This time, they ended up sitting together in an old, velvety armchair, kissing.

Suddenly, Roland pushed her away, got up, and walked across the room. "You know," he said, using his hands as he spoke, "I hope you understand that if I don't go any farther with you, if I don't seduce you, it's not because I don't desire you."

Katherine got up from the chair. She gazed at him for a moment.

"But what if I want you to," she said plainly, looking up at him so his heart jumped.

Teasing her, he replied, "But if I teach you to make love, what will I get back in return?"

"I don't know," she said, all guile, half getting it, but not really.

"Will you let me do a portrait?" the painter asked.

"No! You swore to me!" she cried out.

"Okay. Okay. Calm down. I'm not going to paint you, even though it's my thing, in case you *have not noticed*," he emphasized the last three words. "My God, what you ask is against everything I am," he sighed.

Katherine bit her nail. "I'm sorry, but you can't. You swore. She fell silent, then said brightly, "You said before you didn't know how to swim very well."

He shook his head in amazement, "Yes, I did say that."

"Then you'll teach me to make love, and I'll teach you to swim better."

He burst out laughing. "It's a deal," he said, grabbing for her, adding, "My funny little angel, my Katherine, where in the world are we going to be able to swim?"

"At Tulane. The indoor swimming pool there is beautiful."

He lifted her up and carried her back to the chair, seating her on his lap, his hands more free to explore, his blood surging. For Katherine, he was so warm. When she left, she felt dazed.

Back in school, in French class, Cherie caught Katherine mindlessly doodling R's in her notebook.

"Who's that?" Cherie teased.

"Nobody." Katherine closed her notebook.

Cherie smiled, "Nobody, my butt."

Katherine gave her a look, and Cherie backed off.

On her third visit to Roland's studio, Katherine lost her virginity to him. First, he pulled the shades and darkened the studio, so only a few late afternoon light rays filtered in and highlighted the dust motes. Irma Thomas was on the stereo.

"I love Irma Thomas," Katherine smiled, "You know she's from here."

Roland kissed her. Kissing and touching. "But what if I bleed?" she anxiously interrupted.

"Don't think about it. It's not a problem."

They drank glasses of wine, then more glasses, and he disrobed her very slowly. With each article of clothing that fell to the floor, he caressed her newly exposed flesh with his fingertips as though painting her. He followed every touch with kisses. Inch by inch, the tension in her body gave way to his careful hands and mouth, to the whole of him. He saw that it hurt her when he pushed into her, but seeing her grimace and bite her lip, he slowed down. Afterward, he didn't jump out of bed but let her cling to him through a post-coital nap.

Katherine could never say "I love you" to Roland, but she fell in love with him, nonetheless. She lived for the few hours once a week if she was lucky that she could sneak to his studio and be with him. She thought about him day and night and how they shared true love. At night, alone in her little bed, Katherine dreamed of marrying him and moving far away. She would be his muse, and as soon as they were married, he could paint her all he wanted.

They didn't always make love when she visited. Sometimes, she would watch him paint if he was deep into it when she showed up, as long as he took a few minutes to hold her tight before she slipped away. Marlene covered for her without asking a lot of questions, so Katherine could lie to her mother, "I was studying at Marlene's."

Sometimes, Katherine would ask Roland for advice, and he readily gave it, encouraging her to speak her mind and stand up for herself. She told him about her best friends, what Marlene and her family meant to her, how she and Cherie both had crazy European mothers who hated each other and how much she loved Lila more than a friend.

Even with his back to Katherine as he worked on his portraits of local people and clubs, his eyes lit up at the mention of Lila's name. Roland had noticed Lila at events and parties around town, the slender, vivacious girl with a pixie haircut, chic little dresses, and long, beautiful legs. He wanted Lila to model for him. *Am I hearing her right?* he thought to himself. Did she just say *more than a friend?*

"You know, maybe," Katherine added, "she could come here with me and be with us, you know, make love with us. Group sex. *Menage a trois.*"

Roland started, and he smeared his brush stroke. Again, Katherine threw him completely off guard, that he knew only the shell beyond her need to be loved. Never in a million years would he have expected something like this.

"That would be very nice, yes, but then we wouldn't be such a secret anymore," he tried to keep his cool.

"Yeah. You're right. It's a bad idea. Anyway, I don't think she'd want to," Katherine sighed, thinking Roland would not be handsome enough for Lila's opinionated standards. Roland, for his part, kicked himself for questioning such a possibility.

She walked over and leaned on him, putting her arms around his neck. He let her, rubbing her back, still holding the brush in the other hand. Katherine reveled in his love and kindness. She felt like everything was good, that she, too, was good. The good, whole feelings made her want to cry, but she fought her tears back. Even more than Cherie, who cried in secret, Katherine felt crying was stupid.

Yet after a month of secret visits, Roland became restless and irritated with their routine — she'd show up, they'd drink, make love, he'd take time to let her cling to him, and then she'd look at his art books while he worked.

It was not enough for him. He wanted to paint her, but Katherine refused, nor would she let him take a photo of her. If he held up the camera, she would protest and make an ugly face. Nor did she talk much. If she found an idle sketch of herself, she would throw a fit and tear it up. *Little bitch*, Roland thought.

He began to hate the secrecy. It was against his nature, and it made him nervous. It wasn't just the specter of her mother, Giselle; he had heard her talk about her ex, Katherine's father. Giselle told him everybody loved her ex-husband's soft-spoken, mild manner, but that was a lie. Beneath his sweet public face, she said, was violence. He beat her son, Kaleb, Giselle recounted, her face contorted with pain. Kaleb, the son who ran away.

Roland shrugged his shoulders. *Enough with this baby Katherine already.*

Roland had met someone else. She was a beautiful woman in her late twenties. She was free and wild. He could paint her body and paint her portrait, a real woman. She wasn't a frightened young girl that was sticky like glue.

He justified breaking it off. *I've been very good to her, very sweet. I was her bridge between little girl and woman, and better me than some stupid boy.*

Katherine knew the second she walked in and looked at Roland's face something was wrong. Instantly, fear gripped her, squashing her breath.

"Sit down, Katherine."

"No. I can stand."

"Si tu veut. If you want," he translated even though he knew she knew exactly what it meant. To Katherine, it was another bad sign.

"What's that music?" she frowned, listening to *you can hear the boats go by; you can spend the night beside her...*

"It's Leonard Cohen."

"Where'd you get it?"

"Never mind," he admitted, "it was a gift."

Katherine froze. She looked expressionless, stiff, staring at him.

Then Roland spoke to Katherine in a kind, slow voice. "You are a lovely girl. You have enjoyed coming here, but now it's time to go on with our lives."

Roland fully expected her to start crying, but she didn't. She didn't move a muscle as though nailed to the spot. The blood drained from her face. She stared right at him, her expression fixed like a ghost. She didn't look alive to him. It unnerved him, and he didn't like it.

He looked at his watch. He needed to pick up his new girlfriend in an hour. He exhaled a long stream of cigarette smoke, put out the stub, and lit another. *Better get this over with.*

"You need to leave right now. We're not going to do this anymore."

Katherine pleaded, "What happened?"

"Nothing. Nothing happened! You will always be my little friend, but it's time for you to have a boyfriend your own age and for me, a lady my own age."

Katherine struggled to breathe. She felt as though she might black out.

Roland repeated his dreadful words.

She didn't respond. She stared at him.

He ran his hands through his hair and paced across the room and back, more upset. "Listen to me, please! You must go."

In a small voice, she said, "You don't love me anymore?" Then she answered her own question, "Guess not. Never did, did you?" she added bitterly.

He softened. "You have been my good little friend, and I will always love you, *always*, but for the third time now, it's over."

"I don't understand," she whispered.

"There's nothing to understand! I don't have to explain myself to you. Grow up! This is what happens." He paused, again checking his watch.

Katherine noticed. "You have a date?"

He opened the door for her. "Go. Now. Don't look so pitiful. You're not a baby."

She couldn't move. He put out his cigarette and reached for her. For a second, she thought he would gather her up and kiss her.

"Enough!" he yelled at her.

Roland grabbed her arm tightly above the elbow. At his volume and harsh touch, Katherine went limp. Like a ragdoll, she fell to her knees. In a fury of angry words, he pulled her to her feet and dragged her to the door. He pushed her hard through the frame. She hit her head on it. Awkwardly, he shut the door behind her and caught her hair. She screamed. He opened it, shoved her away from the door, and shut it again.

Katherine rubbed her head. She steadied herself on the landing wall as she got up and slowly headed down the stairs. She started to shake. Trembling, she walked to the end of the block and sat on the curb, afraid her knees would buckle beneath her. She looked down the street in hopes that he would come after her. Instead, she saw him speed away in his station wagon.

No. He's not coming after me, she thought. *He's not coming after me because I was nothing to him but somebody to get. It was all a joke. It was a joke. Little friend, that's the real joke.* She rubbed her arm where he had grabbed her. Two bruises from his thumb and fingers were beginning to form. *I was nothing but a screw to him. Nothing, nothing, I'm nothing,* she chanted in her mind.

She sat on the curb, her arms wrapped around her knees until a shiny black Buick pulled up, and the well-dressed businessman behind the wheel offered her a ride, jolting her out of her reverie.

She tried to yell, "Leave me alone," but the words stuck in her throat. She forced herself to stand and walked in the opposite direction.

Back at home, Katherine tried to ignore her brutal headache. It seemed as though her mother was a screeching harpy. When

Katherine brought her mother a cup of tea to her bedside, she accidentally dropped it on the floor. Broken bits flew everywhere, and Giselle yelled at her for being so clumsy. "Clean it up, idiot!" Giselle shrieked at Katherine.

Katherine swept up the mess and wiped the floor, not daring to raise her eyes to look at her mother or speak. Then she brought her another cup of tea. Giselle told Katherine she was sick of looking at her sad, ugly face and that she looked like one of those stupid clowns painted on cheap velvet. Then she said that Kaleb hated it, too. "No wonder he left us!"

Katherine felt ill thinking that her mother knew about Roland, enraged that Katherine had won the attention, however brief, of a man her mother wanted. Now, there would be punishment.

"You want people to love you? How can anybody love you with that stupid face!" her mother spat at her. "No, they'll take what they want and throw you in the garbage!" Katherine stood there and took it until Giselle snapped, "Go! I don't want to look at you! Go!"

After everybody in her house went to bed that night, Katherine quietly opened the medicine cabinet. She took down the bottle of her mother's sleeping pills. She also took the razor and twisted it open, extracting the blade. With the bottle in one hand and the blade in the other, she thought how quick dying would be if she took the pills and then cut herself open.

She stared at them for a long time. That's all she did. She stared at the bottle of pills and the razor for an hour, going over and over in her head that if she did both at once, she would die a lot faster. She put them back in the bathroom cabinet.

It was a comfort to Katherine to know that she could leave painlessly and forever if she needed to. Mother Mary, her true, merciful mother, would understand. She'd send beautiful angels with sparkling, golden wings to lift her up and fly her away to Heaven. There, she would know pure, true love.

Katherine went on with life like a zombie. A couple of weeks later, Cherie and Marlene finally got her to tell them what was wrong, but only after they took the obligatory oath of secrecy. Even then, Katherine didn't cry.

They entertained Katherine by cursing Roland, cursing him to planet Pluto and back. They cursed him with all sorts of vicious and vile calamities. Marlene's ability to invent killer curses was a side of her personality rarely seen and one Cherie heartily appreciated.

"I hope he folds up an easel and gets his dick caught in it right at the hinge."

"And it's permanently bent, so when he pees, it splatters all over."

"I hope he cuts his fingers off in a meat grinder and roaches crawl up the stumps!"

Despite Cherie and Marlene's best efforts, Katherine still felt a raw jolt in her heart. She felt foolish, so full of love for him when he felt nothing.

"You've got to come to the conference with us in late July. It's going to be great," Cherie entreated Katherine.

"I don't think I can."

"We'll work it out," Marlene assured. "My parents will call your mom. They'll convince her to let you go. I'll get my father to call. You know she won't say no if my dad asks. Don't you want to go?"

Katherine nodded, so Cherie took over.

"We're all going. It will be the four of us, and we can represent New Orleans there."

For a few days, the seeping wounds would be diminished. She'd forget him for a few days—*Roland Le Fartiste*, as Marlene now called him.

"I saw the flyer. It looks so cool." Katherine smiled at the thought. It would be so cool to go to the big Unitarian Church teen conference in the Tennessee mountains. They would attend workshops and discussions, do music and crafts, worship, and dance. For a few days, they would be part of the most exciting thing imaginable, their own little LRY nation, which stood for Liberal Religious Youth.

CHAPTER 21

Chatoyance

ON SUNDAY MORNINGS, Cherie, Lila, Katherine, and Marlene joined their crowd of fellow LRYers at the Unitarian church.

The building was uptown on flower-lined Jefferson Avenue. It was different from any other in New Orleans, built in Frank Lloyd Wright style, angular and filled with light.

The front area was shaded by tropical trees, and its glass portico featured stairs like one half of an X that led up to the sanctuary. The lower level had classrooms and offices. It was adjacent to a small park with large live oaks that served as an outdoor classroom.

For folks that attended, their torch-bearer was Reverend Albert D'Orlando. He moved to New Orleans in 1950 from Boston with a zealous commitment to civil rights. By 1960, he organized integrated sit-ins at downtown coffee shops. When two of his protesters were arrested and sentenced to ten whole years of wretchedness in Louisiana's Angola prison for criminal mischief, D'Orlando went national and raised enough legal funds from other congregations to take the case all the way to the Supreme Court. The Supreme Court tossed the sentences.

D'Orlando never wavered, not when he was ordered to testify before the House Un-American Activities Committee and not when the Ku Klux Klan set off dynamite in front of the church, firebombed his home, and threatened his family.

The NOPD detectives dutifully found the three Ku Klux Klan perpetrators, who were sentenced to five years in Angola Prison.

Services were unpredictable and ranged from soul searching to social politics.

Cherie particularly enjoyed the morning local poet Miller Williams showed up. He was lighthearted and quick-witted, not boring like so many other speakers.

In between poems, Williams stopped and explained, "Sometimes I feel sorry for my family because I never know when I'm going to get hit with inspiration. The other day, I took my son out of the bathtub and thought of something I wanted to write. There he was, cold, wet, and screaming while his dad ran around the house looking for a pen and paper."

Cherie looked over to see Mr. Williams' little daughter Lucinda as she watched him. She stood near the back, lugging a guitar bigger than she was. She was one of those New Orleans kids for whom a musical instrument was an extra body part; it was so often attached to their slight bodies.

She's so lucky to have a dad like that. He's so cool, not scary, Cherie thought, as the envy of idealized fatherhood for those who felt a dad's absence fluttered through her. Marlene looked over, and as if she read her friend's mind, she squeezed Cherie's hand.

The flyer for the midsummer teen conference was posted on the bulletin board. It would take place in the Tennessee mountains. The conference theme, from which the workshops would derive, was Thou Art God.

Thou Art God smacked of Maharishi Mahesh Yogi influence.

It prompted a lengthy discussion among the teens, the general response being *Huh?*

Evelyn, their youth advisor, tried to explain.

"It probably means that we as individuals shouldn't think of ourselves as separate from the spiritual world, but part of it." She looked around at a roomful of blank expressions, ran her hand through her short, curly hair, adjusted her lotus position, and continued.

"Like when we meditate. We become part of the unseen cosmos or spiritual realm in a way that's bigger than just our bodies. In that way, as part of the Cosmos flowing through you, you become a part of God or God-spirit."

"But God connotes all powerful," Marlene pointed out, "and we're not."

"Well, but what if ... if by expanding your consciousness to include the unseen cosmic world, you were able to tap into a little bit of that power, share that power, feel God within you and part of you, as a way to be creative, or make the world a better place."

Finally, some half-nods of understanding. Then, "I don't know, though, it sounds a little bit like when the Baptists yell, 'I got Jesus in me!'" At that, Cherie and Lila at once began to roll around on the floor, yelling, "I got Jesus in me! I got Jesus in me!" It took a few more seconds for the group to catch on, and then they were all doing it.

Evelyn clapped her hands, "Please, let's not be disrespectful!" She waited patiently for the foolishness to die down and continued, "Well, maybe that's their way of connecting. What about you? What's your way of connecting?" More nods and snorts.

"You know," Evelyn continued, "in the New Testament, Jesus states that he is the son of God. But what if that statement was mistranslated or misinterpreted? What if there's another possibility that Jesus was trying to teach people to know that we *all* can be part divine creation or God, that we're not separate from the divine, but that we can share it and be connected in a loving and positive way?"

They all loved Evelyn, especially Katherine, who wished she was her real mother. They thought Evelyn was radical. A former Martha Graham dancer, she tore down most of the walls in her house to create "an open living space" and always wore clunky German sandals called Birkenstocks. The girls thought they were peculiar, but Evelyn just smiled when confronted and posed to show how they balanced her posture. Her three young children were, as almost everyone noted, the sweetest and smartest children one could ever hope to meet.

Because her ex-husband wasn't wealthy, Evelyn had to work. She convinced some of the hospitals in New Orleans to let her develop a new kind of physical "dance" therapy.

A short while later, there she was, teaching hardened guys who had been severely injured on oil rigs to move their limbs all over again as Erik Satie's music played in the background.

The girls ached to get to the conference. They had already attended the Birmingham and Huntsville, Alabama conferences to their infinite delight. The following spring, in their senior year, New Orleans was set to host the regional conference for the Lower Southern District that included far-flung Unitarian youth from Louisiana to North Carolina.

The teens would travel to conferences via VW buses, Greyhounds, trains, or bummed rides from all their various corners called home. They blended in an amalgam of brightly colored jeans, hair, T-shirts, beads, buttons, hats, and bandanas.

The conferences commenced with ritual greetings, chores teams were organized, rules were gone over, often met with disdain, and then dinner. After dinner, there was a guest lecturer or performance. In Birmingham, the first black policeman in Alabama was the guest speaker. In Huntsville, a performer dropped by and demonstrated Japanese Noh Theater. Former Freedom Riders stopped by and told their scary stories about voter registration and civil rights protests. Beyond the games, music, and workshops, it was a love fest. Cherie felt a kind of joyous delirium among the scores of teens, familiar strangers as they were. She pondered the glory of it. *It's another reality, a better one.*

~

"Give me that! I'm sick of you dribbling this stuff in your eyes. You're going to bleach them blind," Cherie grabbed the eye drops out of Lila's hands. "That's how eye drops work. They've got bleach in them."

Lila was crying again. Tears streamed down her face as she whimpered, her body trembling. She covered her face in her hands, and when she leaned forward, she hit her head on the bus seat in front of them and moaned. They were cramped in the fourteenth row of the Greyhound bus, their backpacks under their feet.

Lila sat next to the window, and Katherine was across the row. Lila *had* been sitting next to Katherine, but they were fighting so much Cherie broke them up and took Katherine's seat. Still, Lila was a blithering mass of snot and tears.

Lila blew her nose and looked out the window at the magnificent Tennessee mountains, finally quiet. The August sun filtered through the trees, giving Lila's light blue eyes a teal cast. As Cherie studied them, it reminded her of Vivien Leigh as Scarlett in *Gone with the Wind*. Vivien Leigh's eyes were blue, so the movie people added yellow lights for her close-ups to make them look green. Scarlett's green-with-envy eyes were important.

Cherie recalled seeing *Gone with the Wind* on a movie screen by the lake. It was crowded with fans, even on a Saturday morning. When the theme music filled the theater, and the title stretched across the screen, you could hear sniffles all around. Audience members were crying even before it started. Later on, when Rhett tells Scarlett he'll take her to New Orleans for their honeymoon, the whole audience hollered and applauded with proud satisfaction.

Cherie smiled at the memory.

"What's so funny?" Lila asked.

"Nothing. Your eyes look green in the light, not blue. I can't wait to get to the conference."

"You and me both."

"This one's national, not just southerners. They'll be kids from New England there. I doubt, though, anyone from California. It's too far."

"Maybe from California. You never know," Lila added, "Most of the Merry Pranksters are ex-LRYers from California, and they go all over the place."

"How did they pick Sewanee, Tennessee? It's such a strange place."

"Probably because it's sort of central, and they could rent the military school cheap."

"Isn't there a university there?" Cherie asked.

"Uh huh. University of the South."

"Maybe that's how they knew about it." Cherie smiled mischievously, "We'll have to enchant the military school so when they all come back in the fall, they're anti-war and drop out."

Katherine ignored them from across the aisle. She sat rigidly, holding a dog-eared copy of *The Guardian Angel* by Oliver Wendell Holmes that she had found on the ground.

Cherie wondered if Katherine was reading it or if her mind was far away, thinking about the previous night.

What happened last night? Cherie thought as she leaned back into her seat. She missed Marlene, especially with Lila and Katherine acting so awful. Marlene was driving up with a boy she had met in Birmingham. He was *it*, the boy Marlene picked out to lose her virginity to in Sewanee.

The trip had started with high spirits. Early in the morning, Lila, Katherine, and Cherie caught the crowded City of New Orleans train to Memphis.

The girls fixed the wooden seats, so they were facing each other.

Taking the train was a thrill. As the terrain went from flat to hilly, Cherie gasped at the sight of a group of horses as they frolicked and ran madly across the field, long manes whipping about.

That's when Cherie and Lila got into their first fight. A man wearing sunglasses and carrying a cornet case plunked down in the seat across from Lila. Engrossed in her copy of *A Separate Peace*, Lila went from stretching her long, slim legs across the booth to pulling them up beneath her, sitting cross-legged on the seat. She wore a sundress, and her cross-legged pose revealed her white panties with little blue flowers. Unaware or not, she was flashing him. Katherine pointed it out to Cherie.

Cherie shoved Lila.

"What?" Lila irritably replied.

Cherie whispered, "Pull your dress down."

Shocked that her casual pose on the seat could be misconstrued as indecent, not to mention her resentment over being chastised, Lila audibly concluded with a wave of her hand, "He's not looking at me!" She went back to her book.

Cherie glanced at the musician doubtfully. He smiled at her ever so slightly and turned his gaze out the window like a gentleman.

She went back to her copy of *The Brothers Karamazov*. Marlene and Lila read it at school, and they insisted she read it, too. She had just seen the old film of it on TV. Cherie was shocked to see Captain Kirk, William Shatner himself, in the role of Alexi, the younger brother who is a monk. The book pulled her into its world. Ivan, Alexi's older brother, tells him a terrible story called "The Grand Inquisitor." In Ivan's story, Jesus reappears in a 17th century Spanish town. The Grand Inquisitor arrests him and tells Jesus he's going to execute him in public because he has no right to show up and offer the townspeople enlightenment.

Cherie didn't understand it at all. *Why doesn't he want Jesus to give people enlightenment? Why is that a cruel thing, and anyway, isn't he supposed to worship Jesus, too?* She folded the corner of the page and made a mental note to ask Marlene and Lila about it.

Lila had called a Memphis girl she knew and set up for the three of them to stay at her house overnight. The following morning, they would board the Greyhound bus across Tennessee to Sewanee.

Lila told them a little bit about the Memphis girl, "Yeah, she felt so guilty about being rich that she would starve herself and sleep on the floor without air conditioning. Her parents had to take her to a doctor. She wanted to join the Peace Corps, which upset them."

"That's awful," Katherine said.

"Why doesn't she join LRY in Memphis?" Cherie asked.

"Are you kidding? Her family owns tobacco and oil! Everybody in town knows them. She has to stay Baptist or Lutheran or whatever they are."

Cherie and Katherine nodded with understanding. The family couldn't have their public face smudged by a daughter hanging around with rabble-rousers.

The Memphis girl picked them up at the train station. Cherie's jaw dropped when they pulled into the driveway of the old, four-story, stately mansion befitting a business baron. It wasn't as beautiful as the antebellum houses on St. Charles Avenue, but just as impressive. The roses and hydrangea hedges stretched far beyond the house, framing a garden with a fountain, benches, and a gazebo.

After introductions and some dinner in the kitchen served by the housekeeper, they were ushered to their bedroom up on the top floor on the attic level.

That's when the big fight started. Lila lied to the Memphis girl about her heartfelt desire to visit an elderly great auntie. She talked their young hostess into driving her there. In truth, she was going to visit her former French teacher.

He was an exceedingly handsome young French teacher from France whom Lila met in New Orleans when he substituted for a month at her high school. He was part of a state program to bring real French teachers from France to Louisiana. He left the program for Memphis to teach in a private girls' school. Towing a massive crush, Lila wanted to go see him.

"I want to go, too. You can't just leave me here," Cherie protested.

"No, no, he doesn't want a bunch of people over, and I don't want to go alone, so Katherine and I are going just for an hour, then we'll be back. You'll be okay."

They grabbed their backpacks and left. Cherie took a deep breath. *Something stinks,* she figured, *no doubt about it.*

She hardly slept and roused herself about 6 a.m. Lila and Katherine hadn't returned. She didn't know where to call. They knew the bus for Sewanee left at 8:30 a.m. She dressed, gathered her things, tip-toed down one staircase and another, and made her way across the grand entryway into the portico by the living room.

She stepped out the front door, walked down the long drive to the gate by the street, figured out how to open the gate, and sat on the sidewalk. She waited for Lila and Katherine for an hour, her anxiety increasing. Finally, a taxi pulled up.

Katherine hopped out and yelled, "Get in! He'll take us to the station." Cherie crawled in the back. Lila looked terrible; her knees were drawn up with her arms wrapped around them.

"Are you okay?" Cherie asked.

Lila shook her head no. "My head is banging. I need aspirin."

"I've got some. Here," Cherie dug into her stuff and handed over a bottle of St. Joseph's Aspirin for Children.

"Why do you have these? They're for little kids," Lila asked helplessly. "I need the real stuff." She moaned and grabbed her head with both hands.

"I like the taste, and you can chew them without water. Take six of them," Cherie replied.

Lila poured the orange tablets into her palm and chewed them up. "They taste awful," she complained.

Katherine looked over at Lila, and Lila glared back at her, muttering, "Don't look at me. I feel like killing you."

They arrived at the station to see their Greyhound Bus backing up out of its parking space. They took off after the bus and ran alongside its wheels, banging on the door and calling to the driver. It stopped. As they boarded, Mr. Driver yelled at them, "I darn near ran over you girls! What's the matter with you?"

"Sorry, sir," Cherie said, handing over her ticket, "But we have to get to a church conference."

"Which church?" he asked, softening as he took Lila's and Katherine's tickets.

All three at once, Lila said, "Baptist," Katherine said, "Catholic," and Cherie said, "Unitarian." The driver shook his head, and they stumbled to their seats.

Hours into the ride, the bus stopped in the middle of nowhere, high on a ridge. An old lady got on and sat by the bus driver, using the two-step bus entry as a seat. She chatted sweetly with him about the weather and the state fair.

"Look at that," Lila whispered, "there she is, all old, and still, deep inside, is a young girl flirting away for a man's attention."

Cherie nodded. Once again, she saw Mama Faylene's insight into human folly shining through her daughter.

Cherie felt Lila grab her arm, "My eyes are so sore. I need my drops back," she whined.

"Not unless you tell me what happened," Cherie negotiated. "You and Katherine abandoned me at that girl's house. I listened in on a phone call, and her mother complained about what an imposition it was to have us stay over. What a bitch! Jeez, that house had twenty-five rooms in it. So, what happened?"

As Cherie had imagined, they got drunk, and then, the French teacher rattled Lila when he moved on Katherine. He kissed Katherine, whispered, and led her into the bedroom. Lila was left alone with the TV and a wine bottle, and she could hear them kissing and moaning. It put her into hysterics. After a while, Katherine came out and tried to bring her in with them. "Oh, hurray, now it's my turn!" She kicked Katherine away.

"She made me feel like dirt," Lila whimpered.

"But what did she say?"

Lila pirouetted through her swirling emotions, "She handed me some bullshit like she didn't think it would upset me," adding bitterly, "I don't know, maybe she's so desperate for it." Then, "No, it's not her fault. He's so good-looking, you can't resist. I just didn't think that she could ever treat me that way."

Cherie sympathized. "Look. A few more hours, and we'll be there. It's going to be great. Terry, that boy from Huntsville, will be there. He loves you. He's incredible. You won't even remember what that jerk looks like." Cherie handed over the eye drops.

Lila tilted her head back, and as she squirted the drops into her eyes, she asked Cherie, "Are you going to lose your virginity?"

Cherie had turned seventeen and was determined to accomplish what the girls called Mission-Get-It-Over-With. Nobody wanted to graduate from high school intact.

"If I can," Cherie whispered, "if seeing a boy naked doesn't freak me out."

Lila peered at her through the streaming eye drops incredulously. "You're joking, right?"

"No. Just art pictures, like Michelangelo's *David*, and statues, you know, Captain Beau Scrotie," to which they shared a smile. "I've only lived with Paulette. I remember walking in on one of Paulette's boyfriends once when he came out of the shower. I was really little. It looked like a dark pink hairy worm stuck on him like Pin the Tail on the Donkey. And *Playboy* only shows girls. They never show boys. It's so unfair."

"Yeah, that's totally unfair," Lila agreed, adding with authority, "Well, when you see boys, at first you won't like it, but then you'll love it."

Lila turned toward the window and curled up to sleep. She smiled at Cherie, "I'm so glad you're here. If you weren't here, I'd kill somebody."

"I'm glad you're here too."

"Do my eyes still look green?" Lila smiled impishly, staring out the window.

Cherie leaned over to look and stared at Lila's eyes.

"Yeah."

"*Chatoyance*." Lila yawned and closed her eyes.

"Shatto, what?"

"It means how jewelry and shiny things change color in the light." She fell asleep.

Cherie moved into the empty seat next to Katherine. They whispered.

"Well, at least you're not mad at me," Katherine said dryly. "Do you have any aspirin left?" Cherie handed her the bottle, "Keep it."

Cherie wondered if Katherine was about to cry. The expression on her face was one of profound sadness, but Cherie had never seen Katherine cry, not from slaps and bruises, insults, or rejections. Katherine frequently got sick and got headaches. She sometimes played the same song over and over, and she would stare into space, but she wasn't a crier.

Katherine bit her lip. "It was really late. We drank all this wine and watched an old *Twilight Zone* on TV."

"Which one?" Cherie interrupted.

"The one where the deformed doctors unwrap the girl's face, and she's beautiful, but it's abnormal in their world."

"Oh my God, yeah. That used to scare me so much. I hated the music. I would scream in the closet to block it out."

"I don't know what happened. We drank some wine, and he kissed me. I didn't know Lila would flip out. Then we went into his bedroom. It didn't last long," she shrugged. "It was just a fuck. Who cares? I don't care if he lives or dies. And he doesn't care if I live or die. I'm nothing to him."

Cherie felt uneasy. All of a sudden, her friend Katherine, whom the poet Balladeer referred to as a "fragile fawn," sounded hard-bitten. Katherine went on.

"After we, you know, I *tried* to get Lila to come into the bedroom with us, but she wouldn't. I got down next to her on the rug and put my arms around her, but she got so mad. She kicked me. It really hurt, too."

"You stole her crush. She felt thrown away."

"Then why did she bring me along?"

"Because she didn't want to go alone."

Katherine looked regretful. "I apologized. I love Lila, but what am I supposed to do? Kiss her feet?"

Katherine leaned against Cherie in a momentary show of affection. She opened her book. "I want to forget about it. So, Lila hates me now?"

"No. She'll come around. Is that a good book? Is that the one you found on the ground?

"Yeah. It's around the Civil War. This girl is all messed up, but she has a friend who's a boy who's trying to save her from marrying an evil man, so I guess he's the angel."

Cherie went back to her seat. Even though she knew the Wordless Diary was in her backpack, she unzipped the side and reached in to make sure that indeed, it was there.

Late afternoon's sun flickered through the trees and draped the Appalachian Mountains of Tennessee in shimmering amber light. *So beautiful*, she thought, gazing at their majesty. Cherie decided to draw them for 3-7-7. *August 1969. I only have a year and twelve days left. Then I'm gone.*

CHAPTER 22

Peace and Love

IT WAS the second night of the conference. The four mademoiselles tumbled out of the crowded flatbed of the old truck and ran to the edge of the lake past pods of jeans, shirts, sandals, and underwear. The truck's headlights were finally turned off. It took a few seconds before Cherie's sharp night vision set in. And then it did.

Naked boys. Scores of them. There were so many you couldn't look at all of them at once. Their bodies were glossy from the water and luminous in the moonlight. They were unearthly, kinetic, shimmering beings that bolted out of the water onto the platform in the middle of the lake and dove back in again.

Cherie stood with Katherine, surveying the mythological landscape.

"Girls are in there, too," Katherine said.

It took Cherie a few seconds to discern the girls from all the naked boys that had caught her attention, but sure enough, the feminine lines were there.

Lila was already in the water, her delighted soprano squeals added to the howling altos, tenors, basses, splashing water, and guitars. Group activities at conferences, especially the spontaneous ones, were rarely executed without a music jam. It gave shy kids and sideliners something robust to do.

Marlene was next to take the plunge, but she wouldn't do it alone.

"C'mon! I will if you will," she encouraged Cherie and Katherine, and when they didn't move a muscle, "C'mon, *you know* you're dying to go in."

Lila provided the last impetus, calling from the water, "You're stupid insane standing there. Get in! The water feels so good!"

Katherine stepped back as she shook her head no and headed for the kids with instruments. No one cajoled her.

Marlene and Cherie looked at each other, nodded knowingly, counted off one ... two ... three ... GO! They shed their cotton and denim, every stitch of it, screamed, and ran into the water. It was Tennessee mountain cold, even in August, and with a gasp and a shiver, three mermaids swam like hell for the platform.

As Cherie neared the platform, she stopped swimming and treaded, looking up from the water to take in her first close-ups of the silvery boys.

They were well past the middle school discomforts of voice-dropping and reaching their adult height. Against their lean bodies, their flat torsos, arms, and thighs, their dicks and balls looked like small protuberances, a delicate architectural detail carved on a pillar.

Cherie felt tingly.

Lila and Marlene paddled up next to her. For a second, Lila watched Cherie watch the boys and then sputtered breathlessly, "It's not how they really look."

"What do you mean?"

"Their dicks. They don't normally look like that."

Marlene explained, "The water's freezing. It makes their balls contract, and that pulls up their penises."

In case Cherie didn't understand, Lila translated, "It shrinks them up. They're bigger normally, and erections are totally different." She swam away for the platform and yelled back at her knowingly, "You'll see soon enough, and more than that, too." Lila's laughter blended with the platform's chatter.

Marlene followed Lila to the large lake platform, bobbing under the weight of a crush of swimmers. Cherie, not as strong a swimmer as her friends, struggled. Giving in to an inelegant dog paddle, she finally reached the ladder. She held on to the side of it, gasping.

"Do you want to come up?" somebody asked.

She looked up into a handsome face more round than angular, framed by wide blue eyes and dark blond wet hair. The accent was southern, but not deep southern. He kneeled down and held out a hand to help her.

"Do you want to come up?" he repeated.

Cherie nodded yes and reached up.

She got one foot on the lower step of the ladder, barely beneath the surface of the water, grabbed his hand, and immediately found herself up and standing on the platform. He was a lot taller than she was.

"Thanks," she muttered.

"Where are you from?"

"New Orleans."

He smiled, "Cool."

It *was* cool. New Orleans was magic, and Cherie loved saying it, being from New Orleans, being the strange voodoo princess with dark tresses, at the moment, draped only in its wet tendrils and night light.

The air was warm, but Cherie stood there as if frozen and silent. She was relieved when he spoke again.

"Sit down here and catch your breath," he said, referring to an open space on the edge of the crowded platform.

They sat down together, barely enough space for both of them and the side of his arm and leg touched hers.

"I'm from Williamsburg. My name is Jessy. And you are ... ?"

"Cherie."

"S-H-E-R-R-Y?" He spelled it out.

"No, C-H-E-R-I-E. It means 'little dear' in French."

"D-E-E-R?" he teased with a smile.

"No. D-E-A-R," she said, smiling back.

"I know. I'm just giving you grief," he admitted, and Cherie wasn't sure she'd ever catch her breath again.

One of Jessy's naked buddies lightly punched him on the shoulder, "Hey, we told Paul we'd help him build the bonfire." Jessy gave him a *no-way* look, but his friend insisted, "C'mon, man, he hates it when people fink out on him."

At that, Jessy pushed off into the water, now looking up at her. He asked, "You can swim back okay?" Cherie nodded yes. "Then I'll see you at the bonfire?" She smiled at him, "I promise I won't D-R-O-W-N."

"Better not!" he smiled, shaking the water off his face.

He swam toward the shore. Cherie watched his shoulders, backside, and feet slide along the surface of the dark water away from her.

Thank God Lila and Marlene made me get in, she thought. Jessy from Williamsburg. She wondered how his mouth tasted kissing him. She wondered how much bigger it would look once it warmed up.

Her feet in the cool water, sitting on the edge of the platform, listening to the excited chatter around her, the splatter of it, feeling the drops and sprays of it as people dove in, hearing the soft strains of acoustic guitars on the shore, Cherie felt that everything bad was washed away. All her worry about the world and all its misery, her fights at school and with Paulette, her nightmares, it all felt washed away. And with that, she swooned at every good thing, every good possibility. There was no other place on Earth she wanted to be.

Marlene sat down next to her.

"Who was that?"

"Jessy. He's from Williamsburg. Where's that?"

"Virginia. It's where the College of William and Mary is. Let's go find Katherine. I don't want to leave her all by herself."

"Did you see Lila?"

"She found Terry."

"Guess what! They're going to build a bonfire!"

"I thought so. There was a ton of marshmallows in the truck. Josh went to gather wood for it. You ready? Go!"

And they were back in the water, swimming toward the sweetness of marshmallows, toasted and sticky in the fire the boys would build.

As the clothed-again, lighthearted crowd gathered around the bonfire, Cherie tried to keep her eyes on Jessy. It was impossible. He kept appearing and disappearing in the flickering light.

It was clear that Jessy was a star, one of LRY's envied teen leaders who organized things and was immensely popular. When Cherie did get a glimpse of him, he was busy carrying wood, telling somebody what to do, or talking with one of the adult supervisors. Then he vanished again. Cherie then saw a girl hugging him, greeting him with an ear-splitting "Jeeesssee" that made Cherie bite her lip; it was so grating.

Jessy was on call, but nonetheless, Cherie felt rejected and disheartened. For a moment there, she thought maybe he was looking for her, but the moment passed. Lila sat to her left with Terry, who had evidently shirked his bonfire duties to make out with Lila. At her right, Marlene shared a blanket with her new boyfriend from Birmingham.

Although they had rushed back to save Katherine from being alone, there was no need. They found her among the musicians, a recorder at her lips, improvising with the group. Some of them looked like her: lean, pale, same hair color, making music.

Cherie didn't have the courage to go up to Jessy. If he wanted to find her, he would. She stood up to walk around. She thought, *maybe if I get closer, he'll see me and come over.*

Sure enough, she slowly circled the bonfire twice, and on the second go-round, their eyes met. He smiled and mimicked shooting her, then continued placing marshmallows on long sticks. *Damn, stupid marshmallows!* She hmphed to herself.

Cherie felt like she might burst into tears. She looked around for her friends and didn't see them. *Did they move?* She backed away from the fire so her eyes could adjust to the darkness. She realized she was standing next to several people lying on their backs on a blanket, looking up at the stars.

The man closest to her was pointing out the constellations. His hair was light, reddish brown, and he was good-looking with a face like a Renaissance painting. Cherie noticed that instead of sneakers or sandals, he wore boots made of soft leather cuffed over the end of his jeans.

On the other side of him lay two women, one with her arm around the other's shoulders. Cherie figured they were New Englanders. She knew them to be women who didn't do much of anything to fix themselves up. Even in the dark, Cherie could see they were on the plain side of pretty. One had long hair, and the other had a short haircut in a bob like the boy for Buster Brown's shoes. She had seen lady tourists like that in the Quarter, and some went to their congregation.

Cherie jumped when the man lightly grabbed her ankle, "Hey, didn't mean to scare you, but you're blocking the Northern Cross," he said.

"Sorry," Cherie replied, sitting down on the edge of the blanket, then asking, "What is the Northern Cross?"

"Come lie down, and you'll see it," he said, "I'll point it out to you."

"Come lie down with us. It's so beautiful," the two women on the other side of him said. They ordered, "Mac, move over," entreating Cherie, "Come lie down with us. There's room."

She did. She could feel their warmth. She wanted to look at them, the three familiar strangers with whom she was sharing the blanket, but instead, peered straight up into the stars. She exhaled.

Mac caught it. He took her hand and rubbed and patted it, "Yes, relax, relax. Breathe. There you go. You can't see the stars if you're all wound up. One more deep breath. Yes. Now look straight up. See them? Three bright stars. Deneb, Vega, and Altair. They form a triangle. It's the Northern Cross constellation, also known as Cygnus the Swan, the gateway to the Milky Way."

"Right there. Yes, I see them!" Cherie exclaimed.

As the scent of burnt sugar filled the air, his low voice mixed in with percussion instruments being played by the bonfire, Mac pointed out constellations and even a part of the Milky Way. For a moment, she forgot about Jessy.

The two women left to join in the dancing.

Mac and Cherie now lay on their sides, face-to-face, talking.

Grazed by firelight, she could see how handsome he was and a lot older than she was, maybe thirtyish. She learned that he was from Massachusetts, but he wasn't one of the adult supervisor.

"No, my wife is a supervisor. I just came along for the ride. And I'm doing a workshop on Earth ecology. You should come to it."

He was wearing a wedding ring.

"You're married?"

"You saw her. She was just here with her girlfriend."

"But you shouldn't be talking to me like this if you're married!" Cherie protested.

Mac thought that was hilarious. He laughed.

"You couldn't tell?" he asked her.

"Tell what?"

Mac pointed toward the dancers. Cherie sat up and, sure enough, saw Mac's wife and her friend dancing entwined like lovers.

"She's a lesbian. She just realized."

"You're not mad at her?" she asked.

Mac shook his head, "Of course not. I want her to be happy. Why? Would they get mad in New Orleans?"

"For sure. They'd yell and scream and chase each other around the house with kitchen knives, and the neighbors would have to call the cops."

"I think I'll stay in Stockbridge," Mac replied.

"Will you stay married?"

"We haven't figured that out yet. Probably do a group marriage."

Cherie reached out and took the amulet that had fallen from his shirt. It was a silver pentagram inside a circle on a leather cord. As she picked it up and studied it, he asked, "Do you know what it means?"

Cherie nodded, "It's the witches' symbol, but I've never actually seen anybody wearing one. Does this mean you're a warlock or something? Or you do Black Mass?" She let go of the amulet.

He frowned, and his tone became indignant, "No. Absolutely not. Black Mass is a perversion practiced by Satanists, invented by disgruntled Catholics. It has *nothing* to do with me!" His expression softened. "Sorry, but I feel strongly about that."

"Then what is it?" Cherie asked, dazzled by the revelation that she was talking to a real male witch.

"It means I'm a neopagan. It means I practice traditional rituals with other neopagans. It means I worship the divine Mother Goddess and the sacred Earth, her ultimate creation in consort with Father Sky. I believe in a pantheon of gods and spirit."

"What do you mean by *pantheon*?"

"I don't believe in monotheism, which means one god."

"I know what monotheism is," Cherie said defensively, adding, "but you still go to church with your wife?"

"No. I can't confine my religion to one little building. It's bigger than that. My spirit is bigger than that. It's all of creation, our planet, and the sky, and the stars beyond, and other dimensions we can't see, but we can feel and know if we open up to them."

Cherie's insides surged with heat, and she prayed the blush didn't show. She didn't know what to say. She felt dumb.

His gaze was steady. He didn't mind the silence.

She broke it, chattering, "Well, then, I guess you wouldn't make a very good Unitarian. A lot of them have trouble accepting the idea of one god, much less a whole bunch of them," all the while thinking, *Why am I talking so much?* She continued, "Well, that's not completely true, is it? A lot of Uni's believe in God, especially in the South and Midwest. I guess that's the difference between the secularists and the humanists. And social justice is like God-inspired work, too." Cherie finally shut herself up, drawing in a long breath.

Mac pushed a lock of hair off her face and ran his fingertips down her arm. "You're so smart and ... so pretty. Maybe I should visit New Orleans."

She wanted to kiss him, and she wanted to bolt. Cherie felt herself pulled between two magnetic forces, her desire for Jessy, who glowed with the sun, and Mac, a lunar-driven ebb tide, pulling her underwater. She felt a chill, and she pushed Mac's hand away. He smiled sweetly at her and nodded with a fixed stare as though to say, *It's okay. I know you're a virgin. We can go slowly.* Cherie wondered if he was patronizing her, which she hated, but still, she didn't get up and leave. She felt like she was glued to the blanket.

Suddenly, he stood up and lifted her to her feet. "C'mon, my sweet tooth is howling with hunger. Let's go get some of those toasted things."

By the bonfire, Cherie reunited with her friends. Lila prodded her, "Did you talk to him?" Cherie knew she meant Jessy. "No."

The next day was filled with workshops. Lila and Cherie attended *Creating Political Theater,* Marlene attended *Jesus and Civil Disobedience,* and Katherine went to *Chanting and Music Meditations.*

After lunch, they took an *Introduction to Yoga* class. The woman who taught the class was an Earth mama who had her three little kids and her man with her at the conference. She had a sweet smile and spoke in a soft, warm voice, but much to the quartet's horror, she didn't shave her legs. Lila, Marlene, Katherine, and Cherie thought that was so gross. As they twisted their bodies around, they whispered to each other and made faces about hairy spider legs.

After the class, Marlene cracked them up by commenting, "You know, that's what some Native Americans out west call palefaces that don't shave."

"What, spiders?"

"No, they call them tarantulas."

After yoga class, the conferees were divided into groups to discuss the conference theme, *Thou Art God.* It was pretty much what they thought it would be, whether God was external to humans or lived in their spirits or both.

During the discussion, Katherine had a delayed reaction to "tarantulas" and couldn't suppress her laughter. Then, with her delicate fingers, she perfectly mimicked a tarantula crawling up her leg. Cherie caught on and immediately succumbed. Tears rolled down their faces, and the more they tried to be quiet, the worse it was. Lila and Marlene were able to maintain decorum and chided, "Stop it!" but that only made it worse. It wasn't long before they got angry looks, especially from their group leader, so they had to crawl away from the group. Lila gave Katherine a nasty look, still mad.

"Man, everybody is so damn serious," Cherie commented.

By five o'clock dinner, Cherie made a pact with herself that if Jessy hadn't shown up to talk to her by the time dinner ended, she would forget about him. Five o'clock dinner came and went. She ate with Marlene, Marlene's boyfriend, and kids she knew from the conference in Birmingham.

Jessy-who-shined-with-the-Sun didn't show up at all, not for one second. After dinner, her friends left, and Cherie dawdled at the table. She read the back cover of a copy of *The Harrod Experiment* that someone had left there. For no reason, she angrily ripped it in half and pitched it across the room. She traced an X on the table, which meant *forget Jessy.*

She saw Mac walk in her direction. He held hands with a different woman, neither his wife nor her girlfriend. Cherie figured another New Englander, *but at least she wore long, pretty earrings.* When he spotted Cherie, he bid the woman goodbye. They shared a mouth kiss, and Cherie heard her tell him, "See you later."

He sat down next to Cherie. She felt flattered.

"How are you? How was your day? Did you go to any workshops?" he asked.

They talked workshops and the *God Within.* He invited her to attend his workshop the following day. He said as far as he was concerned, saving the Earth and educating people about it was the only political issue that existed.

"After all, what does it matter if you win or lose a war or distribute wealth without clean water or air? Then we all die," Mac said bitterly, betraying his otherwise easy exterior. "We're made out of the same stardust as everything else on Earth. There's no separating us. That's God within, or as I prefer it, the Goddess within."

"Yeah? What about good ol' Father Sky?" Cherie said sarcastically.

Unsmiling, Mac gave her another one of those searching looks and then declared, "Soul. Body and soul. The feminine and masculine forces of the universe. It's the sacred marriage of body and soul that makes us earthlings tick."

As though in pain, Cherie put both hands on the side of her head, "I've been discussing stuff all day. It's making my head hurt! I'm exhausted."

At that, Mac laughed and moved closer, putting his arms around her and rubbing her neck and shoulders.

"You're right. I'm sorry, Cherie. It's much too beautiful out to get intense. And anyway, I didn't come over to evangelize conservation, I came over to ask you to take a walk with me. It's light for at least three more hours. C'mon, let's climb the bell tower at the University. It's right down the road. And there's a trail that leads back. I discovered it yesterday,"

Cherie couldn't think why not go with him. He was dazzling. Tall, but soft-spoken. The way he thought about things, ideas she had never heard of before. She loved what people called *the old religions*. She loved the gods and goddesses of ancient Greece and the Norse legends. She believed in ESP and paranormal phenomena. She had a voodoo doll at home that she had picked up in the Quarter. The lady who sold it to her drew a star and cross mark on it so it would only attract good and not harm.

She was sure she'd be safe with Mac. He wouldn't try to force himself on her. She figured, *He's so cool. He's not even mad at his wife for being gay.*

Yet despite all the cheerful logic her brain generated, her insides twisted with trepidation. It was that feeling of her feet sinking into the sand as the waves dragged back into the sea, dragging her out until she was too deep to get back to shore. But the call to adventure was greater. She took his hand, and he led her out. "By the way," he asked, "What's your real name?"

Cherie responded with, "What does Mac stand for, MacDonald's?"

The main campus of the University of the South was beautiful; its stone buildings and walkways touched up in Gothic style. They climbed to the top of the bell tower adjacent to the church building. The last few steps felt like being suspended in space, and it frightened and thrilled Cherie. Mac climbed up behind her, reassuring her with every step that she could do it. Despite her fear and misgivings, the view of the mountains beset by the colors of the setting sun was magnificent.

Cherie was grateful Mac didn't make a pass at her. Still, he felt free to touch her, her hair and shoulders, and down her spine. It didn't feel good. She hated it, hands that appeared out of nowhere to push or pull at her hair, pat her back, face, and behind. That's what Paulette did, and that one thought made Cherie seethe. She felt she'd rather jump off the tower than go with a man whose touch reminded her of her mother. Seeing her expression darken, Mac asked, "What's wrong, baby?" he asked. His hand glided over her neck under her long hair.

"Nothing, just don't." She shrugged off his hand, but he didn't seem to notice. He put his arm around her and gave her a squeeze. She pushed him away.

They took the trail through the woods to get back to the conference. The air was fragrant with wild raspberries and blackberries. Along the way, they ran into three local boys who looked about eighteen. The boys stared at them, amazed to find themselves face-to-face with two of the people they deemed to be weirdos staying at the military school.

"Yeah," one of them said, "We were watching y'all last night by the lake." And they all snorted and giggled.

It hadn't occurred to Cherie that locals could be spying on them beyond the trees. As they chatted, she learned that all three boys were drafted and going to Vietnam. They parted ways. She told them, "May God keep you safe."

"Pretty sweet," Mac said unsmilingly.

"I meant it," Cherie replied.

"So did I," he replied.

Farther down the trail, Mac shook his head and let out a sound akin to a growl.

Cherie jumped, "What's the matter?"

"They're probably going to die, all three of them," he said, "and it's so wrong."

She walked more quickly, his footsteps close behind her. It was almost dark when they reached the school's campus and passed by the outlying tennis courts.

"Hey, look," Mac beckoned to her, walking onto the court surrounded by tall fencing, "This would be a great ritual space. We could come here tomorrow night."

"What would you do?" Cherie asked from the other side of the fence.

"We would evoke the spirits to guide us through our sacred communion. It's a new moon, perfect. But I need to clear the energy here. The energy is off. Can you feel it?"

Mac began to walk the perimeter of the court, suddenly calling to her, "Look!" He touched something with his toe, "It's a dead bird. Oh wow, it's a screech owl. Come see it."

"I'm going back," she called.

"I'll come and get you for the poetry service," he replied.

"No, I'm going to skip it."

As she left the tennis court, she could hear him saying a prayer for the dead owl. She broke into a run, her feet flying across the football field. Every stride echoed as her foot hit the ground like something was running at her heels, chasing her, about to attack. She fled toward the gym, which was filled with light.

Cherie found her friends and fell onto Lila, knocking her over.

"Where have you been?" Lila asked, full of concern.

"I'll tell you later."

"What's wrong?" she moved closer.

"I'll tell you later," Cherie replied. "I want to dance. Come dance."

"I'll dance," Marlene joined in.

Cherie danced like hell's bells were ringing—jumping, stomping, screaming—the music couldn't be loud enough or the beat hard enough until her stomach was uncoiled, and she was spent.

Back in their dorm room, she sat with Lila on one of the beds, discussing the day's events. Up and down the hallway, there was a lot of noise as two of the youth organizers, dressed in capes and masks, chased kids out of their rooms to go downstairs to the late poetry service. As the hallway emptied, it grew silent.

Lila cut to the chase. "Typical Yankee. He thinks you're a dumb Southerner, and he can seduce you."

"He doesn't think I'm dumb." Cherie was defensive.

"He's going to press on you until you give in. That's what's coming. Is that what you want? If it is, then hell, you could do a lot worse. He's really sexy and looks like he knows ..."

"No, it's not what I want! I don't want his hands on me. I don't want to feel pressured. I want to feel ... like it's all I want." Cherie brooded, "I guess he is a pig. But he's a pagan, he loves the Mother Goddess. I thought that would make him different."

"Uh, get real," Lila said sarcastically. "Oink, oink, even if he's a vegetarian. Religion has nothing to do with it. Jimmy Swaggart's in New Orleans all the time cruising for you-know-what, and half the priests out there have boys hidden under their altars."

"Is that why they call them altar boys?"

"Haha. Very funny. Mama says, 'You can't blame a man for wanting you,'" She pointed her finger at Cherie for emphasis.

"Okay. I won't blame him for wanting me."

Both Lila and Cherie covered their mouths to suppress their screams when they heard Mac call Cherie's name from down the long hallway.

Cherie peeked into the hallway. "Oh shit! He actually came here to get me!" she whispered.

At that moment, the two masked-and-caped organizers burst into the room, eliciting frightened gasps from Cherie and Lila. Terry from Huntsville removed his mask, and Lila threw herself on him.

"You scared the shit out of us," Lila admonished. They fell on the opposite bed together, Lila playfully beating him up and him loving it.

Jessy, who shined with the Sun, removed his mask.

"Hey! Cherie, where have you been? I've been looking for you. Didn't you see my note? I left it for you on the bulletin board."

"Cherie, are you here?" Mac called from down the hallway. Jessy looked over his shoulder in the direction of the disembodied voice.

Desperate, Cherie put her hands on Jessy's chest, grasping his shirt. She stood on her tip-toes so her mouth was close to his, and looking straight into his eyes, she whispered, "Don't go to the poetry service. Stay here with me."

"Okay," he whispered, "I can do that."

The heavy, booted footsteps in the empty hallway were getting closer.

She put her arms around Jessy's neck, her mouth reaching for his. He gathered her up into his arms. She clutched him and kissed him long and deep. She breathed in the sun and heat on his skin. He kissed her back, each unwilling to let go.

Though her eyes were shut tight, she heard Mac's measured footsteps stop at the door. Then she heard them recede back into the stairwell.

It was perfect. Jessy and Cherie sneaked up to the top floor of the dorm, which was empty. All the rooms had in them were twin beds with mattresses on them, wooden desks, and dressers.

They threw off their clothes and, with no inhibitions, collapsed onto the bed. They grabbed at one another. They kissed and petted. Cherie ran her tongue over Jessy's sweet-tasting palate and felt his erection, indeed a wondrous thing. French kissing and petting, Cherie had done all that already with Thornton. She was ready for cherry jubilee.

Awkward at moments, and despite Jessy's hard work getting into her which wasn't as easy as Cherie thought it would be, it wasn't painful making love with him. It felt more like her guts were being squashed. It took her breath away, the weight of him against her and the compression. Like Lila told her it would feel, the swaying movement was like flying.

Afterward, Jessy slept deeply, not stirring, his arm draped over her. She couldn't sleep at all. Cherie thought how grateful she was that being with him was so all-consuming that nothing else bad flashed through her mind that would take her away from him.

In the morning, he smiled, and they kissed; he noted the morning bell that chimed eight times and left to see to his conference obligations.

Cherie returned to her room, showered, stayed in bed until two in the afternoon, read magazines, and slept just for fun. She had the perfect excuse because now, everything was different.

Lila, Marlene, and Katherine flopped down on the bed with her.

"Well, it looks like we've got two steak dinners coming in this crowd. We'd better make reservations as soon as we get home," Lila announced.

Cherie sat up. Getting a steak dinner was the girls' code for going all the way. Linguini was code for oral sex. Pastry was just kissing and getting basted meant petting. She knew Lila and Katherine weren't virgins, so that meant Marlene.

Marlene tried to stay cool but couldn't and started giggling, her face in the pillow. They pulled the pillow out from under her and hit her with it.

The girlfriends made Cherie get out of bed and get dressed. They wanted to make pierced earrings at the beading workshop. Cherie remarked to Marlene, "I didn't bleed."

"I did. But don't worry about it," Marlene assured her, "Lots of people don't. In some societies, where they display the sheets after the wedding night, the bride will sneak in a chicken to slaughter just in case."

"That's disgusting," Katherine declared.

Late that night, Cherie and Jessy sneaked up to the top floor to make love again. She had counted off the days from her last day on the rag and felt she was safe for one more night of sex. It was only the seventh day, almost a week off from the twelfth to the eighteenth danger zone.

Cherie got on top. Making love was easier and more coordinated this time. They found their rhythm. Afterward, she even slept a little bit, nestled against Jessy's sleek frame that felt so hot next to her cool skin.

It was time to say goodbye. Everyone had to clear out and be gone by high noon.

Much to the chagrin of the conferees, all peace symbols and anti-war slogans had to be removed, and everything had to be clean and left exactly the same. This required the participation of every attendee.

Nevertheless, some of the girls wrote secret notes to the boys returning to their proud military school in the fall. They tucked them under pillows and on the top shelves of closets. The notes read:

Dear Boyfriend, I don't know you, but I slept in this bed this summer when I came to a conference. Please, I beg you to question the war and save your life. Please drop out of this school, go to Canada, and stop the killing. Peace and love from a girl who might be a stranger but still loves you and cares about you.

They were decorated with flowers and peace symbols and kissed with lipstick.

These final hours of the conference were as busy and emotional as its first few hours. Conferees sat in small circles, vowing everlasting friendship in the last few moments of conference bliss. Everybody helped one another pack and clean up. Tears, hugs, and kisses flowed freely as conferees hung on to each other for dear life.

A collective knowledge was shared among the LRYers that wrenching apart was not the hardest part. The hardest part was going back home with all their tender feelings and being back in your other life. Cherie knew that Jessy would go home to his Virginia girlfriend.

The Northerners understood that the Southerners were more vulnerable and isolated in their communities. They graced their goodbyes with, "Be careful. Take care of yourself."

Cherie felt a hand on her shoulder and turned to find herself face-to-face with Mac. She smiled before she could assume a demure posture, amazed that she was, in fact, pleased to see him.

"Are you happy?" Mac asked.

Cherie nodded an enthusiastic yes.

Mac smiled, "That's all I wanted, for you to be happy."

"Then you got what you wanted!" Cherie blurted out.

Mac raised his fist to his heart. He staggered back, making Cherie laugh.

"Oh, so young and already so cruel," he said. He held both

hands out to her, and she took them. He pulled her close, embraced her, and then he whispered, "See you someday at Solstice. Merry meet and merry part. Until we meet again."

He hugged her tightly, let her go, and walked away. Cherie ran after him.

"Mac. Stop. Why do you say that? Do you think I'm a pagan?"

"I don't have to think. I know. I knew the second you showed up that you're one of us. We always find each other. You chose to find me. This may be a beginning, not a goodbye.

"But what if I don't want to be one," she opposed.

"It's your soul, Cherie. The sacred grove will always call to you even as you practice modern religions, and the sacred circle will always be your home. It's just how it is. Don't you get how magical you are?"

She didn't argue, so he went on. "Don't worry, you can still love Jesus. A lot of us do. It's just his followers we avoid."

Cherie pushed him away, "Shut up! Go chop some wood or something!"

She ran off.

Terrific, Cherie thought. *Now, along with bad hippie, bad daughter, bad atheist, bad all religions whatever, I can be a bad pagan. Well, yuk, yuk, and goodie gumdrops.* She could feel him watching her as she ran off.

CHAPTER 23

Queen of the Road

THE GIRLS WERE GETTING HOME every which way. Lila flew out of Chattanooga to Florida to join her grandmother and sister for a cruise leaving from Miami, and Katherine left with Marlene and her boyfriend, squished in the back seat. Cherie bummed a ride with a girl from Birmingham whose friends called her Maddie Granola.

Cherie could stay overnight with her. The next day, Maddie Granola and her family were headed to the beach in Biloxi, and they could give her a ride. From there, Cherie could catch an afternoon bus back home. It was ninety-five miles from Biloxi, but the bus ride, being as it was local along Rt. 90 with beach traffic would take five hours.

They yelled and waved as they drove away from the conference. Soon, they were on the highway. Maddie Granola's best friend was driving. They were perfect best friends. They sang along to every song the radio played, and they knew every lyric, be it Stevie Wonder or Patsy Cline.

Cherie leaned against the back seat and stretched her legs and arms. The wind blew her hair wild. As if the conference wasn't mind-blowing enough, she now thanked her lucky stars for being in a big, old, roomy red convertible, Detroit's version of a magic carpet.

Cherie hovered between sleep and reality and thought about Jessy and her first boyfriend, Thorn. They were both Aquarians. A warm satisfaction swept over her that she knew her type. From then on, she would only be attracted to winter souls, born between January and February twenty-first, *Well, maybe back to November,* she figured, *just in case a Scorpio or Sagittarius crosses my path.*

She made a note to honor this profound revelation with a small altar on top of her dresser with an Aquarian astrological symbol and flowers.

She opened her eyes just enough to take in the blue skies, puffy white clouds, and treetops along the highway. The cotton fields were threshed, and the leftover cotton bolls looked like snowflakes that had lost their way.

"Hey, look!" Maddie Granola started from the front seat.

Cherie looked. Ahead in the right lane, for as far as one could see, was a slow-moving Army convoy of Jeeps, all filled with troops. It formed a massive caterpillar that lumbered slowly down the hot highway. Cherie looked over at Maddie Granola, who gazed at the soldiers with a psycho look as though tales of the Merry Pranksters danced in her head.

"Speed up!" Maddie Granola said to her friend.

The next thing Cherie saw was Maddie Granola up on her knees in the front seat, facing backward as the car zoomed by the convoy. She raised her right arm, shot the bird at the soldiers, and shrieked, "Out of Vietnam, mutha-fuckas!" Then, she repeated it as they sped by a dozen more.

Cherie gasped with horror, her dreamy ruminations about love drenched with ice water. She looked over. The soldiers yelled back terrible things. Despite the convertible's speed, Cherie spotted one guy, his face contorted with fury, pointing his rifle at them.

She reached for Maddie Granola's arm and, missing it, grabbed her shirt so hard it ripped, "Shut up! They're draftees, they don't have a choice!"

Maddie Granola yelled back, "There's always a choice!"

"Stop yelling at them!" Cherie yelled as loud as she could.

Her friend suddenly hit the brakes, which caused both Maddie Granola and Cherie to sink down hard on their seats to keep from being thrown out of the convertible. Back on their derrieres, the argument continued.

Cherie fought back, thinking about the three boys she saw in the woods.

"Draftees don't know how to get out. They don't know about deferments. They're not in college. They just go. That's why it works."

"So how do we know this crowd didn't volunteer?"

"We don't, but either way, they're facing hell, and we should be blowing them kisses."

Maddie Granola thought about it for half a second, turned back to her friend, and said, "Okay, speed up!"

As though a switch turned from OFF to ON inside Maddie, she spent the next few minutes speeding past the convoy, blowing kisses, waving and yelling, "Peace! End the War. We love you!" to the soldiers. Cherie joined her. Maddie Granola lifted up her peasant blouse and flashed her braless beauties, an extra thrill for both her and the boys off to war. They roared with approval. No Mardi Gras Queen could have outdone her.

As they receded from sight, her eyes welled with tears. She sighed, "I don't think the war will ever end. We'll be there forever, and a million people will die."

"How many dead so far?"

"About 40,000 and 240,000 wounded," Cherie said, "and

that's just the Americans. Vietnamese aren't included in the numbers." Granola looked back at her, impressed.

"It was in one of the workshops," Cherie confessed.

The conference was indeed over. Like the name of the herbal tea with the Mad Hatter from Alice in Wonderland on the box, it was *Back to Reality*.

Cherie was seized with sadness. She curled up on the back seat and covered her head with her black zip-up sweatshirt. In this dark place, she could grasp the last sensation of Jessy's hot body, his arms tightly around her, the weight of him a luscious, breathtaking crush. She wanted to hold on to the thought before the slog of school and Paulette's snare drum made it vanish.

She recalled a fancy, embroidered pillow she had seen in The Lemon Tree shop on Royal Street. On the pillow was stitched a Tennessee Williams favorite saying: *There's nothing more important in life than enthusiasm.* She pretended she clutched the little pillow and reassured herself as she chanted silently, *It's okay. One more year. It's going to be good, fabulous even. You've got friends, you can earn money, you can apply for college, the spring conference will be in New Orleans ...*

Cherie thought about Mr. Grunewald. It genuinely cheered her up. Mr. Grunewald was the senior English teacher at Fortier High School. This year, she'd have him for two advanced classes, English Lit and World Lit. He was a rare powerhouse of a teacher, funny and passionate. He publicly counted down the years to his retirement. He also read aloud to his classes, waving his arms about — Milton, Dante, and Shakespeare. His loud, dramatic intonation echoed along the gray concrete hallways, coloring them with life. Cherie remembered the first time she heard him. She was sitting in Algebra when Mr. Grunewald's disembodied voice, deep into Lady Macbeth's soliloquy, bounced into the room, *I, who have given suck ...*

Not only that, Mr. Grunewald lived in the Quarter. He lived

in one of the exclusive Pontalba apartments that overlooked Jackson Square.

The Pontalba was the oldest apartment complex in the United States, built in the 1840s by an enterprising widow, Micaela Leonarda Antonia Almonester, Baroness de Pontalba. She introduced the idea of apartment complexes to America.

Delta baby Baroness Micaela married into minor French royalty and moved to France. Not long after her father-in-law's failed attempt to shoot her dead for her family's fortune, the old man committed suicide with the same dueling pistol. Her husband died soon after. The Baroness returned home and used her money to buy real estate and transform the square between the St. Louis Cathedral and the Mississippi River. She contracted the city's favorite architect, James Gallier, to build practical, Parisian-style apartments around the square. The ornate, wrought iron balconies of the Pontalba Apartments even featured her initials.

One time, Cherie saw Mr. Grunewald on his balcony smoking cigarettes with his boyfriend, classical music blaring out of the apartment. Despite how much she hated school, Cherie felt better knowing she'd spend two entertaining classes a day with Mr. Grunewald.

Cherie boarded the bus in Biloxi, tired to the bone. It was a hot and humid August day on the Gulf Coast. Even though folks opened all the bus windows that weren't jammed, it must have been more than a hundred degrees inside the bus. The driver had a fan going by his seat, but that was it.

The bus was packed, and there were no seats left. Cherie went to the back and stood next to the last rows, where several older ladies sat.

They were energetically fanning themselves with folded-up newspapers and chatting about the weather, the rigors of church committees, and recipes. They were wearing their summer dresses, the scent of their hairspray and cologne piqued by the heat. All of them had shopping totes crammed with belongings.

Cherie felt safer being by them, less likely to be bothered by a pervert. She held on to the sweaty, metal pole with both hands, backpack at her feet. The bus pulled away.

An hour into the ride, Cherie felt sick. She closed her eyes. She tried not to pass out from fatigue and the heat. She leaned her forehead against the pole to steady herself and tamp down the nausea.

No. I will not faint, Cherie repeated to herself.

Suddenly, as though it was someone else's voice, Cherie heard herself moan, "I can't breathe." The surrounding passengers struggled to find her space. She felt somebody take her arm and direct her to a seat by a window that some merciful body vacated for her. "Sit here, honey," a voice said. She felt people fanning her. Another lady handed her an empty paper bag that smelled of fries, "Here, sugar, if you're going to throw up, do it in here."

Cherie nodded and held the paper bag close to her mouth. She drifted off for a while, her head leaning against the side of the bus. She woke up to indignant and horrified voices.

"Devil Hollywood. I'm telling you, it's devil Hollywood out there! The place is filled with devils crawling all over."

"The world is going to hell!"

"It's a crying shame. Look at that poor thing."

"So pretty, too. Texas girl."

"Can you imagine anybody doing that to a pregnant woman eight months along?"

"Breaks your heart clear through."

"The sickness of it!"

"May the Lord mete out his justice."

Cherie leaned over to look at the newspaper, the late edition. On the front page was a large photo of one of the most beautiful women she had ever seen, startlingly beautiful. Her name was

Sharon Tate. In a fancy mansion up in Beverly Hills, some people so rotten they made diseased rodents look good knifed her and her friends dead. She was the wife of Roman Polanski, the director of a horror movie called *Rosemary's Baby*.

Cherie had seen that movie with Marlene, Lila, and Katherine. It upset Katherine terribly, "I'm sorry I ever saw it," she whimpered.

To Cherie, what happened to beautiful Sharon Tate was far more frightening.

A woman on the bus summarized the whole sordid event, and Cherie took to heart the wisdom of her words. The woman shook her head sadly, pointed her finger, and said with conviction,

"It's just another reminder to *never, ever, ever* covet somebody else's life. Beautiful, famous, and married with a baby on the way — and look, just look, what happened to her!"

CHAPTER 24

Hoot and Howl

As Cherie had predicted when she toasted her imaginary champagne glass in the red convertible in Alabama, senior year in high school was the best year yet. It seemed filled with daily ease and advantages, both expected and unexpected.

Cherie went to school for only four hours a day. She discovered that she had already fulfilled her requirements for math, science, and gym. She only needed to take what was left of her A-track: World Lit and English Lit with Mr. Grunewald, French with Madame Delacroix for a third happy year, and an elective. She chose Study Hall so she could read and sleep.

The big bonus to this minimal-effort schedule was that she could leave school at lunch and not return. Sometimes, she walked over to Tulane after school.

Setting foot onto the campus, it appeared to Cherie to be buzzing with life. She learned how to sneak into the theater department and watch whatever Richard Schechner was directing, hang around the new Jazz Archives and listen to old recordings, be a volunteer model for art classes, watch sports practice, read flyers in the cafeteria, hang around the bookstore, or sit under a tree and look at everybody.

Cherie received a notice at school to meet with her new guidance counselor.

She walked in, and even though she tried not to appear surprised, she was. Her new counselor was a black man who looked to be in his early forties. His very presence at Fortier High School meant that at least one of the promises made after the Black Student Walkout had been fulfilled. She stood in the doorway, and he gestured her in. His name was Mr. Alphonse.

"Sit down. You go by Cherie, right?"

Cherie nodded and smiled, amazed he didn't call her by her dreaded real name.

Mr. Alphonse asked her if she was thinking about applying to college.

"Well, yeah, I do want to go to college, but I didn't think I could get in anywhere."

He looked over her records.

"Why would you think that? Your grades are good, your SAT scores are above average, and you made it into the National Honor Society."

"Well, I did think maybe I could apply around here. I thought I could ask some of the professors I babysit for if they would help me get in."

"Is that what you want? Go to college here and live at home?"

Cherie was caught off guard. No one had ever talked to her about it. There was an assumption between her and Paulette that she would go to college unless she went to work, but where and how was never broached.

The reality was she dreamed about going far away to college. She wanted to go north, way north, where it snowed, where everything was happening. It was that or stay stuck at home and get a job.

Cherie sighed sadly. Her grades were good, but that was only half of it.

Cherie knew her records were filled with notes about her bad attitude, sass, insubordination, cursing in class, the time she shot the bird at a cheerleader, absences, detentions, and all kinds of stuff. The icing on the cake was the mammoth six-week suspension for the Walkout.

Cherie flashed back to the time she told Señor Deloro, the Spanish teacher who wore lots of jewelry, that she was not going to attend the induction ceremony for the National Honor Society. Right in the hall, he pushed her against the wall and held his fist to her face, his big, shiny rings inches from her nose.

"Do you know how hard Madame Delacroix fought for you to be included?" he blazoned at her. "Almost the entire faculty was against you, but she and Mr. Grunewald fought for you and convinced them to let you in. You're going to the induction ceremony! You got that?"

"Okay, I'll go!" she pushed his fist away and walked off. *Jeez. Okay. I didn't know about the faculty meeting. No one told me. Oh my God. No, I can't insult Madame Delacroix and Mr. Grunewald. Still, Señor Deloro didn't have to be such a merda about it either.*

Mr. Alphonse studied her disciplinary record. He frowned. "What's this about refusing to march in gym?"

"Oh, that was awful," Cherie groaned. "The boys needed the whole field, so the girls were confined to the little corner by the gym. Coach Simmons was in the army, so she decided we would spend the whole semester marching military style in a little square back and forth and back and forth in the hot sun every day. I told her I burned my draft card and refused to do it. I still passed the final just from watching them, so I didn't get an F."

Mr. Alphonse nodded at her and hmphed.

Cherie shook her head and bit her lip, "I didn't think I could get in anywhere, you know, because of the six-week suspension and other stuff."

Mr. Alphonse closed the file. "I suggest you think about where you'd like to go to college. There are a lot of catalogs from different universities here in the office. I'll help you get applications to a few of them, and you go ahead and apply."

Then, he added, "I'll take care of your disciplinary records."

The next student knocked on the door.

"Be right with you."

Cherie got up to leave. She tried to say, "Thank you, Mr. Alphonse," but the words croaked out.

"You're welcome."

"No, I really appreciate it."

Mr. Alphonse opened a door she thought was closed. The crisp autumn breeze of a New England college blew in and encircled her. Cherie walked out of his office dazed, light, buoyed on the zephyr and a whole, new possible future. *Tufts in Boston. Wasn't that where Reverend D'Orlando went? I can get a job there and help pay for it.* She felt grateful. *Thank you, Mr. Alphonse.*

That evening, Cherie sat down on the couch with Paulette to watch the news. She stared at her mother as Paulette took a long drag on her cigarette.

"When did you start smoking?"

"I have to lose some weight. This will help me lose weight."

"Today in Los Angeles," the WDSU reporter announced, "a break in the Tate/LaBianca murders." Cherie turned her attention to the TV. *Tate, Sharon Tate, that I saw on the bus.*

After months of searching and pouring over every possible lead, the police in Los Angeles arrested a hippie freak named Charlie Manson. They also arrested a bunch of his followers, who used to be normal but had become his psycho-slaves. The local news reported a New Orleans connection.

It was a spirit cult that had a storefront at one time in the French Quarter on Royal Street. They called themselves the Church of the Final Judgment, recognizable by their long capes. After they left New Orleans and moved to Los Angeles, Manson glommed onto them.

An icy shiver ran through Cherie from the top of her skull to her soles. *The purple people eaters. Those pasty-faced, bony people with British accents! She and Thornton had hung out there on Lower Royal. The workshop on psychometry! The lectures on Armageddon and the end of everything.* It didn't make sense. *Loons, for sure, but they weren't killers, they wanted love and kindness!*

Love and kindness notwithstanding, in Charlie Manson's bad, drug-soaked brain, it all became twisted.

Why do people listen to people like that? How can they be so flimsy? Cherie's eyes flooded with tears as she watched the news report. She began to cry for Sharon Tate.

Paulette's laughter split the atoms in the air. "What is the matter with you?" she shouted. "What are you crying for? Crap like this happens every second all over the world! Don't you know how primitive humanity is? You're going to cry every time? You'll be crying all day and all night. You think because there are books and buildings, people are advanced? Humans are savages! People are stupid and cruel. They kill for nothing."

Paulette made a crying face, "Ohh, boo hoo, boo hoo." Then she laughed, delighted with herself.

Cherie ran out, got on her bike, and headed to Lila's house.

As she left, she could hear her mother's sarcastic tone behind her, "Oh, excuse me, she's so sensitive, poor thing. I have to walk on eggshells around her ..."

Three. Two. Seven. Boobs and arrows. That was Cherie's irreverent numbers for the Wordless Diary that night.

It was a relief to be with Lila. She'd been gone for days at the Poetry Symposium at Tulane. She was the youngest person on the steering committee, tasked to help with logistics. Lila explained to Cherie that logistics was nothing but a fancy term for picking up famous poets at the airport and running them around town.

"It was me and a Tulane photography student from Moon River, Georgia."

"Moon River? Like in *Breakfast at Tiffany's?*" Cherie interrupted the story.

"Yes, Cherie, there really is a Moon River," Lila replied. Without an iota of prompting, they sang *"Moon River, Wider than a mile."*

"So Audrey Hepburn, the Holly character, is from Georgia, and she sings about her hometown?" Cherie jabbered.

"No, no, she's from Texas. Don't you remember?"

Lila's first task was to drive to the airport to pick up living legend Allen Ginsberg, who wrote the famed, banned book of poetry, *Howl*.

Cherie was awed, but Lila related the story with the same nonchalance she displayed when she described the Warhol party. Cherie knew Lila believed it was her destiny to spend her life with notable poets, artists, and movie stars. To her, she was one of them.

Lila and the photographer from Moon River drove out to the airport in her red Volkswagen Beetle.

Allen Ginsberg came off the plane, impossible not to recognize. He sported his trademark beard and long hair, sandals on his feet, thick glasses, and he wore a light blue India-style shirt with embroidery over his loose, cream-colored cotton pants.

"He was so cool. We waved him over, and he greeted us with such a warm smile. Everybody stared at us like crazy when we walked through the airport. I know that some people recognized him. I'm sure of it because they got really excited.

"When we got to my car, I told him I used to have a VW hippie bus, but it shrank due to Zen meditation, which Allen loved, and he laughed. He was in a really good mood and happy to finally visit New Orleans. He asked us all sorts of questions, like where to eat and listen to music. Anyway, we drove to the Beau Jardin Hotel in the Garden District, which is so beautiful. Do you believe it? The steering committee actually reserved a suite for him because we were all so honored to have him here."

Lila described the luxurious Beau Jardin lobby. It had Persian carpets and antique furniture. Along the walls were big, framed mirrors which reflected the light from the huge crystal chandelier.

"But get this. As soon as we entered the hotel, the vibes went to miserable. The hotel staff stared at us with ugly faces, and the other guests in the lobby did too, including two couples with golf clubs and a man in a cowboy hat."

"But people stared at the airport, too," Cherie interjected.

"No. Listen. It wasn't like that. They weren't nice, excited staring. They were disgusted staring. I swear, one man even snarled!"

Lila related that Allen Ginsberg appeared oblivious to their unfriendly expressions. She told the young man behind the desk they were there to check in the poet, Allen Ginsburg, and his reservation was confirmed. She said Mr. Ginsburg was tired from traveling and wanted to check into his room.

The young man started to fumble around with the registration book. After a few minutes, he told Lila that there appeared to be a problem.

Ginsberg turned to Lila with a knowing smile and softly said, "They don't want me to stay here. He's stalling in hopes that I'll leave."

Lila told Cherie, "I wanted to kill somebody! This is the kind of hospitality he gets in New Orleans? It was shameful. I was so embarrassed. Then, the manager of the hotel showed up. His name was Mr. Schutt. He's one of the real Schutt family that runs, I think, Comus Krewe? He was so snooty."

Cherie loved Lila's storytelling. She differentiated between the two men in accent, tone, and gesture as she related their conversation.

"How can I help you?"

"I'm here to check in, thank you."

"Well, there seems to be some kind of problem."

"What kind of problem?"

"We can't find your reservation."

In her own voice, Lila continued, "I got so frustrated, I butted in, That's impossible! I confirmed it yesterday afternoon, and everything was in order!"

"I'm so sorry, Miss, but that was false information you received. I realize this is awkward, but we simply cannot find a room reserved for Mr. Jensburg."

"I totally freaked out, I yelled at him, 'That's Ginsburg, you idiot!' I was ready to jump over the desk and punch him in the face."

She defended her bad behavior to Cherie, "Here I am standing next to a man whose poetry is hailed as some of the best of the century, in my hometown, which has given birth to so many great writers and musicians, and I have to listen to this shit? But Allen was so cool. He thought it was funny, and he kind of gestured at me to shut up."

Lila described that Ginsberg approached the desk and began to talk to Mr. Schutt very quietly at first. Allen Ginsberg told him how much he'd like to stay at his esteemed hotel, that he had heard such wonderful things about it. He told him that he knew many famous people who were waiting to hear how much he liked it.

"You could see Mr. Schutt soften up. I swear, Allen molded

that man like clay. He lectured about the importance of the Constitution and individual rights of expression. He even quoted the Bill of Rights and went on about how all Americans must be treated and served equally. The staff and people in the lobby gathered around to listen to him. And he quoted other laws, too, and how the law of the land must be followed. He completely bamboozled him. Finally, finally, Mr. Schutt looked through the registration book and said, 'Well, Mr. Ginsberg, it does appear that there's been a cancellation, and we will be able to accommodate you in a lovely suite. We can have it ready for you in fifteen minutes.'"

"Then, Allen stepped back from the desk and announced, 'No, thank you. I've changed my mind.' He walked out. I nearly fainted, except I had to follow him out."

"You should have seen the expression on Schutt's face! It was, *Oh shucks, I'm a schmuck!*" Lila laughed.

"So where did y'all take him?"

"All I knew to do was drive to the Quarter, and then ... it was a miracle. I remembered that the Olivier House was renovated a while back. You know, it's on Toulouse Street right off of Bourbon. I remembered because the owners bought one of Roland De Veer's paintings. I was at the gallery opening when they bought it. It was perfect. They flipped out when we walked in. They were so honored to have him. It worked out perfectly."

"You're brilliant! You saved the day."

Lila glowed at the compliment. Her expression became more playful, and her eyes sparkled. Cherie knew the look.

"Okay. Who was it?"

Glitterati groupie that she was, Lila had left Ginsburg at the Olivier House and returned to the poetry symposium to seek out the mesmerizing poet, Merlin Weyword, so he could autograph her book.

She handed Cherie his book of poetry and commented on

how celebrated he was for his ultra-consciousness. "He's so amazing. He's the poet of the future."

Cherie focused on his photograph on the back cover. He was very handsome and had a mischievous expression.

"But he looks so much older than us," she protested to Lila, "How old is he?"

"I don't know, maybe forty. Forty-five."

Cherie made a face. "What did it feel like?"

"Well, I could tell he was older," she gestured a hand job. "Compared to Terry or John, I could tell it was an old dick."

"Get out!" Cherie screamed.

CHAPTER 25
Angels. Garrett

FAR FROM THE laughter that sparkled out of Lila's well-appointed blue and lavender bedroom, Garrett flopped down on his cot in Juvenile Lock-up.

He'd been in there for months. He stared blankly at a lazy cockroach slowly working its way up the wall. He hit the wall to see if it would run. It did not. Every day, he asked for a newspaper, but nobody would give him one. He had finished all his books.

Garrett learned the previous day that the State of Louisiana declared him an "Ungovernable Minor" due to his arrest record and unrepentant attitude. It was the worst thing the heavy hands in charge could do to him. It meant that Garrett would be taken away from his family and locked up in an isolated prison for violent youth in Missouri until the age of twenty-one. This was the judgment, even though he had not destroyed any public or private property, nor thieved, nor committed any act of violence against another person.

He did the math in his head. If indeed he was condemned to the reform jail, reputed to be a true hell, it would be more than three years before he was free again.

His last and only hope was if his father could persuade Ben Smith, the radical lawyer, to step in and try and save him. Garrett knew who he was, that Ben Smith was not only brilliant, he believed in truth and justice. He and another radical lawyer, William Kunstler, founded the Law Center for Constitutional Rights to help protect civil rights workers in Mississippi. *Maybe Ben Smith will help me too,* he prayed.

Garrett ran down the hall to meet with his father in the Visitor's Room. The second he saw his dad's pale and sad face, his heart imploded.

"Ben Smith won't help us?" he groaned.

"No, it's not that," his father replied and reached for him.

The gesture startled Garrett. "Dad, what's wrong?" He felt an unfamiliar pang twisting through his body. It was fear. His dad held onto him and wouldn't let go.

"Your mother's gone."

"What are you saying?"

His father's lip quivered, and his voice barely broke a whisper, "She fell down the front stairs and hit her head. The neighbors helped her inside and put ice on it, but ..." He shook his head sadly.

"But what? But what, Dad?"

"It was a slow bleed. And she died."

The breath knocked out of him. Garrett fell to his knees.

Bettina, Garrett's extraordinary mother, died way before her time. She died like a character in the southern novels she read as a girl. Bettina took a mortal fall down the eight stone steps that extended from the front porch to the sidewalk.

"Was it possible?" everybody wondered.

"Did it rain, and the steps were slippery?"

"Maybe she had a migraine, and she wasn't watching her step."

"Had she drunk too many?" They hung their heads. "You know, she never was the same after the divorce."

"Who could blame her? Home with all those wild kids and no help?"

Salting the wound, Garrett learned the night before her funeral that the authorities would not allow him to attend unless he wore chains accompanied by two policemen.

"Burn in hell, you bastards. No! No!" he cried. He would not be a spectacle at his mother's memorial service, the son people pointed fingers at.

"Oh, look at him," they would whisper, "Look how he went bad and broke his mother's heart."

The night of her funeral, Garrett fell into a raw, tear-stained sleep in his Spartan cell in Juvenile Hall. Outside the small, barred window, the rain had stopped. Trains chugged along on the nearby tracks, and a foghorn sang its grand bass note on the river. Crickets and cicadas added their chants to the hymn of darkness.

Garrett's mama came to him. It wasn't even like a dream; she was so real. In another kind of reality, she was with him so sweetly. Bettina stayed at the side of his cot, and she told him she was so proud of him.

She spoke to him in a calm voice, so full of love. She reassured him, "Everything is going to work out fine, honey. Don't you worry." She leaned over and kissed him. "I love you, son."

Garrett opened his eyes, aware of her presence. She had come to him. He touched the side of his face where she had kissed him. Wrapped in the sensation of her love, his racing heart slowed down, and peace filled him. "I love you, Mom. I love you," fell from his lips.

One week later, true to his mother's words, he was released. In short order, the great attorney Ben Smith showed up to rescue Garrett pro bono and show Louisiana the error of its ways.

Garrett was free again, but not really. He felt haunted by the entire experience.

He decided to stuff his backpack and leave New Orleans and all his family and friends and hitchhike to the Pacific coast.

CHAPTER 26
Angels. Katherine

ON THE SANCTUARY floor at church, Marlene, Lila, and Cherie sat in a circle. They stared at a few sheets of notebook paper between them, each covered with lists and notes for the spring conference in New Orleans. Outside, it was an early March monsoon. Waves of wind and heavy rain beat against the tall glass walls.

"Good thing we didn't get this last week," Marlene observed, "or it would have totally ruined Mardi Gras."

"It never rains on Mardi Gras, never," Lila countered. "On the news, it said it hadn't rained on Mardi Gras for a hundred years, no matter how cloudy."

"It's because everybody is so happy, it holds the sky up," Cherie concluded matter-of-factly.

"Yeah, it does."

"Yeah."

Marlene looked at the schedule. "So, on Friday afternoon, we have gobs of adults signed up to bring food platters for dinner. We just have to pick up soda and dessert."

"How many people so far?"

"About eighty plus all of us. It's going to be about a hundred."

"Wow. Anybody from Huntsville?"

"Seven so far. Justin's desperate for that red-haired girl to show up, but she's not on the list yet."

Chortles all around. They knew what *desperate* meant.

"Hobbs is coming."

"Ohmygod, Hobbs? That's great!"

"You're in love with him."

"We're all in love with him."

"What time do we go on the Riverboat?"

"Eight o'clock."

"Do you think we need one more workshop?"

"No! We almost have too many as it is. We've got Yoga, Political Theater, Feminism, and all the rest. Look." Lila held up the list.

"Where's Katherine?" Cherie asked Marlene.

"Remember? I told you before Mardi Gras, but it didn't sink in. She's dropping out."

"She's finking out on us now?" Cherie responded frantically.

Marlene nodded. "She knew you'd freak out, which is why she didn't want to tell you herself."

"But why?"

"I don't know why you're surprised. She barely shows up anymore," Marlene stated irritably.

"I don't get it. She hates us all of a sudden?" Cherie knew, however, that it was not *all of a sudden*. Katherine had been drifting away all winter.

"I don't know, you ask her!" Marlene snapped with hurt in her voice. "It isn't like she talks to me either."

Cherie pressed on, "But you're her closest friend."

"Maybe I'm not anymore!"

Lila finally weighed in.

"She's sick, y'all. Don't you get it? John and I ran into her at the Thoth parade on Magazine. She was all broken out from hives and puffed up. It was an allergic reaction to medicine or something. It's all the time. She wanted to hug us. John hugged her, but I didn't want her to touch me." Lila shivered, recalling Katherine.

Cherie nodded, "I saw her from the streetcar before Mardi Gras. She cut her hair. She was with an older girl, like in college."

"So, what if Katherine has a new friend? We all have other friends." Marlene's voice broke, and she started to cry. "I'm still her friend. I'm still *me*. I called her, and we talked about the allergies ... but she doesn't want to be around us anymore."

"Guess not," Lila confirmed.

"Maybe she'll change her mind," Cherie said hopefully.

"Why don't you call her up?" Marlene suggested. "If you call her up,"

"Are you kidding? Cherie shouldn't call her up and beg," Lila responded heatedly.

"No, but you can ask nicely," Cherie replied.

"Fine, call her!"

Cherie exhaled and turned her attention back to the conference. "The lady who's doing the women's liberation workshop wants it to be girls only. She doesn't want boys in there at all, even if they take a vow to be quiet."

"Oh c'mon, what does she think they will do? Throw a hissy fit?" Marlene asked.

Cherie nodded. "Yeah. Exactly. She says they only show up at women's lib talks to fight about it. They hog the space and won't let girls talk, and also, she said that girls act differently when boys are around, that they're not themselves. Except she didn't use the word *girls*, she said *women*. 'Women act differently. Women aren't themselves.'"

"Let's ask Evelyn. Put it on the Ask Evelyn list."

Down by the river, in Iris Gardens Center for Mental Health, confining chair far behind her, Elaine cut out a photo of crotchless red panties with white lace from *Cosmopolitan Magazine*. Then she cut out a photo of Richard Nixon's head and pasted it in the middle. Indeed, as Dr. Welder promised her, her world post-chair would expand.

Her roommate was a law student who suffered from feelings of failure and worthlessness. Together, they gathered furniture from nearby junk piles into their little room and proceeded to paint the pieces in garish colors and reconstruct them into odd shapes. They collaged their bedroom with photos from *Cosmo* and *Playboy* – the only magazines around.

The vast collage featured a Statue of Liberty in the center with a man sitting on the torch. They ensured its longevity by covering it with a polymer gloss. The collage became the talk of fellow "mates," the shrinks, and hapless visitors — *What did all those images mean?*

Elaine became a studied patient. She learned how to sneak out and back unnoticed before curfew, how to unnerve visitors with drooling, and joined with her fellows in terrifying the volunteer dance teachers. There were erstwhile boyfriends among the staff and patients to hug, kiss, and make love with. She went beyond the desire to merely stop the pain. She wanted to revel in being alive.

Elaine looked around at everybody. A doctor was having an affair with a patient. There was another doctor who sat in his car in the parking lot and cried. There was another one who smelled of alcohol. Suddenly, the shrinks didn't look so all-knowing. They didn't look tall anymore, like when she was chained to the chair. They weren't that different, these keepers. Elaine thought, *They're probably just as messed up, which is why they want to spend their days around whackos. It makes them feel superior.*

She was eighteen now, and she knew she was extra pretty.

Elaine asked herself, *So, you want to go to California and work on movies? Do you want to go to New York and be an art dealer? Do you want to go to college and then get married?* She closed her eyes with the last thought. *Marry someone wonderful. We'll travel around the world."*

Without any muss or fuss, Elaine gathered a few things, cleaned up her half of the room, and checked herself out of Iris Gardens. Nobody tried to stop her. Elaine walked out toward her future with a bounce in her step, snapped back into society by the hippest, most state-of-the-art mental facility in New Orleans. She skipped as she headed to her friend's house, a former fellow patient who was waiting for her with a bottle of champagne to celebrate.

In her little room less than a mile away, Katherine looked in the mirror. She didn't see herself in it. In her eyes, the person who stared back at her was grotesque, heavy, wearing baggy, raggedy clothes. Her hair wasn't silky and long like it used to be but chopped short. Her haircut wasn't chic like Lila's elegant, short haircuts, but uneven and ugly. Also, her hair was falling out; her hairbrush was full of hair.

Her thighs were big and pressed against the denim cut-offs she was wearing, emphasizing her knock-kneed posture. Her feet and ankles weren't little anymore but thick and swollen. Her cheekbones had become indiscernible under puffy flesh. Her eyes were bloodshot from lack of sleep. Her skin wasn't porcelain like it used to be in winter, like Cherie's skin, or golden and tan like it used to be in summer, like Marlene's skin.

Most people would tell her, "C'mon, it's not that bad." But not that bad wasn't what she saw.

All Katherine saw was an ugly, misshapen creature covered by reptilian skin, covered with red blotches and pus-filled zits, and scratches and scabs from picking at it. She wanted to tear her own face off. Most of her fingernails were gnawed to the nubs. Her brain hurt, and her bones hurt. They hurt all the time. In her mind, her ugliness seeped right down into her core. She felt like she was rotten.

Katherine felt only her soul was good and pure, not part of the cruel bodily existence, but aloft in the spirit world. She felt her soul was a little pearl detached and lost from the Queen of Heaven's crown.

The conference last summer had proven to be a short respite. Over and over in her mind, she replayed Roland throwing her out, banging against the door, her hair getting caught in it. *Thank God Roland moved away*, Katherine thought. *If he saw me now, he'd throw up.*

For months, she didn't want to be near anybody, she was so ashamed. When she ran into her friends, she didn't know what to say. Marlene kept badgering her about doctors, Cherie asking her to do stuff, and Lila wouldn't talk to her. Mostly, they just ended up staring at each other. *They hate me*, she thought.

Her new older friend got rid of her, too, telling her, "Sorry, babes, but you're going to have to find somebody else to be your mama 'cause I'm tired of it."

There was nobody else.

She missed her brother Kaleb so much that it made her stomach tighten up when she thought about it. *I don't even have an address for him. He's forgotten about me. He's forsaken me. What if he's dead?* Katherine moaned as if in pain and slumped over at the thought of Kaleb dead.

Like Roland, mama Giselle threw her out of the house. In a

frenzy, Giselle told her she was sick of looking at her and sick of the expense. So now, Katherine was back in her father and stepmother's house. She avoided them as much as she could.

Katherine figured the doctors she saw all hated her, too. They couldn't diagnose her, and nothing they did worked, not the hormones, the allergy shots, the iodine, or the painkillers. It all made her sicker. She was constantly nauseous and had more headaches than ever. She hurt so badly and felt exhausted, as though at any given moment she could fall asleep, except that the migraines didn't let her.

Not even the Missionaries of Charity in India with Mother Teresa wanted her. She had filled out the forms, but they expressed concern due to her poor health. Katherine told herself, *They're afraid I'll end up another sickie needing their help.*

Katherine got down on her stomach next to her neatly made bed that had an old cotton bedspread on top of it. She reached underneath to grab a blank book and a pen from a pile of stuff. She flipped past pages of her own scrawl where she had written the same hopeless, miserable rants over and over, along with prayers that begged Mother Mary to rescue her.

She held the pen in her hand to write more, but instead of words, she stared at the pages. She hung her head as she sat on the floor, her knees drawn up and one hand over her mouth to stifle the low croak of her groans. She weakly let her pen and notebook drop to the floor. She kicked them back beneath the bed.

Katherine crawled onto the bed. As she had done many times before, she laid on it as if in a coffin, on her back, feet together, hands crossed over her heart. She was barely breathing. She imagined what it would be like to go to Mother Mary, her true mother.

She closed her eyes and imagined flying out of her body, healthy and beautiful like she remembered. Angels, scores of them, descended upon her, circling her, and she could feel herself floating away with them. There she was, Mother Mary, Queen of Heaven in all her glory on a high cloud surrounded by vibrant, moving golden light, a loving and merciful expression on her face. Mother reached out to Katherine, her whispery, gentle voice beckoning her, "Katherine, my beloved child, thou art forgiven your sins. Let me end thy suffering. Come to me now."

Mother Mary felt closer every day, so much more real to her than her everyday life. Katherine gasped for air, unable to make her lungs immobile.

"But you know I can't, Mother. I'm afraid," Katherine said aloud with a miserable groan.

She heard noises. She sat up and opened her eyes. There, against the ceiling and gathered by the walls, she saw angels right there in her room. Katherine looked all around. From head to toe, she shook with joy and fear all at once.

They smiled at her and held their arms out to her. "Don't be afraid. We love you. We've come for you."

Katherine heard Mother Mary's voice again, "You will know mercy, my child. I won't condemn you. I will bring you to heaven." The angels all around the room shimmered and stirred restlessly.

An angry angel burst forth among them. Her wings fluttering in agitation, she spoke to Mary, Benevolent Mother. "Our Lord commands, Stop!" The Angry Angel protested, "It is His will she should suffer in this life. She's too young. She cannot be part of this."

"She has suffered enough. It is time for mercy," the Queen of Heaven replied.

"No!" Angry Angel flew towards Katherine. Katherine shut her eyes. She felt a heavy weight on her chest, pushing her back down onto her bed. Her soul that had hovered on the edge of life now felt trapped, locked back into her body. Her heart beat loudly. She could hear it drumming in her ears, a loud, relentless pulse.

Angry Angel attacked her. She stuck her needle-like claws deep into her. "No, you will not go. I forbid you!" Katherine went limp in submission; *I should be punished for such longings. I should pay.* Katherine twisted about and bit down hard on her hand to keep from screaming aloud from the painful torture.

A flash of light flared beyond her tightly shut eyes, and she heard the Angry Angel shriek and flap her wings.

Katherine felt the weight on her lift, and the pain stopped. She steadied her breathing and opened her eyes. The Angry Angel flew wildly about the room like a panicked caged bird and then settled in a corner of the ceiling. She glowered at Katherine, her head wavering back and forth. Katherine looked down and saw blood where Angry Angel pricked her with her claws.

The Holy Mother spoke again, "Fear not, my child. There is forgiveness for you. You are loved. It is time. Come to me."

At Mother's words, Katherine shuddered, and everything went black.

When she came to, all was dark and quiet in her little room. She was alone. She realized she didn't feel anything. The fear was gone. The blood, torment, and pain were gone. Even the purple indentations in her hand where she had bitten herself no longer hurt.

Oh, merciful Queen of Heaven. Katherine realized she was already halfway out of her body. Instead of misery, Katherine felt the Holy Mother's pure glory all through her. She wrapped her arms around herself and rocked back and forth, awash in the feeling. Gentle Mary's words chimed in her head, celestial music, "Fear not. Fear not. Come to me."

Katherine whispered aloud, "Yes, Mother. I love you so much." She reached under the mattress for a medicine bottle. It was filled with the secret, sacred sleeping pills she had painstakingly collected one by one over the years from her mother's stash. Mixed in were painkillers she had received from doctors. Attached to the bottle by a rubber band was a little matchbox that contained two new razor blades, the one-sided kind used for arts and crafts. She opened it.

Thank you, Mother. Yes, I will come to you. I'll do whatever you say. I love you so much. I can feel you holding me. Holy Mother, hold me.

CHAPTER 27

Enlightening

KATHERINE'S FUNERAL WAS AWFUL.

It took place at St. Vincent De Paul Catholic Church. Mama Giselle lied to the clergy and told them it was an accident, an allergic reaction, an anaphylactic episode, not a suicide. If the priests learned the truth another way, they didn't let on.

Cherie and Lila entered the church, followed by Lila's family. Lila touched a drop of holy water and crossed herself. Cherie followed suit.

Mama Faylene whispered at them, "Cut that out now!"

"That's what you're supposed to do," Lila protested sotto voce.

Past her sunglasses, Faylene gave a look that prompted obedience.

Marlene sat with her family, leaning against her older sister, who kept her arm around her. She wept inconsolably. Her father handed her a handkerchief and gently pushed golden strands of hair off her face.

Cherie filed into the pew, sitting closest to the side wall. Lila, Faylene, Lila's little sister, and her father followed her in and took their seats. For the occasion, Cherie wore all white instead of her usual black. She did it in honor of Katherine's desire to go to India. In India, people wore white for funerals. That was Cherie's thinking on the matter, and as usual, she stuck out from the sea of mourners dressed in black.

"This isn't real," Cherie whispered.

"I know. It's a bad, bad trip," Lila replied.

Lila and Cherie looked around the crowd. Garrett's brothers and sisters were there, but he was not. He had already left home. Devin sat with them.

There were other people from school, and they recognized adults who were friends with Katherine's father and stepmother. Estelle stood near the back with her boyfriend and two of her brothers. Cherie and Estelle's eyes met until Cherie turned away. She bit the inside of her mouth to shut off the painful feeling. Evelyn arrived with her children. The atmosphere was heavy; nobody waved hello at each other.

Cherie turned her attention to the church. It was decorated in pink and gold. It looked like a smaller version of the magnificent St. Louis Cathedral, a symbol of New Orleans, presiding over Jackson Square. The St. Louis Cathedral was Rococo, not Gothic, and very sweet to the eye.

"So pretty in here," Cherie commented dully.

"I love St. Vincent de Paul," Lila whispered. "I was here when I was little for a wedding. Did you sleep last night? No, you don't look like you slept."

The previous night, Cherie had almost fallen asleep at one point but had a horrible nightmare. In her dream, she saw Zeus standing over her bed. As she sat up to scream, he grabbed her throat with one hand. In his other hand, he held a sizzling lightning bolt. He held it over her forehead. And Zeus said what the Grand Inquisitor said to Jesus, "Tomorrow, I will burn Thee."

Cherie couldn't breathe with his hand on her throat and struggled to scream.

She woke up. Cherie sat up in bed. She tried to get out of bed but couldn't because the thick tentacles of the Monsters in the Floorboards had risen and were latching onto the legs. She slapped them off her legs, and despite the tentacle reaching down her throat, she forced out a loud, guttural scream. This time, she woke up for real. She looked around. The tentacles were gone. She bit her hand hard to make sure. Yes, she was awake.

She got up to get some water. As she opened the door, a figure appeared in the dark on the other side. Cherie shrieked again and staggered backward. It was Paulette. She hadn't bothered to turn on a light.

Cherie switched on the light. "You scared me."

"You scared me, too. You had a nightmare?"

"Yes."

"You were dreaming about Katherine?"

"No. Something else."

"Do you want to tell me?"

"No. It's okay."

"Hmph. Poor thing. But I'm not surprised she did it. Why should I be surprised?"

"Do you want to come to the funeral with me?"

"Are you crazy?" Paulette raised her voice, "You think I'm going to sit there in a Catholic church of all places and watch that bitch Giselle make a spectacle of herself?"

Cherie hung her head and nodded. *How could I be so stupid to ask?* The slight sensation of a tentacle was wrapped around her windpipe.

Paulette moved on, "You know, I always dream something is chasing me."

"Yeah. I know."

"I guess I told you already."

"I'm thirsty."

"So? Go get something to drink."

Paulette went back to bed.

Cherie got some water. She returned to her room and did something she hadn't done for a long time. She played her Eric Burdon albums. She wanted to hear his voice. She remembered seeing him at City Park, one of the best nights of her life. Devin showed her where to sneak in through the fence.

The volume was soft so Paulette wouldn't be disturbed. She played them over and over until the sun rose. She dozed off a little, lying on the floor, her head on the album covers. When she tried to lift her head, they stuck to her face.

"Look, there she is," Lila nudged her. Cherie and Lila hissed like cobras under their breath as Giselle took her seat near the front of the church. She was followed by Katherine's beautiful little sister, who looked so pretty despite her tear-stained face.

Giselle looked devastated and old beyond her years. Cherie and Lila's eyes met when they heard her moan to an acquaintance, "We took her to the best doctors. How could she do this to me?"

During the service, Cherie's mind wandered. She nudged Lila.

"What?" Lila whispered.

"Did you read *The Brothers Karamazov*?"

"Yes. Don't you remember? We made you read it."

"But we never talked about it."

Lila turned and stared at Cherie for a second to make sure she was in her right mind. "Not now. Later."

Following along, they knelt, closed their eyes through the prayer, and sat back down.

A few seconds later, Lila whispered to Cherie, her curiosity piqued. "Why? What don't you get?"

"I don't get why the Grand Inquisitor kills Jesus if he worships him."

"Okay. Later."

A few minutes later, Cherie nudged Lila again, who leaned over to listen. "He was right about Katherine. He was the only one who understood her."

"What?" Lila whispered.

"B'Lordy Michael."

"Who's that?"

"Ohmygod. You don't know."

Lila gave her another *shhh* look. Faylene did, too.

Still, Cherie's mind wandered. *Fragile fawn. How did Michael know? He barely even knew her, knew us, but he saw it; he knew it. He called her fragile fawn. She should have stayed with him, run away with him, maybe if, then she would still be alive. He understood her. He saw it. He would have loved her and taken care of her.*

Cherie whispered to Lila, "Kaleb's not here. I wanted to see him."

"You, me, and everybody. No one could find him."

"Wow. Kaleb is like gone forever."

"Shut up. You're driving me nuts."

As the service ended, they passed by Katherine's open casket surrounded by white lilies and roses. The body in the casket looked nothing like her, past or present. Her face was caked with a layer of make-up, and her lips were painted pink. It struck Cherie as sick funny. Katherine never wore make-up.

As Cherie and Lila walked back into the bright sunlight, they flinched and covered their eyes.

"Oh, for crying out loud," Faylene huffed.

They followed the hearse to a cemetery. There, Marlene

started to cry again, as did Katherine's family and other people, too. At one point, after Katherine's coffin had been lowered into the ground and was being covered up with dirt, Giselle reached for Marlene and hugged her tightly. Marlene graciously let her do it, even though Cherie and Lila knew that for Marlene, it was horrendous.

"Look how superior Marlene is," Lila whispered, "because I couldn't take it if she grabbed me. I would knock her teeth out."

Everybody else left the cemetery, but Marlene, Lila, and Cherie dawdled. They wouldn't leave.

Lila's father and Mama Faylene, in a rare display of mutual cordiality, tried to bribe the three girls into the car with a promise of a fancy hotel brunch, but they wouldn't budge. They wanted to stay longer with Katherine. He gave up, and they drove away.

They sat in the grass together by Katherine's gravesite. A massive, ancient live oak with its low, twisted branches gave them its embrace of leafy shade. They rambled on about the funeral, how freaky Katherine looked in her coffin, the prayers in Latin that they liked, and how stupid they all were not to see it coming.

Then they fell silent, a wave of drowsiness overtaking them.

"Listen to all the sounds," Lila interrupted the quiet.

"Birds singing," Marlene added.

"And those bumblebees," Cherie added.

"The wind."

"The wind and the leaves."

"Traffic far away."

"Shh, I can hear a radio."

"No, that's somebody playing piano."

"A door just slammed."

"I can hear us breathing."

"Do you hear the dog?"

A sudden loud crack of thunder in the distance made them jump. They nervously burst into laughter.

"And I didn't think anything would make me laugh today," Lila declared.

"I need to ask you guys something," Cherie interrupted her.

"Now?" Lila confronted back.

"Why not?"

"What is it? Now's okay," Marlene decided.

"I don't understand why the Grand Inquisitor wants to kill Jesus if he worships him. Why doesn't he want his people to have the freedom Jesus will give them? I don't even understand what freedom he's talking about."

"In the *Brothers Karamazov*?"

She nodded yes. Marlene mulled it over for a few seconds.

"Well, I think if Jesus gives them enlightenment or freedom, then they have a choice. They would know an additional way of thinking besides all the dogma or whatever the Grand Inquisitor shoves down their throats. They wouldn't need him anymore."

"So, the Grand Inquisitor is going to kill Jesus so he can stay in power?"

"That's part of it, but it's more than that. He's also trying to protect all the people, his followers."

"Protect them from freedom?"

"Yeah, because he doesn't feel they can handle it. The Grand Inquisitor knows that most people don't want to be in charge of themselves."

Lila translated, "He knows they're happier being sheep and being told what to think and what to do. Hey, in religion, they don't call them flocks for nothing."

Cherie looked at them, completely befuddled.

Marlene continued, "Or like cults. All those people join cults because they want to be told what to do. Being free out in the world is too much for them. Look at religious fanatics. They'd rather kill people than think for themselves. It's why almost no countries on Earth have democracy, even though our democracy has been here for two hundred years. It scares them. That's why dictators stay in power."

Cherie nodded tentatively. She remembered when Mr. Verett said that.

Marlene went on, "Don't you see? Our American forefathers, well, a lot of them were really radical. They maybe were closer to Jesus than anybody because they weren't afraid of free-thinking, you know, Enlightenment. They based a whole new country on it."

"Yeah," Lila agreed, "Everybody thought we'd go running back to the King in England begging him to take over and order us around, but we didn't."

"Do you get it now? Why the Grand Inquisitor has to burn Jesus at the stake and make everybody hate him?"

"I don't know." It was beginning to click in Cherie's brain:

The Grand Inquisitor was protecting his people because they wouldn't be able to handle the freedom Jesus would give them. It would bring them misery. Most people need to be sheep. It's easier for them to just go along and be told what to do and what to think.

Is that why Katherine died? Because she was told her life wasn't worth it, what a nothing she was, and nobody, not even her friends, could break her out of that? That there was no freedom for her, only the misery of family dogma carved into her, and a mother Grand Inquisitor, and a society Grand Inquisitor, and finally, a self-Grand Inquisitor that makes us kill ourselves?

Cherie's heart quickened. Her skin felt prickly, hot, and cold at the same time. She wanted to run and run. Get out of her head.

"Are you okay?"

Cherie started to sob.

"It's all over. We're all going to different places. It's what I've wanted so much all these years, and now I'm scared. I feel like I can't do it. I'm the same as one of the stupid flock people, afraid that I'm just going to fall apart out there. It's too much for me. But I can't stay here either. You know I can't."

Lila and Marlene started crying, too, "I know, I know."

They put their arms around one another and cried. They leaned on each other and leaned on the low-lying oak next to Katherine's grave. They fell to their knees, their hands in the dirt.

Marlene cried to the grave. "Oh, Katherine, I'm so sorry. I'm so sorry we didn't stay close."

"Me too, I'm sorry, Katherine. Please, please forgive me," Lila sobbed. "I'm sorry I was mean to you. I'm sorry I hurt you."

"I'm sorry, Katherine. We miss you so much," Cherie cried.

Clouds rumbled overhead, and the sky cracked open. It drenched away the mud from their hands and the voluminous tears down their faces. They didn't stop. They shrieked with the downpour. They screamed back at its earsplitting, spasmodic thunder, "Katherine! Katherine!" No one ran for shelter but stayed by the grave as they defied the lightning and its danger.

The storm ceased. One by one, as they sniffled and sputtered, Cherie, Lila, and Marlene pulled themselves up to sit on the grass instead of lying on it.

They caught their breath and looked around at one another.

"We look like drenched rats," Lila whimpered.

"It won't be so bad. We don't have to lose each other," Marlene assured them with a croak in her voice. "We've got phones and mail."

"Of course, we won't," Lila agreed with conviction. "I mean, we all like to write, and we all like to talk on the phone, so it will be okay."

Cherie wiped away some of the grass and dirt off her face. She nodded yes. They helped each other up to their feet, bid goodbye to Katherine, and blew kisses to her grave. They removed their stockings and shoes and walked barefoot out of the cemetery toward the bus stop.

"You know what?" Cherie sniffed, "The Grand Inquisitor is a coward and a whiner. He's the same as the most sheepie scared person in the village because, just like them, he only does what he's been told and then complains about it—how hard it is to burn people and torture them—but he does it anyway. He doesn't even try to be anything else. He's stuck in his dark hole. I hate him! He's the one who should be burned."

Past midnight, past the gossip, past pecan waffles at Camellia Grill, they stayed together at Lila's. Lila sleuthed out Roland De Veers phone number in New York.

"Why are you calling him?" Cherie spat at Lila as she dialed the phone.

"Don't tell me what to do! I want to stick it to him."

Roland's star had risen, and he lived in Manhattan. He already knew. Bad news travels fast. They chatted briefly. Lila told him she was going to college in New York.

They hung up. She reported, "He already knew. And he invited me to his studio in Manhattan. He said, 'Yes, please come see me. Anyone from my precious New Orleans is welcome here. Especially you.'" Lila made a face and rolled her eyes.

"Lordy be. What a surprise," Marlene replied.

Cherie felt too raw to sleep. She thought about Roland and the aftermath of Lila's call. Undoubtedly, it revved him up, and he hoped she would visit. Lila was an excellent model. Roland once told her she looked like a Modigliani.

Cherie imagined Roland's woman, barely awake, calling from their bed, "Who was that?" and his reply, "Oh, someone with the news about that girl, the daughter of a friend."

"That's two calls already. Maybe she was more than a *petite amie*?"

"No, nothing like that!" Roland would defend, then catch himself, "I'm sorry. I feel terrible for her poor mother. We were good friends. Go back to sleep. Go to sleep."

In her mind, Cherie could hear a grandfather clock in his building sound two a.m., and Roland would begin to sketch Katherine. His eyes would fill with guilty tears as his pencil skirted across the paper. He would think, *You poor thing. If only I had known you were so messed up, I never would have ... I never would have ...*

Cherie thought about his excitement when it hit him that he could now paint Katherine all he wanted, anyway he wanted. Even nude. This way and that. The Katherine paintings.

She heard noises and walked down the hallway. It was Lila throwing up. Marlene was helping her, holding a wet washcloth against her face.

Cherie retrieved her Wordless Diary and held it tightly. Then she drew her 6 and 1 as a medieval sword with an ornate handle. It was June. She would graduate from high school even though she wouldn't attend the graduation.

CHAPTER 28

Reckoning

IT WAS a lazy dog day in early August. Cherie woke up from her drop-dead afternoon sleep hot and groggy. She looked at the clock and smiled to herself. The party was in two hours, the last party. Friends would have a chance to hug, kiss, and say, "I love you. I'll miss you." It was at Lila's grandmother's house, which had a pool.

Cherie went to the fridge and pulled out a tray of ice cubes. She banged the metal tray on the counter. Ice cubes flew out of it every which way. She piled a few into a glass and pushed the rest into the sink. She added two spoons of sugar, water, and squeezed in a half-lemon's worth of juice. The lemonade cleared her head.

Paulette watched her unsmiling as she sat at the kitchen table, various papers strewed about. Paulette announced, "I think now that you are going to college, I'm going to go back to France."

"Really?"

"Yes, really." Paulette mimicked Cherie with an exaggerated expression of surprise.

"Your old Paris boyfriend wrote you back?"

"Yes. Of course, with my lousy luck, he just got married again, but he said I should come. He has people to introduce me to."

"What about your job?"

"What do I care? I can work for bastard lawyers in Paris, too."

Cherie took it in. *That's right. Wow.* She was eighteen now. She was going to college. Tufts University was giving her a loan, a work-study job for fifteen hours a week, and a National Honor Society grant toward her first year of tuition. But she wouldn't have a home anymore. It would disappear.

Oh my God. This is it. It's over.

Paulette interrupted her reverie. "Are you sleeping all of a sudden? Am I boring you? Did you hear what I said? When you get there, tell them to check your hearing."

"What did you say?"

"I told you. I need you to give me the four hundred dollars your grandmother gave you for college."

"No. No! I need it. I need it for books. I don't even have a way to get up there. I need to buy a coat and boots for winter. It's cold there almost all the time."

"They're giving you a loan. Ask them for more money in the loan."

Frustrated and anxious, Cherie explained, "They won't do that. It's only for the dorm. It's not for books or a coat!"

"Lower your voice at me," Paulette hissed through her teeth.

"Grandma warned me about this. She told me not to tell you about it. She made me promise not to tell you, and if you found out, she made me promise not to hand it over to you. You want to know what she said? She said, 'Don't let your mother take this away from you!'"

Paulette yelled back, "She gave that money to you just to slap me in the face. That money belongs to me! That bitch has never done *anything* for me, and nothing for you for that matter."

"It's the only graduation present I got. Grandma wants me to have it. She wants me to get what I need for college."

Paulette stood up, her voice loud and shrill. "I don't ask you for anything!"

"And I don't ask you for anything! All my clothes, everything, I paid for myself. I even paid for my own college applications."

Paulette smiled and curled her lip with a sneer. "Anyway, it doesn't matter. I already took it out of your savings account. I just wanted to see what you would do."

Cherie stared at her mother. Something shifted inside of her. She could feel the monsters rising out of the floorboards, poised to strike.

"Don't look at me like that," Paulette warned.

As if nailed to the spot, Cherie continued to glare at Paulette, but she didn't see her mother. She saw the Monsters in the Floorboards slither up the walls. She had to get out. A voice inside her shrieked, *Get out now!* Cherie turned away to leave and stopped in the doorway. She held on to it as if to keep her balance. She couldn't find her voice or catch her breath beyond the tentacle that gripped her throat.

She rasped to Paulette, "Fine. The money is yours. Go to France and leave me the fuck alone."

Paulette flew across the room at Cherie. "How dare you! You, you selfish little bitch!" Paulette shoved her against the doorframe and slapped her hard across the face. Cherie crumpled to the floor as blood spurted out of her nose. Paulette hit her again and again. "Stop it!" Cherie screamed.

"You have everything!" Paulette shrieked, "You are going to college. They're giving you money. You. You with that stupid look on your face! And what do I have? I don't have anything!"

Paulette vented her rage at her, screamed at her, hit her, punched her, and pulled her hair. Cherie curled up and took the beating.

The voice inside Cherie begged her, *Get out, get out!* Cherie balled up her fist. Her whole body tightened behind it, and as she uncoiled, she let her fist fly with a guttural yell. It found its mark hard, squarely in Paulette's stomach. Paulette reared up with a groan, glared down at Cherie, and raised her fist. Cherie pulled herself to her feet and, with full fury, shoved Paulette back.

Paulette croaked and staggered backward. She slumped to the floor by the cabinets under the kitchen sink as she held her stomach. She caught her breath. Softly at first, she began making a peculiar noise as she breathed.

Cherie couldn't tell what the noise was and then realized that Paulette was half-laughing and half-crying. It was maniacal. Cherie felt frightened like Paulette was truly insane.

Cherie pushed her hair out of her face and wiped the nosebleed away. She helped Paulette to her feet and over to the kitchen table. Paulette continued the sickening, laughing-crying grunt, "Henh, a-henh, a-henh."

Cherie got her some water and grabbed the prescription bottle on the counter. "Here."

Paulette took four pills from the bottle. She staggered over to the couch and flopped down on it. Cherie waited, watching Paulette. The crazy noise ebbed to silence. Her eyes were closed. It was over.

Cherie went to the bathroom and locked the door. She held a cold washcloth to her nose until it stopped bleeding and inspected the red streaks on her face and body. She rinsed off in the shower, cold as she could bear it to minimize the bruises. She brushed her teeth. She combed her hair, reapplied black liner to her eyes, and silvery frost on her lips. She dressed, wrapped her swimsuit up in a towel, and put it in her bag. She carefully opened the door and looked around.

Paulette was asleep on the couch. Cherie tip-toed past and quietly closed the door behind her.

Halfway to Lila's house, when she got to the neutral ground in the middle of Claiborne Avenue, she let her bike fall over and sat on the grass until she could mash her tears back down. Cherie decided to lie to Grandma about how much the money helped her and what it paid for. No. That wouldn't work. No doubt, she figured, Paulette would tell Grandma that Cherie willingly handed over the money to her. She would gloat and stick it to Grandma.

She could already hear Paulette's voice rattle in her head as she told Grandma, *Of course, Cherie gave it to me because she loves me, that's why. I didn't even have to ask.*

"You'll be out of there in a few more days," Lila concluded as she pinned a red hibiscus into her hair. "As soon as we get to the party, you'll forget about it. My Granny, she's such a honey sweetheart, was so cool with all of us at her house decorating. She even helped!"

"Promise?"

"What?"

"That I'll forget about it?"

"I promise," Lila crossed her heart. "Wait 'til you see what we did! Marlene and I did most of it, but everybody else helped, too. The guys got really inspired with the crepe paper."

Lila did not exaggerate. At her grandmother's lovely, Spanish-style house, the decorations began right at the garden gate that led to the pool and cabana area. Next to the gate was a poster with a peace sign draped by daisy chains of Black-Eyed Susans and a sign that read, "Enter here."

The pool area was adorned with Chinese lanterns and twisted crepe paper ribbons in bright colors that extended clear across the pool. In the cabana, there was a four-foot-high stack of fluffy, white towels. Nearby, trays were piled high with luscious food. This included pigs-in-blankets with Creole mustard, little artichoke pies, large pink shrimp on ice with remoulade sauce, and pecan-stuffed olives wrapped in bacon. Vases were filled with daisies.

The bar offered beer and soda. The centerpiece, on a separate table all its own, was a blue sheet cake decorated with plastic alligators and boats. "See you later, Gators" was written on it. Music blared from the speakers, mixed with joyous screams coming from the pool.

Cherie took it all in. "Y'all, this is stunning! It's so, totally gorgeous!"

Cherie felt the fight tentacles begin to slink off into another part of her brain. Within minutes, after Marlene pushed her into the pool, fully dressed, she felt normal again.

Within an hour, after sneaking some scotch into her club soda, after she danced holy hell to the boys' music, hugged, drank, and danced some more, she forgot about it.

"See? I told you," Lila teased.

"Told me what?"

The last hours of the party were spent hanging around and talking. When they were sure Lila's grandparents had fallen asleep, they shared some weed.

Cherie gave and received a great, tight hug and kiss from every person that departed. Finally, everybody was gone except for Lila, her boyfriend John, Marlene, and Cherie. They returned to Lila's house and fell asleep together like puppies in her room as Missy Ruby Dawn peaked over the horizon.

CHAPTER 29

August. 1970. Wonders Never Cease

GARRETT HAD BEEN HITCHHIKING for six days, and he was already hundreds of miles away from New Orleans. His older brother's little back-to-the-earth farm in Oregon was closer than ever, but to Garrett, it felt farther away than ever.

The dry New Mexico air seared his throat. He was thirsty and starving. He even asked the strangers with whom he bummed a ride if they had any food.

"No, but there's a commune about two miles down the road called Lower Farm, and they'll feed you. Do you want us to drop you off?"

"Yeah. Please."

They left him on a dusty dirt road that looked like it went nowhere. He watched the Ford disappear. He felt grimy and beat, his gear woefully heavy. Dizzy, he stopped to rest. He spotted a bunch of field rats running into the brush. A lone buzzard looped overhead. The sight spurred him to keep moving.

What a different world, he thought. *I'm not at home here, not like I was even in Arkansas or Georgia. It's a different planet.*

Garrett noted a deepening orange in the eastern portion of the sky as the merciless desert sun began to set. He wandered into the commune. He was grateful to get there before dark before any rattlesnakes found him attractive.

The commune looked to be an enclave of several dozen tents and shacks. Men, women, little children, and a few babies hung around.

Garrett introduced himself to a hippie guy and his Earth mama. Sure enough, just like the strangers said they would, they led him to the ramshackle kitchen.

The kitchen area was a group of picnic tables by a creek beneath a couple of cottonwood trees with a shed and a grill for cooking. There, they served him a bowl of meatless, mushy hominy corn stew. It was tasteless. Garrett ran through his head the ingredients it needed to be good: peppers, tomatoes, garlic, and hot sauce. Nevertheless, he gobbled up the generous portion and washed it down with a glass jar of warm, minty tea. They asked him lots of questions, "Where are you from? Where are you headed?"

"Can I crash here tonight?" Garrett asked.

"Sure, man," they told him.

"I can't pay you for the food. I'm sorry," Garrett apologized.

"Hey, we're here on Earth to all take care of each other. You know what I'm saying? Smog is the only evil."

Garrett smiled, "Thank you. I appreciate it."

They led him to a lean-to where he could sleep. He laid out his bedroll and flopped down on it. Instantly, he began to drift off.

He heard footsteps in the dirt walk up to him. *Oh no. Now what?* Garrett thought sleepily. He reluctantly opened one eye. A skinny commune guy, a different one, kneeled on the ground next to him. His clothes looked like rags. His angular face was shadowed by the neon colors of the New Mexico twilight behind him.

Garrett sat up and rubbed his eyes. He could make out the

young man's scraggly, thin beard and stringy hair that fell far past his shoulders. A ray of light reflecting off the metal pole of the lean-to revealed for a split second a turquoise stud in his ear and his green, almond-shaped eyes as they peered at him from the mass of hair. His nose was sunburned, and his lips were chapped.

The young man stared intently at Garrett until his searching expression broke into a big smile and revealed his perfect teeth.

"Fuuuuuck, man, Garrett. Where Y'at, you southern piece of shit?" he declared with amusement, "I don't believe it!"

Vague recognition of the voice came into play. Garrett gawked at him, jaw agape, astounded. And then it hit him.

"Kaleb?"

Lila and Marlene waited downstairs to drive Cherie to the airport. When Lila learned that Cherie was going to take a thirty-two-hour Greyhound bus to Boston, she appealed to her father, and he gave Cherie the money to fly one way. Lila would head north in a week, followed by Marlene a few days later.

During Cherie's last days at home, not a word was mentioned about the fight. She and Paulette carried on as before in their respective spheres.

Cherie gave away most of her meager belongings. Still, she kept her Wordless Diary, now done, with nothing else to add except for a zero. She felt it was sacred, a touchstone that had helped her get through everything. She'd leave home forever with a duffle bag and a box of favorite books that included her cherished *Greek Myths and Legends* that had already been mailed up north by slow boat.

Cherie took a last look at her empty room. "Thank you for being such a good room."

Lila honked the horn. Cherie smiled. It's what they had

arranged. They determined that Lila should honk the horn every three minutes so Paulette couldn't detain her.

"I'm leaving now, Mama," Cherie called out.

Paulette came out of her bedroom to say goodbye. She wore the kimono her old friend in the Quarter had given her years before, the same one when her swine boyfriend Wayne ... Cherie stopped herself. *No. I won't think about it.*

"Okay then. You write me," Paulette declared, "and if things go well, you'll come to France next summer. Okay?"

Cherie nodded. "Super good luck in Paris."

"Okay, okay. Give me a kiss." As Cherie reached out, Paulette grabbed her and hugged her tightly. Finally, she let go and, in a jokey tone, "You know. I think I'm going to miss you."

Cherie saw tears running down her mother's face.

"It'll be okay, Mama."

Paulette wiped her tears away, "Wait. There's one more thing." She handed Cherie an envelope. Cherie took it and stared at it as though its white exterior would suddenly reveal its contents.

"What are you looking at? Open it."

Cherie tore it open and pulled out a check for four hundred dollars made out to her from Paulette's checking account. She was incredulous. "Are you sure? I thought you needed it."

"I'll manage. I always do."

"Thank you, Mama."

"Well, you know," Paulette shrugged, "I may at times love you badly. But I still love you."

Cherie was stunned. "I love you, too." Tears fell. Cherie did not try to hold them back.

"Look at us. We're both crying now. Okay, go already. Go. Go. Don't miss your plane. Go. Call me when you get there. Go." Paulette retreated to her bedroom. Cherie could hear her blow her nose on the other side of the door.

Lila pressed on the horn again. A neighbor yelled out the window, "Knock it off with the horn!"

Cherie crawled into the back seat of Lila's car. Settled in, she took a deep breath and exhaled, "Whew." She held up the check. "Look, do you believe it?"

Lila glanced at it in the rearview mirror. "Well, well, well. Will wonders never cease."

"It's probably going to bounce," Marlene added.

"Lila, I can pay your father back for the plane ticket."

"Don't you dare!" Lila snapped. "He'd be insulted."

Lila turned up the radio. "Celebrate" by Three Dog Night came on. The little car traveled down Carrollton Avenue.

"Do you know how they got that name?" Marlene turned to Cherie in the back seat.

"I can't imagine."

"It means that if it's freezing, you have to sleep with three dogs to stay warm."

"Or one boy," Lila grinned. She turned onto Airline Highway.

Marlene turned back to Cherie again. "Speaking of, are you going to call what's his face when you get to Massachusetts?" she teased.

Cherie put her hands on her face, "Shut your stupid trap."

Lila sang, "I think somebody's getting a phone call."

"Yeah," Marlene chimed in, "It's holy communion time."

Marlene and Lila both oohed ghostly sounds and kissy noises. "Merry meet. Merry meet," they chanted.

"Shut up. I'll meet somebody new," Cherie decided.

"Who are you going to meet?"

"I don't know. Let me think for a second. I'm going to meet, uh, somebody named Charles, like the river."

They hooted and hollered. "Charles! Charlie River!"

"Hey, Marlene. Are you going to do it with a Dartmouth

Dog?" Lila grinned. "Didn't you tell me that's what the Smithies do? Have a Dartmouth Dog Night?"

"To the airport, Jeeves!" Cherie yelled.

"Yes, ma'am! At your service," Lila yelled back.

Waiting to board at the airport, Cherie pulled out her ragged, glued, and taped-up Wordless Diary and drew her last entry. It was a blazing sun. Zero. She closed her once-blank book and whispered, *Don't worry. I'll never throw you away.*

As the plane lifted off, Cherie leaned into the window, taking in the curve of the river and the whole city. She imagined the Delta Lady, a beautiful woman wearing a crown of diamonds and a flowing gown, camellias, roses, and magnolias at her feet, rising up from the land below to wave goodbye. Cherie blew her a kiss. "See you later."

Acknowledgments

I cannot thank the following people enough for their unyielding encouragement in the writing of CAMELLIA SEASON. It's been a journey in the most universal sense and would not have been possible without their generous spirits.

To the New Orleans krewe be they near or far: Grant Cooper, Nathalie Musson, Maryanne Fischer, Lisa Lawrence, Dave Clements, Ann Asprodites, Alan Gerson, Vicki Heymann, Ramsey McLean, and *in memoriam* Christine Pleasonton and Keith Pleasonton.

Heartfelt thanks for all the advice and editing to: Maxine Herman, Philip Messina, Helene Chirinian, Paul Taylor, Reidar Jonsson, and Miranda Peterson; my readers Ann Simon, Linda Prather-Johnson, Mitchell Haymes, Lynn Fleetwood, Evlondo Cooper, Deb Fox, Nina West, and Charles W. Bailey, Jr.; and to Rosemary James along with the Pirate's Alley Faulkner Society conferences for all the encouragement. Loud cheers to Team Paper House for putting together a beautiful book.

Big thanks to my husband, Scott, and my family who were

with me all the way. And the dogs, here and gone. The comfort of pets is no small thing, especially when you're working on a novel.

About the Author

CAMELLIA SEASON is Natasha Peterson's first novel. She co-authored MEMOIR YOUR WAY, and wrote the graphic novel, THE 9-11 STORY BOOK, illustrated by Alan Gerson. Her first nonfiction book was SACRED SITES.

Email: natashapetersonauthor@gmail.com

Printed in the USA
CPSIA information can be obtained
at www.ICGtesting.com
LVHW091941170824
788567LV00028B/397